Also by Neil Robinson

Sebastian Friend Thrillers
The Other Side of Trust

Non-fiction
Long Shot Summer:
The Year of the Four England Cricket Captains

TENGIZ KHAN

by

Neil Robinson

SAFE HOUSE BOOKS

www.safehousebooks.co.uk

Safe House Books Ltd
London, England
www.safehousebooks.co.uk

Published by Safe House Books, 2026

TENGIZ KHAN

Cover design by Emily Dinsmore

A catalogue record for this book is
available from the British Library

9781739754051 (paperback)

This novel is entirely a work of fiction.
The names, characters, and incidents portrayed in it are
the work of the author's imagination. Any resemblance to
actual persons, living or dead, events or localities is
entirely coincidental.

Typeset using Atomik ePublisher from Easypress Technologies

For Kate and Elizabeth

Slender daughter of Shatili,
I have chosen you,
and will take you from Shatili to Tusheti
on a horse, flying over giant rocks.
I will hold you on the top of Borbalo mountain,
and protect from the rain with a shepherd's cloak.
Wash your eyes with morning dew,
and dress you in a dress made from dandelions.

Erisioni: Shatilis Asulo

PART ONE

ELIF

CHAPTER ONE

HOSTAGE

The Café de Paris is not the most well-known or frequently patronised establishment in the Georgian capital of Tbilisi. It is just a little too far from the main shopping streets and has always disdained the sordid business of advertising itself. But it is among the most civilised. Its quiet backstreet location, well-spaced tables and discreetly attentive service have long made it a favourite meeting place for behind the scenes scheming among the power brokers of the city's elite.

At a little after noon on a dull Tuesday in the middle of February it was quiet even by its own standards. The man at the small corner table diagonally opposite the entrance sat rigidly upright, the small glass of cognac at his elbow still untouched, although it had been brought to him more than ten minutes ago. He was clean-shaven and well-groomed and his expensive looking black shoes were well-polished. But the dark grey suit looked rumpled and old; it had either seen better days or he was simply one of those men who manage to make even the best clothes look untidy. He wore his stiff-collared white shirt buttoned up and tie-less, Persian style. He was visibly tense, his teeth clenched so hard that the corners of his jawbone jutted out beneath his cheeks. When a slim, immaculately dressed young man in his early thirties, his fair hair just beginning to recede, entered the café and walked across to his table with no gesture of greeting, the man's eyes flickered in his direction, but the expression on his face did not change.

The newcomer slipped a pair of leather gloves from his hands and laid them down flat beside the other's untouched cognac. Then he unbuttoned his camel-hair overcoat and sat down, summoning the waiter with a click of his fingers.

'Oui, Monsieur?'

The Café de Paris took its pretentions seriously.

'Double espresso.' The younger man looked at his companion but got no response. 'And another cognac for my friend.'

'Certainement, Monsieur.'

'I hope I haven't kept you waiting too long,' said the younger man, slipping out of his coat and laying it carefully across the back of his chair.

'Does it matter?'

'I suppose not. But we may as well observe the civilities.'

'You can do so, if you please.'

'Oh, don't worry, I'm not going to insult your intelligence by trying to make friends with you. What we are here to discuss is purely a business matter.'

'I don't see what business there is to discuss. I have already said everything I want to say to you people. My position is unchanged.'

'Nevertheless, our mutual friend felt that our meeting…'

'That man is no friend of mine.'

His voice was a growl, as if the words needed to be drawn out forcibly through a jawline set with tension. It carried with it an undertone of violence. For a moment the younger man looked discomfited. Was there to be a physical outrage in Tbilisi's most exclusive establishment? The waiter's arrival with coffee and cognac defused the situation. The older man relaxed and sat back in his chair, resuming his contemplation of the door.

'I've no desire to upset you,' said the younger man, once the waiter had departed. 'My purpose in arranging this meeting was to set your mind at rest.'

'And how do you propose to do that?'

'By meeting your terms. In part at least. My employer recognises that you must have some proof of our good faith.'

'Good faith!'

'We are honourable men. Even if the business we are in is not always an honourable one. Neither is yours, come to that.'

'Which is why you want it.'

'As you say.'

'So, what happens now?'

'You must understand this. Whatever happens in the next few minutes, you are to say and do nothing. Remain seated in your chair; drink your cognac if you wish. If you fail to obey these instructions I cannot answer for the consequences. Agreed?'

The older man signalled his assent with a shrug.

The younger man pulled out a phone from the pocket of his blue sharkskin jacket and made a call.

'Are you ready?' he said. 'Good. Then bring her in now.'

For two minutes they sat in silence. Then a party of three entered the café: two thick-set young men, with close-cropped hair, their muscular arms bulging through the fabric of their heavy winter coats. They looked like the kind of men whose appearance was crafted to intimidate; bodyguards or gangsters. Between them entered a woman. A wealthy woman, too, by the look of her; her black hair expensively curled and falling in locks about the collar of a grey sable coat. The low-heeled black boots were in good taste, as was the jewellery: a simple yellow gold necklace worn above a black woollen roll-neck sweater and a matching wedding band on the third finger of her right hand. Her face, modestly enhanced with make-up, was striking. There was strength to be seen in the long, straight nose, the high, prominent cheekbones, the sharply defined jawline and the upright carriage of the head on the still slender neck. She was no longer young but had reached that age when a face can acquire a dignity it might have lacked in youth. The lady seemed interested neither in her companions nor her surroundings. Her expression was neutral; her eyes focused on nothing in particular, her mind on some internal object. The three had already sat down near the door before her vacant gaze panned across the corner table. There it stopped.

At once she was alert. She made to rise from her seat, but a restraining hand on her arm recalled her to her position. She looked briefly across at her companions, seemed to recover from whatever impulse she had experienced and sat back in her chair. Her eyes looked again towards the corner table, locked with those of the older man, and stayed fixed upon them.

'Ten minutes. No more,' the younger man said.

To the casual observer there was little in the faces of the man and the woman to betray the thoughts behind them. Neither attempted to communicate with the other, by word or by gesture. But their eyes remained fixed upon each other with a focus that went clearly beyond the visual. It was absolute. As long as it lasted, nothing else in the world existed for them.

Perhaps the attitudes of the three other men offered the best guide to the solemnity of the occasion. A pot of black tea was delivered to the lady's table. Her two companions silently poured themselves a cup each; hers remained untouched. The well-dressed young man at the other table flicked through some messages on his phone, studiously ignoring his distracted neighbour, his mind counting down the minutes. In all three there was a restraint of gesture, a minimisation of movement and sound. The Café de Paris seemed possessed by a great stillness and at the heart of this stillness were two people whose whole world was to be seen in the eyes of the other.

All too soon it was over. The young man returned his phone to his pocket and signalled to the two on the other table. One reached over and gently placed his hand on the woman's forearm. Very quietly, he said something to her and slowly, keeping her eyes all the while on the other table, the woman began to rise. The older man kept watching her as she moved away, her head turning once and again to glance back over her shoulder, and then seeming to trust the two men to lead her correctly she kept looking back as she walked, until after a few seconds they led her through the door and out of sight.

For some time the older man remained still, his eyes staring at the door, while the young man summoned the waiter and paid the bill, before slipping his coat and gloves back on.

'Well?' the younger man enquired. 'Are you satisfied?'

The older man sat back in his chair and looked across at him. His look gave the message clearly enough: satisfied was entirely the wrong word.

'You can see at least that she is safe and well. She is being well looked after. She wants for nothing.'

'Except her freedom.'

'Except that of course. Well, now you have the proof you wanted, I assume there will be no further issue with your co-operation?'

The older man signalled his assent with the faintest of nods.

'Good. We will make the same arrangement every month. The same day, the same time, the same place.'

'I understand.'

'In the meantime you will stay where we want you.'

'Yes.'

'You will come when we summon you and do whatever we ask.'

'Yes.'

The young man smiled in relief. 'I'm so glad. Well, in that case I see no reason to detain you further.' He buttoned up his coat and turned for the door.

'Feels good, doesn't it?'

The old man's words hissed with venom. The young man paused in mid-step at the sound of them and turned around. An unfamiliar chill seeped into his bones. The older man had raised the cognac to his lips but wasn't drinking. His eyes were not raised from the golden liquid while he spoke.

'The power. You feel it coursing through your veins, I can tell. It's exhilarating. There's nothing else like it.'

He paused, as if shrugging off the thought.

'Well, enjoy it.' He tilted the glass and took a small sip of liquor before he looked up and into the other man's eyes as he spoke again.

'As long as it lasts.'

The smart young man put up a good show. He tried to dismiss the implied threat with a smirk, but the way the colour drained from his cheeks and the faint quiver in his twisted lips showed that the resolution in the old man's voice had found its target. The old man had almost a lifetime's experience of fear and intimidation. He knew what they looked like.

CHAPTER TWO

BOSPHORUS

She had no time to wonder why he had hit her, or even to register the source of the blow. A moment earlier she had been standing there on the empty deck, alone and confused, her body swaying on uncertain legs as the ship made a tight turn around a headland, shivering slightly in the cold, pre-dawn light. There had been no sound, so it must have been the faint smell of sweat and brandy on the sea air that caused her to her turn and see with surprise his dirty, unshaven face. He didn't hit her with his fist, but whatever he had in his hand thudded into the side of her head before she had a chance to see it coming. It almost knocked her clean off her feet; sent her staggering away in a dizzy whirl of blurred vision and rising vomit. Any moment, she thought, she would be on the floor and then more blows would come. She felt her hip come into contact with something hard, her head pitched over and now she was falling. Rolling and tumbling, she thought, head over heels. Why not heels over head? Any moment there would be the crunch of the deck boards; her arms refused to be thrown out to cushion the landing. But the crunch never came, she just kept falling, falling until her body hit the water. By which time she was too far gone to notice.

The sailor glanced briefly over the side: white water churned up by the ship's passage but no sign of the stowaway in the grey overalls and baseball cap. He shrugged, tucked the cosh back into his trouser pocket and lit a cigarette. Ahead of him, windows on the European shore winked back a reflection of the rising sun.

* * *

Dawn had yet to break when the chirping of the morning alarm rang through Altan Karabeg's modestly-sized flat on the Asian side of Istanbul. There would be twenty minutes yet before the first rose-gold rays of sunlight began to flicker between the old city's minarets and ramshackle rooftops, but already a pale blue light had begun to soften the edges of darkness and the first stirrings of life were prodding away at the slumbering consciousness of its inhabitants. In the streets below, the aroma of baking bread and fresh, sticky, baklava pastry filled the air, mingling with the first promise of bitter black coffee from the cafés that would be filled within the hour with eager patrons loading up with caffeine and carbohydrate before a hard day's toil.

Food and drink were not among Altan Karabeg's major passions, but breakfast was still his favourite time of the day. Within ten minutes of the alarm going off he had showered and dressed - smartly in a meticulously ironed cotton shirt and navy chinos - and was preparing himself a light repast of creamy plain yogurt with fresh green figs and half a ripe mango, while the coffee was quietly brewing in its metal pot on the stove. When it was ready, he placed his breakfast on a wooden tray and took it out through the sliding doors to a small, circular table on the balcony. Then, observing that the mornings were still cold at this time of year even though it might be 22 or 23 degrees by midday, he went back inside to fetch his laptop and equipment and put on a cardigan of heavy grey wool.

It had been the balcony that first attracted Karabeg to this apartment. As a well-paid freelance network engineer he could easily have afforded a place offering far more generous internal proportions. Instead, he had opted for this simple studio; a reasonably sized living/bedroom with a small galley kitchen tucked away at the back and a tiny shower room off to the side. But what sold it to him was the balcony, running the whole length of the property and broad enough to accommodate a table and chairs. It offered outside space and cool air above the heat and pollution of a city that could be stifling in summer. And what really made the balcony was its location: on the fourth floor of an apartment block at the southern end of Körfez street, near the old Anatolian fortress. Facing west, it offered a breathtaking view over the Bosphorus at its narrowest point, almost directly opposite the Rumeli Hisar fortress on the European shore.

As his laptop flickered into life, Karabeg checked his watch. He was in no particular hurry that morning, at least not now that he was enjoying his breakfast on the shaded balcony. It was more a case of knowing how long he would need to wait. The password prompt appeared on the screen. He entered it, then turned his attention to the mango, carefully peeling and slicing it before dropping the pieces casually into his yogurt. He wiped the juice from his hands and took a sip of coffee. A ping from the laptop announced its readiness. Karabeg opened his internet browser and made his way to a private forum, used by himself and a couple of dozen friends in and around Istanbul. Checking the latest posts he quickly found what he wanted.

The Turkish Frigate *TCG Istanbul* had contacted Turkeli Control Station on VHF channel 16 three and a half hours ago and requested permission to enter the Bosphorus. The ship was at the time some thirty nautical miles north-east of the Strait of Cannakale. Permission was granted. Thirty minutes later, the captain had switched to channel 13 and submitted his SP-2 sailing plan, giving his ship's name, call sign and flag; his current position (now some twenty nautical miles away) and expected time of entry into the straight. He reported no damage or defect on board the ship and declined the service of a pilot. This was confirmed directly to the Kavak pilot station on channel 71.

It was less than an hour later that the next report had come in;

the *Istanbul* reported that it was passing the Anadolu lighthouse and entering the Strait. Turkeli control acknowledged the message and instructed the Captain to switch to VHF channel 12 and stand by. Barring emergencies, there would probably be no further radio communication before the Istanbul passed through the Strait and into the Sea of Marmara.

The *Istanbul* had entered service in 2023; the first of four new multi-purpose frigates commissioned by the Turkish Navy. Boasting 50% greater fuel capacity and operational range than its predecessors, the Istanbul was 113 metres long and was equipped with a MIDLAS vertical launch system, 16 ATMACA surface-to-surface guided missiles and powerful 76mm naval guns, offering impressive anti-air, anti-submarine and surface warfare capabilities. For such a large vessel, the Bosphorus could be a tricky passage, with several difficult turns to navigate; it was not a route any sensible skipper would rush. Checking his watch again, Karabeg calculated that, travelling at a steady eight or nine knots, the *Istanbul* would probably come into view of his balcony in around twenty to thirty minutes. When it did so, the captain would be slowing down to begin the 45-degree course correction between Asiyan and Kandili Point. That, Karabeg knew, would give him the perfect opportunity to get a few good shots in before her skipper could swing the helm around Kandili Point and disappear towards the Sea of Marmara.

Karabeg leaned back in his chair and relaxed, watching the morning light across the city turn slowly from the waspish, insubstantial thing that came with the dawn, towards the harsh, solid glare that it would be by afternoon. He drained the last of his coffee and carefully peeled another fig, rolling it piece by piece around his mouth until the flesh was almost all juice. Every so often, he checked his watch, counting down the minutes until the ship's arrival. With five minutes to go he picked up his camera, double checked the battery life and took a few practice shots of the many small boats now plying their morning trade up and down the strait, and of the cityscape on the opposite shore.

And then there she was, grey and sombre as the waters sparkled around her. Amid all the colours and noises of the waking city, she was a dark, silent bullet cruising slowly through its heart. She seemed to be coming straight at him, her prow a finger of denunciation at the sight of his raised camera. Karabeg clicked the shutter, a dozen times perhaps, and then more as, slowing almost to a halt, the *Istanbul* turned hard to starboard, broadside on to him now in grey silhouette. He followed her, clicking intently, until, with what might have been a last wiggle of her tail, she passed behind the headland and was gone. Karabeg placed his camera down on the table and checked his watch. He had no sense of the passage of time from the ship's appearance to this moment. It might have been an hour, but his watch told him it had been less than five minutes. Such anticipation for such a brief reward. Was it worth it? No question. No point even asking. The thrill of that moment of first sight, the glory of the view, the slow, majestic passage of this great ship of war through the heart of a peaceful city; it was unbeatable. He would still be living off the thrill come the evening, only then looking forward to the opportunities the night, and the next morning, might bring.

He flicked open the catch on the side of his camera and ejected the memory card, slipping it into a USB adapter already plugged into his laptop. As the images uploaded he thought again, as he did almost every day, how much he wished he had found this flat at the beginning instead of spending months cycling up and down the shores of the Bosphorus looking for the best spot. Still, it had been fun in its own way. They had been a small band, all competing to find the ideal vantage point, the most dramatic photographs. That had been their happy time, the first years of the conflict in Syria when it seemed half the Russian Black Sea fleet had transited through the Bosphorus each week on their way to Mediterranean patrol. Then one of their number, Yoruk, had lucked out, capturing the moment when one Russian warship had passed through the centre of Istanbul with a marine standing on deck, a missile launcher balanced on his shoulder aimed at the heart of the city. It had been a perfect shot, the marine clearly outlined against the background of the minarets of ancient Istanbul. Practically every newspaper and TV station in the world had featured it. The Turks had just shot down a Russian fighter jet which, they claimed, had strayed into Turkish airspace. Yoruk's picture of this gesture of Russian defiance had captured the imagination of the world and, for a few brief weeks, that little band of friends, the ship spotters of Istanbul, had become headline news across the world.

The media attention had been a bit too much, and Altan Karabeg was not alone in being glad it was over. He had found his flat, his vantage point, just too late for this burst of activity, but he had no regrets. There was still plenty to be seen.

The upload complete, Karabeg went back to the forum and posted a selection of low-resolution images. Then he closed down his laptop and stowed it away in a canvas shoulder bag next to his front door. He spent a few minutes clearing away his breakfast things, then swapped his woollen cardigan for a zip-up suede jacket, stuck a pair of shades into the top of his shirt and headed for the door.

He was spotted as he came out of the street door less than three minutes later, slipping the shades on to shield his eyes from the glare of the low morning sun. The relaxed, tough-looking man in the mirrored sunglasses idling at the wheel of his car raised a phone to his ear and spoke calmly.

'He is on his way. Looks like he's got the laptop in a bag over his shoulder.'

'Understood. Stand by,' said the voice at the other end of the line.

The man put his phone back down on the passenger seat beside him and waited.

* * *

For the past month Altan Karabeg had been on a contract job for a small media company on the Asian side of Istanbul. They were relaxed about their working hours and it was only a short tram ride from his home, so he had ample time to enjoy his balcony at the beginning and end of the day. Sometimes, it was true, he would meet up with friends for a drink after work, but he much preferred those evenings when he could be home by about five-thirty and enjoy the last hours of the day watching the traffic along the Bosphorus before the sun sank down behind the rooftops of the west. Those sunsets could sometimes be as enjoyable as watching the boats, but he had never quite mastered the art of photographing them.

His was a life of routine, to be amended only when the arrival of something special in the waters demanded a change of schedule. Timings were of little importance to him as long as the order of things remained unchanged. Each day he would rise, wash, dress, breakfast on the balcony, upload his morning's work to the forum and then tidy the flat before leaving. He hated to come home to dirt and disorder. Leaving the flat he would head to the same tram stop, headphones in his ears, checking the latest news on his phone. His surroundings, known instinctively but unconsciously, made no impression on him. It would be hard to think of anyone easier to follow than Altan Karabeg.

That was certainly the thought shared by the man and the girl on the motorcycle parked across the road from the tram stop. Karabeg didn't notice them when he arrived at the stop, nor did he look up from his phone while waiting, until the tram approached and blocked them from view. They saw him climb aboard and then pulled slowly out into traffic as they followed the tram down the hill, slowly weaving between the cars. They were in no hurry; a young couple in jeans and dark jackets enjoying a city ride in the morning sun. That particular morning, Altan Karabeg was one of many Istanbul commuters distracted by the news that the body of a young woman had been pulled from the waters of Fenerbahçe Marina. According to a brief statement by the local police, the woman appeared not to have drowned and her body had been in the water for some time. Unlike his fellow tram passengers, however, Karabeg's years of observing the varied currents of the Bosphorus had given him a fair chance of estimating where the woman's body had entered the water, and how long it might have stayed there before floating up among the yachts. It only took a few minutes of pondering the question for him to conclude that it could well have happened fairly close to where the water was overlooked by his own balcony.

Within ten minutes of Karabeg boarding the tram, his apartment block was the centre of chaotic scenes. A van full of officials and workmen from the Istanbul Gas Company had arrived and informed the building manager that a serious leak had been reported. The building would have to be evacuated while the matter was investigated. If the apologies were a little abrupt, that was only to be expected in the circumstances. And it seemed of little importance that the senior official, rather than arriving in the van with the rest of his men, had emerged from a car already parked across the street, slipping a pair of mirrored sunglasses into his breast pocket before composing his face into an expression of compassionate seriousness. The building manager wasted no time. He led the gas men from floor to floor, knocking on doors to rouse the inhabitants and using his pass keys to admit them to apartments that failed to reply. Within fifteen minutes a group of twenty people were huddled together on the pavement outside, while two of the junior officials from the Gas Company quizzed them about any unusual smells, and the age and condition of their domestic appliances. They were soon joined, to the confusion of all, by several curious bystanders.

Mercifully, it was all over very quickly after that. The senior official emerged from the building, with the rest of his men in tow. He told a relieved building manager that the readings they had taken were reassuring and that only normal trace amounts of gas had been detected. All residents were free to return to their apartments, but he recommended that windows should be left open for the remainder of the day and that everyone should remain alert for unusual smells, which should be reported at once to the number on the card he handed over. With more apologies for the inconvenience – which were instantly dismissed in the relief of the moment – they were gone. Some irritated, some just bewildered, the residents trooped back into the building leaving only the building manager on the street outside. He shook his head and slipped the card into his pocket. In the urgency of the situation it had barely registered on his mind that the official from the Gas Company had spoken Turkish with something of a foreign accent, and that the majority of his men had been of too pale a complexion to be local. But then, Istanbul was full of foreigners these days, and always had been. Syrians, Armenians, Russians, Levantines, Jews, they all came and went. Even Atatürk had been of mixed blood. What should it matter to him?

Nevertheless, he did notice that while the rest of the men drove away in their van, the senior official was sitting in a smart Mercedes coupé parked across the street, talking into his mobile phone. It was fortunate for him that he did not hear the official report the taking of two hard drives, several memory sticks and other sundry items of electronic equipment, or acknowledge the report from another team of the capture of a laptop.

It had happened within two minutes of Karabeg stepping off the tram. As it pulled away the music in his headphones had obscured the sound of the motorcycle accelerating towards him. Only at the last moment had a sudden movement among his fellow pedestrians, a woman's eyes staring over his shoulder as she lurched away from the edge of the pavement, a shrill nearby scream, alerted him to danger. He was halfway through a turn to the left when he felt the strap of his shoulder bag come away from his body, a sudden flash of pain as the knife slashed through the strap, nicking his upper arm on the way. Then he was alone, standing on the pavement watching the girl's dark hair flowing out from beneath her helmet as she placed his bag carefully between her body and that of the rider.

CHAPTER THREE

BIRDCAGE WALK

In London, spring seemed to have taken a single, furtive glance at the future and decided it would be better off reverting to the safety of youth, when it had only just grown beyond the infancy of winter. Those heady, sunny days of February, when all the city discarded its winter layers and rushed as one to the parks and heathlands that interrupted its endless suburbs, were a distant and perhaps unreliable memory. Now, as April turned to May, the mercury remained stubbornly stuck around eleven degrees Celsius and bitter easterly winds cut through a despairing population and had them digging into forgotten cupboards for the hats, scarves and gloves they had so wantonly put away weeks before.

The strollers in Green Park tucked their chins into their collars and hunched their shoulders in protection from the wind. A party of Italian teenagers, hushed in unaccustomed silence, huddled together for warmth. Half a dozen young Australians equipped with only shorts and flip-flops shared the sudden, horrible realisation of why their ancestors had fled to southern climes. If they had made their planned pilgrimage to Lord's or the Oval that day, they would have found cricketers clad in multiple sweaters, hands stuffed deep in their pockets and with only two hopes between them: that the ball might come nowhere near them and that rain or bad light would soon have them back in the blessed warmth of the pavilion.

Two middle-aged men walking side-by-side nearby offered a further case in point. Both had retained their heavy, and notably well-cut, winter overcoats and topped them with cashmere scarves in sober shades of grey. Both wore expensive-looking leather gloves and while the shorter man was bare-headed (and lucky enough that his ample dark locks offered sufficient insulation for his head), the taller wore a black bowler hat and carried a neatly-furled umbrella in expectation of more of the icy rain that had plagued the city in recent days. An uncharitable observer might have found in the pair a hint of Laurel and Hardy, although there was little comedy to be seen in them. It was merely that there was a good eight inches' difference in height, that the shorter man was slightly built and the taller boasted a midriff of quite admirable girth.

Closer observation might have revealed that the taller man, while heavy about the middle, walked with a curious lightness of step; his long, slender legs - at odds with the bulk of his upper body - moving elegantly, his feet placed with a precision that would not have disgraced a ballet dancer. Only the more practised eye could have spotted that the large midriff was as solid as the basketball it resembled, or guessed how many knuckles had been bruised against it in the past.

While everyone else in the park was evidently in a hurry to be somewhere else, preferably somewhere with four good walls and an efficient heating system, the two men were ambling along without any apparent destination in mind or any sense of urgency. They had greeted each other on Birdcage Walk with no more than a nod, and strolled off towards the Palace, before rounding the Victoria Memorial and heading across the park in the direction of the Bomber Command Memorial at the far end of Piccadilly.

Although it was just possible that the pair were old school friends catching up (and there could be no doubt what sort of school it had been), there was little sign of either man enjoying the other's company. And yet, if this were not a social stroll then what else could it be? It was decidedly odd weather to be discussing business out in the open air, even if one wanted to avoid prying eyes and ears. Perhaps the answer might lie behind the wheel of the large, black Jaguar with the mirrored windows that had dropped the shorter man outside the Guards' Museum; the same black Jaguar that was now parked illegally, and without official interference, on Constitution Hill.

The car was the official vehicle assigned to Sir Richard Graves, K.C.M.G. Sir Richard's name was not widely known beyond the more discreet corridors of Whitehall, since the Secret Intelligence Service, or MI6, had, in a climate of ever more diverse threats to national security, decided to reverse its recent policy of greater openness. But within those discreet corridors Sir Richard was the safe pair of hands who for more than four years now had occupied the post known traditionally as 'C'; the Head of SIS.

Sir Richard's career had progressed along conventional lines: Oundle School, Brasenose College, Whitehall. He had never been a field agent but he was an SIS man to his core, with all the experience that a quarter of a century in the service had brought him. His companion that day had followed a far less predictable trajectory to his current position, and the preconceptions about his background that might have arisen from his appearance, or the company he kept, would have been very wide of the mark indeed.

From a minor Grammar School in mid-Wales, he had joined the Royal Air Force at the age of eighteen, without bothering to acquire a university education. An excellent record of service in the first Gulf War, and in other theatres, had seen him rise to the rank of Wing Commander before, to everyone's great surprise, he had resigned his commission and entered the City, where his military connections had served him rather better than his school affiliation.

For the past five years Wing Commander Alun Rhys Owen had been the Chairman, and sole Director, of one of the oldest and most exclusive private banks in London. Willoughby & Co. had a history stretching back to the seventeenth century; they had made their name with perfectly-timed trading around the south sea bubble, before losing it in the twentieth century in the years that followed the Wall Street Crash. That disaster had cost them their place in the heart of the City, from where they had moved to more discreet premises in Mayfair. Ever since, City gossip had held that Willoughby's was a shadow bank; no longer a living entity but an empty shell propped up by the loyalty of a decaying establishment. It was not so far from the truth. Since the late 1930s, Willoughby's principal activity had been as cover for one of the most secretive branches of Britain's security establishment. Its staff had been carrying out operations on foreign territory and at home ever since.

Sir Richard had not called this meeting in the interests of fresh air and exercise; it was simply that he found meetings with the Director to be generally uncongenial and best conducted away from the prying ears of colleagues, and that for security reasons neither man was permitted to be seen entering the other's lair. So neutral territory it had to be, and far better in the open air than in one of the West End clubs or restaurants where the staff, usually foreign these days, were entirely unvetted. That, at least, was Sir Richard's current attitude. To the Director's despair he seemed to flip-flop between the two with little warning. They were halfway down Birdcage Walk before Sir Richard broke the uneasy silence.

'I wanted to see you in person, Director, to ask for your help with a rather sticky problem.'

The Director smiled. If it were not for the world's sticky problems he would be out of a job.

'Go on.'

'How much do you know about human trafficking?'

'Not much. It isn't something that my department gets involved in as a rule. More of a Home Office matter, I should say.'

'On the face of it, yes. But the criminal networks involved in that trade operate worldwide, well beyond the remit of the Home Office and our friends across the river. And we have to acknowledge that as long as undocumented migrants are landing on our shores and evading our border controls, the criminal and terrorist networks of the world are bound to take advantage of the fact. Among all those thousands who arrived across the Channel last year, we identified nineteen who had previously come to the attention of ourselves or allied agencies, and no doubt there were many more among those whose identities could not be confirmed.'

'I concede the security aspect of course, but surely this is an issue that requires a political solution. You can't expect the intelligence services to solve it.'

'The politicians don't dare touch it. For a start, they probably worry about alienating half the electorate as soon as they open their mouths on the subject. Then, to be fair to our political masters, the problem itself is almost intractable.' He looked up for a reaction but there was no expression on the Director's face. 'Take, for example, a boat-load of migrants arriving on the coast of Kent. Even if they're picked up by Border Force, the traffickers will have made sure they know at least one word of English: "asylum". Now as soon as anyone lodges an asylum claim it has to be investigated properly. That takes time. Then there's an appeals process; more time and a well-funded legal industry determined to prevent any removals. And even at the end of the process there are problems. Let's say our migrants from that boat are refused asylum on the basis that they should have lodged a claim in the first safe third country they passed through. The boat came from France, we all know that, and France is a safe country. But how do we *prove* it came from France? There's no documentation, the boat isn't registered anywhere, so the French won't accept it. Let's say for argument's sake that our migrants are Albanian – roughly half of them are – and their applications are turned down because there's no war going on in Albania, nor any persecution. But how do we *prove* they're Albanian? Their passports - if they ever had any – are at the bottom of the Channel. All right, they speak Albanian, but they might be from Kosovo, or parts of northern Greece or half a dozen other parts of the Balkans. *Where's the proof these are our citizens?* asks the Albanian government, quite legitimately. So, we end up with a massive bureaucracy geared towards an end it can't possibly achieve. Faced with that, what can the politicians do? They make a few bullish speeches to please the readers of the *Daily Mail*, come up with the odd radical but completely unworkable project – like that Rwandan nonsense – and hope the issue stays out of the media. No, there's only one way to deal with the problem. At its source.'

'You mean in the countries of origin?'

'Good heavens no, that would be an even more difficult problem to solve. No, I mean by tracking down and dealing with the criminal gangs who control the traffic in human beings, who make fortunes out of the suffering of others and help to jeopardise our national security at the same time.'

The Director nodded and Sir Richard felt a small surge of relief. He was beginning to get through. It was time to take the personal approach.

'Of course it's not just about security,' Sir Richard continued, 'the problem is also a humanitarian one. The people who are being brought here, they dream of a bright new future for themselves, but end up little more than slaves. The poor devils are left to paddle across the channel in dinghies I wouldn't trust on the boating lake in Hyde Park, or they're crammed into shipping containers with no sanitation and barely enough food and water to last them through the voyage. And when they do get here, what's waiting for them? Indentured labour as domestic servants, agricultural work on much the same terms, the sex trade. The Albanians now control cocaine traffic in this country and many of their newly-arrived fellow countrymen are forced into working as couriers or low-level dealers. Only the other week a nice young woman from the Home Office came to HQ to give us a briefing on this; she said that they simply have no reliable estimates on the number of victims of human trafficking or modern slavery in the United Kingdom today. In the last calendar year, well over ten thousand suspected victims were referred to the care services, and that figure was likely to be the tip of a much larger iceberg. It's a scandal, really.' He looked upwards cautiously, into the Director's stern, unflinching gaze. 'Well, that's only my opinion, of course. You may think differently.'

'Scandal,' said the Director dismissively. In his opinion the word clearly didn't do the subject any kind of justice. 'If you ask me, it's the modern face of imperialism.'

I suppose I did ask for this, mused Sir Richard silently as he braced himself for the explanation. None came. He waited for what seemed an age as the two men trudged along side-by-side in cold silence. When at last the Director spoke again, he still offered no explanation for his remark.

'Look, Sir Richard, if you want my sympathy for the poor exploited masses, you have it. If you want my understanding of the implications for national security, you have that too. But I'm not sure why you think it should be my job to do something about it, because that is what we're talking about, isn't it?'

Sir Richard offered the only answer he could. He reached into his coat and brought out a small manila envelope. Inside was a series of photographs, their heavy pixilation suggesting enlargement from wider originals. The Director flicked through them: a small cargo vessel sailing close to an urbanised shoreline, its registration details just about visible; a closer view of the superstructure showing two figures close together; two more views showing the same figures, seemingly exchanging blows; one last image of a sole figure leaning over the far side of the vessel.

'Just as Britain has its train spotters,' explained Sir Richard, 'so Turkey has its own class of hobbyists whose idea of fun is tracking all the shipping to pass through the Bosphorus. Mundane as it sounds, they can be quite a useful source of minor intelligence, particularly so when Russian involvement in the Syrian conflict was at its highest. So we've been monitoring their output on a little private forum for some time.' He smiled. 'I keep a small team of low-achievers on the books for just this kind of thankless task. They're inexpensive and occasionally productive. Well, a few days ago something rather curious happened. A young woman's body was washed up on the Asian side of the Marmara strait, at the southern end of the Bosphorus. Twenty-four hours later, all of the posts and images uploaded by one of these ship spotters, a young man called Altan Karabeg, suddenly disappeared from the web. Our local station found out that his apartment had been stripped clean of all electronic devices. A whole squad of men pretending to be from the gas company sealed off the entire building and went flat to flat with the concierge. At the same time our keen ship spotter himself had his laptop stolen by two young hoodlums on a motorcycle.'

'Rather an excessive amount of trouble to go to just to cover up a simple case of manslaughter on the high seas,' commented the Director.

'Indeed it was. Luckily our useful no-hopers routinely archive everything on that site, so we were able to recover these images, among others. Karabeg himself probably had higher resolution versions on his own hard drive, but these were just about good enough for us to identify the ship. She is the May Rose, Panama-registered but owned by a Georgian company. She mostly travels the Black Sea-Mediterranean route, carrying cargo out of Trabzon in north-east Turkey and Batumi in Georgia through to ports in Greece, Italy and France. On this particular voyage she was listed as departing Trabzon with a mixed cargo of textiles and foodstuffs, dried figs, that sort of thing, en-route for Marseilles. But she never reached Marseilles. She put into Piraeus reporting engine problems that required urgent repairs just a day after passing through the Bosphorus. Her cargo, whatever it really was, was taken off there.'

'What do you think they were carrying?'

'Most of it probably was t-shirts and figs, that's certainly what Greek customs recorded. But we are confident that a proportion of the cargo was human.'

'I see. You have evidence of this, I presume?'

'Circumstantial, mostly. We have analysed the movements of the May Rose and her sister ships over the last two years and found a correlation between them and incidents of newly arrived undocumented migrants picked up near ports like Marseilles and Bari. Enforcement units from Border Force have uncovered related information in interviews with illegal workers picked up in raids on various premises as well as many migrants using the Channel route. Syrians, Iraqis, Iranians, Afghans, Pakistanis, all telling similar tales of boarding cargo vessels in Turkey or Georgia, bound for the west. Our European partners also have evidence of new migration routes across the Black Sea to Constanta in Romania, which is another port served by this company's ships.'

Sir Richard saw the doubt written plainly across the Director's face. He ploughed on.

'Then there's the identity of the woman they fished out of the water in Istanbul. She was a local journalist, Elif Çalışkan. Now we both know that journalism can be a dangerous profession in Turkey these days, but this particular journalist made her reputation by exposing the people smuggling operations controlling the flow of migrants through Turkey into Greece during the early years of the Syrian conflict. So, we ask ourselves, what was Elif Çalışkan doing on board a cargo vessel out of Trabzon heading for southern Europe? Well, we know that one of the principal migration routes runs from Aleppo in northern Syria across the Turkish border to Gaziantep. There is another route into eastern Turkey from Erbil in Iraqi Kurdistan. Now, if you were to draw a triangle with Aleppo and Erbil as its base points, Trabzon would as near as damn it be at its head. The western routes to Greece from Gaziantep to Marmaris, Izmir and Cannakale are well known now, and Turkish security keeps them under close surveillance. We believe that there is a new route running out of Trabzon and depositing large numbers of migrants on European shores, and that this Georgian company - Guria Shipping & Trading - is controlling it.'

The Director allowed his eyes to wander across the park to the grand buildings lining the north side of Piccadilly, to the buses crawling up the crowded street and the pedestrians shuffling along the damp and glossy pavements; to an ordinary life that his world was extraordinarily removed from. He and Sir Richard were walking, rhythmically in step, directly towards it, but he knew they would never get there.

'How was the woman identified?' he asked.

'Like many Turkish journalists of her generation she was not unknown to the authorities. They had her fingerprints on file.'

'And who is behind this shipping company?'

'On the face of it the company seems to be a normal family business. We know it was first registered in 1992 by a Georgian businessman. He died two years ago and control of the business passed to his daughter. She has no known criminal connections, but then neither did her father. There is nothing suspicious about the ownership of the business, but ownership and control are sometimes two different things. Our analysts suggest, and I agree with them, that this could well be a case of someone else pulling the strings behind the scenes. The only way we can be sure is to put someone in play to find out.'

'By 'someone' I presume you mean one of my people.'

'Yes,' said Sir Richard, as confidently as he could, only to immediately offer a concessionary 'if, that is, you choose to accept.'

Sir Richard felt a distinct sensation of pain somewhere around the top of his chest. He could not order, he had to ask. The Director's department was nominally part of SIS, but it was operationally and financially independent. Each year, when he received his budget templates for submission to the Treasury, they came with an entry attributed to 'audit services' already filled in and greyed out. His own financial team believed this to be for some form of official scrutiny of the service's budgets, but Sir Richard knew it was not. For each of his four years in charge, he had seen the figure rise, apparently without effort and at a level frustratingly above the current inflation rate, even as he had to fight for every penny of his own operational funds. He was reminded of the fact in every conversation he had with the Director; reminded that his technical seniority meant almost nothing in terms of practical authority.

A brief, perhaps contemptuous snort came from the Director's long nose.

'Whether I accept or not,' he began, 'depends upon whether there are any reasonable alternatives. Why not use the local station in Istanbul, for example? Or even hand over the information to the Turks? They're supposed to be a NATO ally after all.'

'I am sure you're aware that relations with Turkey are not what they might be at the moment. And as for our local station, well, highly as I rate them, they are completely overstretched dealing with the situation on the Syrian border and all the other fall-out from that unholy mess of a civil war. I expect that enquiries will need to be made not just in Turkey, but also in Georgia and perhaps even Ukraine or Armenia. That's more than one station could handle even if they weren't already over-committed.'

The two men had reached the Bomber Command Memorial. They both paused for a moment in silence, before Sir Richard led the way between the classical columns of Portland stone and stood staring up at the giant sculpture of the seven-man aircrew. Behind him, the Director respectfully removed his hat.

'Do you like it?' asked Sir Richard. 'I think it's very moving. It's reassuring to know that we can still honour these men who sacrificed so much for our freedom. I come here quite often. It helps to remind me that what we do, whether tedious or stressful, is also important to the future of this country. Your grandfather was one of them, I believe.'

'Yes, he was.'

'What did he fly?'

'He was a rear gunner in a Wellington. Shot down over Bremen in '43 and spent the rest of the war in a camp. He survived, but it ruined his health. He died before I was born.'

'I'm sorry.'

The Director nodded. He held Sir Richard's gaze for a moment, then turned again to face the memorial. He stood there in silence, as though Sir Richard were no longer there and no response were required.

This is all back to front, thought the Head of the Secret Intelligence Service. *I'm supposed to be intimidating him, not the other way round.* The Director simply radiated a kind of natural authority from his person, even when silent and motionless, that Sir Richard Graves knew he himself could never achieve. He glanced irritably at his watch, waiting for the Director to say something. He was damned if he would resort to begging for an answer. Nevertheless, since he preferred to conduct his business on a human rather than geological timescale, he decided to make a final appeal.

'Well?' he asked. 'Will your department accept the job?'

The Director gave a long sigh. 'Very well, I accept. My department will handle the case providing that you can give me a defined objective and appropriate terms of engagement.'

'You'll have them. Do you have anyone free at the moment?'

'Yes I do. In fact I have someone in Georgia at this very minute.'

'You never cease to surprise me, Director. Who is it?'

'Sebastian Friend.'

'Friend?' Sir Richard's mind flew back some months to an awkward briefing in his office and a discreet conference of war weeks later at his private residence to sort out the hornet's nest young Mr Friend had stirred up as a result. 'I remember him, of course. What on earth is he doing in Georgia?'

'Trekking in the mountains, from what he told me. That and visiting an old friend.'

'It's a little early in the year for mountain walking, I would have thought.' Sir Richard mused. 'Who's this old friend of his? Do you know?'

'As it happens, I do. His old commanding officer from his army days.'

'Not the mad major?'

'The very same.'

Sir Richard gave a sharp laugh. 'Major Stephen Magniac, well well.'

There was a certain irony in Friend – a man whom even his strongest allies would admit could not be trusted to take an order – forming a lifelong bond with his old army commander.

'I think that's everything settled then. I'll have all the relevant information sent through via the usual channels. Thank you, Director.'

Sir Richard stood and waited. The Director did not move except to turn once more and face the memorial as though it held some fascination for him. Was there a resemblance in the faces of one of the airmen to his dead Grandfather? Sir Richard bristled a little at his inability to dismiss an underling from his presence. He wanted to stick it out, but he was cold and he had a warm car waiting to take him to more comfortable engagements.

'Well then,' he repeated, 'I have to be at the Foreign Office in fifteen minutes. Please keep me informed about the operation.'

Without waiting for an answer, he strode off through the colonnade and down the long, straight, empty path to where his car was waiting on Constitution Hill.

The Director watched him go, wondering which faction of government had instructed the head of SIS to direct his resources against this elusive and ill-defined target. What would success in the mission look like; would it really make any kind of difference? Perhaps only to his department, or to Sebastian Friend. Turning down work was no way to justify the department's existence; accepting an ill-conceived mission was a poor way to risk an operative's life.

He looked up again at the memorial and thought of his grandfather crashing down to earth in a flimsy silk parachute, starving and freezing in a prison camp for two years, marching, at the point of an SS rifle, two hundred kilometres in broken boots. What would he have thought of the battles being fought now? There was no front line, there were no safe spaces, no way of telling when you might see the tracer rushing up at you from the blackness below. Where before there had been nations and armies to battle against, now there was only lawlessness and anarchy. The soldier defending free people had become a policeman enforcing an ever stricter and more complicated law. And for what? Did the politicians really care about people smuggling? Did the public? Corporate interests certainly didn't and therein lay the issue, the Director mused. In the days of Empire, Britain had invaded poorer countries to exploit their resources. You couldn't get away with that these days, but it was perfectly acceptable to lure the youth of these same countries to Britain and exploit their cheap labour here, stunting the development of their homelands while depressing wages and increasing profits here. Tackling the smuggling gangs was nothing more than window-dressing. That, he reflected again, was the modern face of imperialism. He shook his head but failed to dislodge the thought. It stayed with him as he crossed Piccadilly and wandered back through Shepherd Market to his office in Mayfair.

CHAPTER FOUR

WOLF

There is a wind, far up in the High Caucasus, that is as feared and legendary in its own way as the *mistral* of southern France. It first draws breath in the distant wastes of central Siberia, before sweeping across the steppes of Kazakhstan, skirting the northern shores of the Caspian Sea and battering the wild hills of Dagestan and Ingushetia. There it meets the high peaks which guard the ancient Kingdoms of Kartli and Kakhetia, the forerunners of modern Georgia. At its worst it blows clean the caps of mounts Shani and Kazbek, sending flurries of snow down into the valleys from otherwise clear blue skies. The hardy local sheep huddle together for warmth and comfort, and even the mountain goats seek shelter from its path; to be caught exposed on a north-facing slope when it finds you means, in all probability, a slow and lonely death.

For as long as anyone can remember this wind has been known to the locals as *mglis suntqva*, or *The Wolf's Breath*, and it is when the wolf comes howling down the flanks of the mountains and rushing into the valleys below that they fear it most. For then it darts hither and thither, seeking any gulley, alleyway or street into which it might pour its icy breath. The people bar their doors and secure their windows at the first sign of its approach, but with devilish tenacity it rattles their shutters, tugs at their roofs and whistles down their chimneys, bringing clouds of freezing soot. Any gap beneath a door frame, any ill-fitting window, even an empty keyhole allows it passage and in the older houses, where drafts are a fact of life, any bit of surplus fabric or cladding is saved for those occasions when it might be needed to plug a gap and keep the wolf from the door. For those stuck inside it is a waiting time, a watching time, like submariners under bombardment from a surface vessel, waiting in silence to see which seal will break first, from where the icy stream will begin to pour in.

The wolf never breathes in summer, only in the colder months of the year, but once it starts there is no way of telling how long it will last. It might be only a few hours, but more commonly it endures for several days and some of the older locals still speak with awe of the terrible winter of 1947 when it blew for three straight weeks and several villages were entombed by the blizzards it brought in its wake. It was only with the personal intervention of Stalin himself, never normally one to take much interest in the internal affairs of his home republic, that battalions of *Komsomol* volunteers were despatched to dig out the buried houses and restore life to the upper reaches of the Teleki valley.

The wolf drew its last breath late in this particular year. It was the beginning of May, and a prolonged spell of spring-like warmth had already melted the snows beneath the treeline, exposing the mountains' green flanks and banishing the ice to the highest peaks. At first it blew gently, a mere breeze to take the edge off the warmth of the sun, but already in the villages there was the sound of shutters being slammed tight shut and a flurry of activity in the houses as people stuffed old socks and sheets wherever drafts had shown themselves in the past. Far above them, on an east-facing slope on the edge of the Tusheti National Park, Sebastian Friend felt the wolf's damp tongue gently licking the exposed skin above his shirt collar.

For an hour or more before he first felt the wind at his back, Friend had found his eyes drawn upwards to where a golden eagle seemed to be tracking him, drawing wide, lazy circles in the clear blue sky. Friend was four days out of Omalo and heading north-west towards Khevsureti. His original intention had been to take in some low-level walking in the forests between Omalo and the Babaneuri State Reserve to the south, beyond which lay the Telavi vineyards and the soft, rolling country toward Tbilisi. Nevertheless, he had decided to stuff his crampons and winter clothing into the bottom of his rucksack and, later, when some whim had drawn him north towards the mountains, he had done little to resist. It was a weakness of his, he knew, this habit of giving in to whimsy, of surrendering to his instincts. It had a way of getting him into trouble. It had another of getting him out of it.

He was halfway up the eastern face of Chanchakhistma when the wolf breathed upon him. His legs were still aching from a run of steep ridges and gullies and he had grown hot walking in the sunshine. But the wind blew a chill through his bones and in just a few minutes all the heat of the day had dissipated. He sensed the daylight dimming and turned to look at the sky behind him. There was no sign of the eagle. It had flown off at the first breath of wind from the east; the warm thermal currents it had been floating on no match for the Siberian wolf. A curtain of grey-white cloud was sliding across the sky and already several of the peaks he had passed earlier had been swallowed up by it.

Friend dug into his rucksack and pulled out a compact hooded parka, a beanie hat and some gloves. He needed to think quickly; already he could feel wisps of icy sleet pricking his face. He had a choice of losing some altitude and finding a path lower down that would take him around the mountain, or of following the path he was already on and carrying on to the summit. It didn't take long to decide. The odds of finding his way down to the lower path in these conditions were slim. He was on the summit path already and should be able to follow it as long as visibility remained above a couple of metres or so. His mind made up, he pulled the hat down across his brow, lifted the rucksack onto his back and plodded uphill.

He was still a good fifty yards short of the summit when the cloud enveloped him. He had watched it building as he glanced up every few steps. Now, the summit was no longer visible; a white shroud cloaked the mountain and instead of the wet, unpleasant sleet he felt a storm of icy shrapnel all around him. He could feel it striking the stiff cloth of his coat, its sharp edges cutting at his legs. It swirled around in all directions, tiny shards of it somehow making their way into his hood and nipping at his face. Visibility was down to about ten yards and getting worse. He closed his mind to it all and focused on the picture he retained of the last few yards towards the summit and on the only goal that now mattered: making sure the next step was a safe one.

He must have gone twenty yards beyond the summit before the gradient told him that he had passed it. He didn't pause to consider his achievement, just ploughed on, away from the gathering blizzard. The going was tricky on this side of the mountain; a rocky slope strewn with boulders. He remembered from his map that the trail led away to the left, in a south-westerly direction, and that if he missed it there would be a treacherous drop awaiting him. Although sheltered from the worst of the wind Friend was still in the cloud layer. The summit was three thousand metres above sea level, so he might have to lose a lot of height before visibility improved. Larger flakes of snow were beginning to settle on the slopes, but Friend could still just make out the path. Fifteen minutes later he had lost it completely.

The mountain was now covered in a thin layer of white. Friend told himself to stay calm and tread carefully. He would just have to follow the contours of the hill and keep heading down into the valley. There should be a pass, a narrow dirt track, between two peaks before the valley floor. But by the time he crossed it this too was obscured in snow. By the time he realised he must have passed it, it was too late to go back.

Somewhere on the valley floor, Friend remembered, he would find a stream. When he reached that, he could follow it along the valley until he found shelter. He kept going downhill, the occasional stumble not disturbing him. Instinct told him his route was taking him away to the south, away from the western slope that would give him the greatest shelter from the wind. He shrugged off the thought. There was nothing he could do but follow the mountain wherever it led. And then, without warning, he found himself looking down a sheer cliff from the top of a ridge. The drop beneath him was no more than twenty metres, but quite enough to be fatal. He looked either side of him for a way down, but as he peered through the mist and the snow what met his eyes was the last thing he expected. Barely visible in the low cloud and fading light, hanging over the southern flank of the mountain where the drop to the valley floor was at its most sheer, was the low, dark shape of a shepherd's hut.

* * *

'You're lucky to be alive,' said Tamara Magniac, her dark eyes wide with amazement. 'No-one treks in those mountains much before the end of June.'

'I probably wouldn't be if I hadn't stumbled into that hut,' replied Friend. 'God alone knows how I found it. It was an almost total white-out by that stage. I'd been walking practically blind for half an hour and nearly fell on top of it. I managed to scramble down the cliff somehow and then nearly froze my fingers off trying to get a padlock off the door.'

He took a sip of wine and warmed himself with the memory.

The meaty palm of Major Stephen Magniac came down on the table with a slap.

'Captain Friend,' he said, 'I've told you before to be more concise in delivering your reports. Get to the bloody point, Laddie.'

'Yes, Major,' replied Friend, putting his wine glass down and flashing a grin at his old commanding officer. The three of them were seated around a circular table in the small, cosy dining room of Tamara's family home. In the warmer months, dinner would be eaten outside on the broad, lantern-lit terrace that commanded a view of the family vineyard and the high country beyond. But spring evenings are chilly in the foothills north-east of Telavi and here inside, amid the plain whitewashed walls with the heat from the fireplace ruddying his face, Friend could still imagine himself back on that mountainside with the blizzard raging all around him.

'Well, there wasn't much inside apart from a stove and some firewood. The back wall was stacked to the ceiling with wooden crates, so I pulled one down thinking there might be some tinned food inside if I was lucky. I was down to my last few dried figs and a bit of cheese.'

'And were you lucky?' asked Tamara.

'Not really. It was loaded with half a dozen AK-101 assault rifles and a few boxes of ammunition. The next one I tried was full of mortar shells. *Podnos*, Russian-made, like the Kalashnikovs. I looked through six crates and five of them were enough to start a small war.'

'What about the sixth?'

'Two dozen bottles of Armenian brandy. Seven-star *Ararat*. Good stuff. There's a bottle in my kit somewhere.'

'Intriguing. So, what happened next?' asked Major Magniac.

'I was stuck in that hut for two days, more or less,' Friend continued. 'Just me, my thoughts and an unlimited supply of brandy.'

'Oh, the hardship!' said Magniac.

'On the second morning it was clear and the snow was beginning to melt away. I still had some rough terrain to cross but I made it to a nearby village by midday. Typical highland place, quite large and probably thriving once, but most of the young folk had left for the city and there were just a few old families hanging on and keeping the place going. Most of the old boys seemed to end up in the local bar by lunchtime, chatting and playing cards or dice.

'That's where I ended up too, and they seemed to think me some sort of wonder, walking down from the mountain after a snowstorm that had kept them in their homes for two days. They took me to the bar and gave me bread and wine and gazed at me as if I was a human miracle. Even the women came down to have a look. Of course, they all wanted to know how I came to be there and so there we were, one Russian-speaking Englishman surrounded by a couple of dozen villagers hanging on his every word and it was just fine until we came to the part where I broke into the hut. I didn't mention anything about the weapons, just the hut itself. That was enough. The atmosphere in that bar changed like someone had just flicked a switch. I swear to you, it was as if I was a wild-west gunslinger who had just strayed into his rival's favourite saloon. People literally began to turn their backs on me.

'Well, I figured by now that I was unlikely to get a bed for the night in that village, so I had better get moving and pitch my tent somewhere else. I spent a few minutes finishing up the food and drink they had given me then lifted on my pack and made for the door. I hadn't got more than a few yards down the street when a car pulled up alongside and the local policeman got out and beckoned me over. I waited while he consulted his notebook, then he looked up at me and said in Russian "I'm told you broke into a local property a day or so ago." I couldn't believe what I was hearing. But I told him that I had simply been caught in a storm in the mountains and had taken shelter in a shepherd's hut. Yes, I had to break into it but if I hadn't done that I might have died up there. I was sorry for any damage caused and was perfectly willing to compensate the owner if he would be so kind as to put me in touch with him. He scribbled away in his notebook while I was talking, barely looking at me. Then when he'd finished writing he said "the owner's identity is not the question here. Destruction of private property, whatever the reason, is a serious offence, and I must ask you to accompany me to the nearest police station."

'Well, I didn't like the sound of that, so in my most ingratiating manner I suggested that no real harm had been done, nothing that couldn't be put right by replacing the broken padlock. Wouldn't it save us all a lot of trouble if he simply let me pay for a new one?'

'Did it work?'

'No. And as it turned out he didn't drive me to the police station either. We spent a couple of hours bumping along mountain roads in complete silence with me wondering what the hell was going on, until he finally pulled up on the main street of a much larger village on the Stepantsminda highway. He kept the engine running and said that the overnight bus to Tbilisi was due in just under an hour. I should get on it and go home. That was it. I got out of his car, grabbed my pack off the back seat and watched him drive away.'

A short bark of laughter escaped Magniac and he gave the table another slap with one meaty hand.

'Talk about being a gunslinger in an unfriendly saloon, Laddie,' he said. 'You just got run out of town by the sheriff!'

'I know. And I'm embarrassed to tell it to an old comrade. So that's why I ended up in Tbilisi a few days earlier than expected. What do you make of it?'

'What do I make of it? I think you lead a charmed life, Laddie. You always did.'

'So you've said before. But what about this hoard of guns and booze in the shepherd's hut?'

'Oh, it's always been bandit country up there. That village you stumbled into was probably the home turf of some local chief or other. In fact, now I come to think of it you remind me of something Tamara told me about a while ago. The legend of the greatest bandit who ever lived in those parts. What was his name again, darling?'

Tamara Magniac smiled affectionately at her husband. He rarely remembered the details of anything she told him.

'People called him the Khan,' she said. 'Tengiz Khan.'

* * *

The Magniacs' house was a low, broad, modern building cresting the top of a hill and commanding fine views of the surrounding land. And land it was, rather than countryside. On each side, sweeping away towards the valley floor, stood row upon row of vines. Only the winery itself, a squat concrete rectangle overlooking the north-eastern slopes, broke the symmetry of the view. Tamara loved to begin each day on the terrace outside their bedroom, her arms resting gently on the railing, breathing in the clean country air that three generations of her family had grown tall and healthy on and marvelling at the fact that this all now belonged to her. This vast - well, it seemed vast, being pretty much as far as she could see to the nearest boundary - wonderful tract of land, fertile with life and memories, was all hers. Down there was the rutted track along which she had bicycled to school, a skinny, gangly thing all knees and hair; there was the pond where she learned to swim and beside it the old tree where the remains of her childhood swing still hung from a gnarled branch by one tattered rope. At times it seemed to her that she had sprung from this land as organically as the vines that thrived upon it; having come back to it now she struggled to account for the fact that she had once contrived to leave it.

She had spent years away from this place, years in far-off countries surrounded by misery and want, knowing all the while that one day she would come back for good, never dreaming that when she did she would have an English husband in tow. No, not English, he was quite touchy on that point. British was fine, Channel Islander was better. A Channel Islander with such a funny name. She had seen the name before she saw the man; typed on the transport manifest of an aid shipment she was responsible for delivering to a group of villages in the remoter parts of southern Iraq. Major S.P. Magniac, in charge of military escort. She had got the pronunciation completely wrong when they met: Mag-nee-*ack*, she had said. No, he had corrected her gently, 'the "g" is silent.' She still remembered his half-puzzled smile when, thanks to her reasonable command of French, she had chosen the correct option for her second attempt: *Mah*-nee-ack. That, he told her much later, had been the moment when he felt the first stirrings of love. He was, like every born romantic, frequently ridiculous.

Why had he done it? How could he so easily have given up his comfortable army life, responsible for his men but not for a home and family, to come so far from his own country to a land he didn't know, a language he didn't understand and a life he must barely have been able to imagine? She had always thought it would be she who made the sacrifice; that she would end up tucked away in some bland house on a soulless estate somewhere, surrounded by other army wives. She had toyed with the idea that whenever Stephen had an overseas posting the agency might find a place for her with her some aid mission nearby, but she knew at heart that this would never work. Her commitment would need to be to her own job, not his, and the last thing he would need would be the additional worry of knowing she was in a war zone too, and he powerless to help. And so she had raised the subject with him one evening and was astounded when he at once declared that he would resign his commission and come and live with her wherever she wanted to be. Still more astounded when she had spoken with her parents and heard them say that they had been thinking of retiring for some time, had even found a nice little house in a quiet part of Tbilisi, and would she consider coming home to take over the winery?

It had taken a little time for Stephen to sort things out with the Army. Resigning his commission had involved giving a year's notice and then there had been the question of his automatic transfer to the reserve. This would have lasted for another six years and might well have seen him being called up for service for weeks at a time. When Stephen had pointed out to them that this was hardly compatible with his desire to begin a new life on a vineyard in the Caucasus they had just shrugged. Not our problem, they said. If it's worth it, you can wait for it. And so, reluctantly, they had prepared to wait. But then, quite unexpectedly, a bargain had been offered. A quick way out: immediate release, and while service on the reserve list would remain at six years, he would only have to commit to one week's 'training' per year. There was, however, one condition. A condition it had taken them some time to accept.

That had been almost six years ago. Stephen must have only a few months left on the reserve list, and that training week he had been on two months ago must have been his last. The short separations hadn't been too bad for her. They had managed to arrange them for winter, when the vines needed little attention and there wasn't much work to do outside of bottling and distribution. Most times she had shut up shop completely and gone to spend the week in Tbilisi with her parents. Then, when he flew back in to Tbilisi, they would all meet him at the airport and a full-scale family celebration would ensue, as though the prodigal son had been lost to them for years rather than away for a glorified week-long adventure break. Nothing made her happier than those times when she could see that Stephen was not just her loving husband, but a loving and beloved member of her family.

But in one respect Stephen had never left the army behind. Tamara knew nothing about Sebastian Friend except that he was an old comrade. They turned up from time to time; tough-looking, hard-drinking chaps who preferred Stephen's whisky to her family's wine and spent the evenings laughing about the same old stories or getting maudlin and depressed about the fate of former comrades who hadn't fared so well. She didn't mind. Stephen had given up so much to come and live with her here on her little patch of Caucasian paradise, the least she could do was accommodate his family and friends. She had grown quite fond of some of them. Especially those who volunteered to help at harvest time.

Friend was not of the usual type. He neither looked tough nor drank hard. He was average sized, neat and well-groomed with hair and clothing that seemed undisturbed by hours in a stifling car jolting along bumpy roads. He had a broad, charming smile that might have been issued with his uniform. Tamara found it easy to laugh with them as they talked about old times and just as pleased as Stephen was to hear what his men had felt for him, that they had loved him then as she did now. Watching the two men talk she was struck again by how unexpected her love was. Everything she had thought as a girl about love, about the man she should be with, was contradicted by her husband and represented by Friend. The latter was slim, neat, polite, deliberate in word and action; the former large, wild, demonstrative, prone to outbursts of passionate opinion and verbal rage, and to overindulgence on days like these where old love and new came together like a collision of stars. Yet for all this she loved him. Even in his ramblings and rantings when she scolded him and saw him off to bed on the living room sofa only to hear his cavernous snoring vibrating through the fabric of the house for hours through the night. And then in the morning when he came to her sore-headed and sorry and folded her in his arms and pressed her to his grape-soaked skin, then she loved him most of all. Tonight, she knew, would be just such a time, and as always her anger would be no more than theatre, a part she played in a shared game that they both enjoyed.

* * *

Friend said: 'Tell me about the Khan.'

Tamara thought quietly for a moment. It had been many years since she had heard anything of the Khan. When she had been a little girl, he had been the bogeyman that mothers would threaten their children with if they misbehaved. There had been stories of him shared by all generations, stories of great crime and wrongdoing, but with a kind of heroism too. The stories had been told all over Georgia, but to the people living north of the Alazani river they were more personal, for they had the clear air of the hills within them and they told of deeds as grand as the mountains of Tusheti and Khevsureti. Legends of course, and like all legends obscured by mist and misapprehension, each tale with its own variety numbering dozens in the telling. But they were legends of her own past and her own people, and improbable as they might seem when told around a well-laid dining table among civilised company, each time she looked north and east to the great peaks and passes that guarded the border with Chechnya and Dagestan she knew them in her heart to be true. Which is how she began to tell it.

CHAPTER FIVE

LEGEND

'I suppose all legends,' Tamara said, 'are built upon a core of truth. So, if Tengiz Khan is the greatest legend in these parts, he may also be the greatest truth. If there is truth in his story it is the truth of the highlands. You cannot imagine more remote places anywhere in European civilisation. Up in Khevsureti they were still worshipping at pagan shrines when the Russians arrived in the eighteenth century, and these are the places where our civilisation has retreated to when invaders came. Every time a wave of invasion has passed through between Asia and Europe, in either direction, they have come through Georgia. Alexander the Great on his way to India, Pompey and Ghenghis Khan, then later waves of Mongols like Tamerlane. All our history is a tale of being trapped between Byzantines or Turks to the south-west, Persians to the south-east and Mongols or Russians to the north. All of them have used Georgia as a stepping-stone to get to their enemies and each of our leaders has had to strike a balance between upsetting any or all of them at one time or another. We have seen our cities razed to the ground, our civilisation and culture burned to ashes, our populations deported, forcibly converted to Islam, or exterminated, our kingdoms splintered into rival principalities, our very existence pushed to the brink of extinction time and time again. Through all those times the highlands have been our refuge, the last redoubt of our culture, a symbol of our freedom and the wildest and most essential part of ourselves.

'This has been as true in the last hundred years as it was in any other. When the communists took over it was a mixture of royalist freedom fighters and bandits who led the resistance. There was Prince Choloqashvili - people called him *Kakutsa* - who led the Band of Sworn Men, and another man called Laskarashvili who joined up with the Khevsureti highlanders and held out against Stalin's men for years. These men became folk heroes. And then after communism ended the same thing happened; we were on the brink of civil war, ambitious men with private armies tried to carve out power for themselves. They gave themselves all sorts of fine names: the White Eagles, the White Legion, the Forest Brothers, but in reality they were just bandits proclaiming some sort of bogus political agenda. They were horrible people and it was a horrible, insecure time to be Georgian. But if one of these bandits stood above the rest it was the Khan. I don't mean to say he was necessarily more successful or notorious than the rest, but there was a sort of mitigating humour, a sense of mischief about the stories surrounding him that the others never had. And there was also the fact that no-one seemed ever to have seen him or to know who he really was. The mystery added romance to his tale.

'Most of the other warlords were public figures to some degree, a couple even served in Shevardnadze's cabinet for a while, until he got tired of their antics and threw them in jail. But with the Khan there were only ever legends. Everybody seems to have agreed that his first name was Tengiz, which is a fine old Georgian name very probably derived from Ghengis, but nobody could ever say what his family name was. I did hear it said that he was the son of a good Tbilisi family who had rebelled against his parents and run off to join the bandits in the hills, but others claimed he was some sort of primeval hill-god, come down from the high passes to torment the peoples of the valleys and cities, a vengeance brought upon us by God, or the Russians.

'It was known that the Khan controlled the highlands of Khevsureti and Tusheti just as Kakutsa had done in the 1920s; that he was the cleverest smuggler, the most daring bandit, the most beloved leader of his men and that he looked after the peoples of the highlands as no government in this country has ever done.'

'Something of a Robin Hood figure then?' put in Magniac.

'Very much like that,' continued Tamara. 'But can you imagine a Robin Hood existing in England in the 1990s? Of course not. This is a purely Georgian story. In many respects he was like the other bandits. At the time there were lots of Russian and western businessmen in the country, trying to carve up its assets just as they did in Yeltsin's Russia. Sometimes these men would find themselves held up by local police, who would kidnap them and sell them on to one of the bandit groups for ransom. Some of these people were never seen again, but a handful came back after the ransom was paid telling stories of a kingdom in the clouds, where they were treated as honoured guests and assured that no harm would come to them. Everything said about the Khan was on the grand scale. It was even thought that he was behind the theft of the great icon of Davit the Builder in London. Perhaps you heard about it?'

Friend and Magniac shook their heads.

'The icon was an eleventh century painting in oil on wood of our most famous King, Davit IV, a companion to the fresco in Gelati monastery. It went missing from a palace in Imeretia, in the west of our country, sometime in the eighteenth century, only to turn up again in St Petersburg in a private collection just before the First World War. Nothing more was heard of it until twenty years ago when it was put up for sale at an auction house in London. There was a big outcry here, everybody thought it was a Georgian national treasure and should be returned, but of course none of our museums could afford it. About a week before the sale one of the major American museums arranged for their conservators to conduct an assessment of the icon's condition. They arrived on the day agreed, bearing all the right credentials, inspected the icon and left. It was only a couple of hours later, when the real conservators turned up having been delayed at the airport, that the auction house realised that the previous pair had been imposters and the icon was missing.'

'What happened to the icon?' asked Friend. 'Did it ever turn up?'

'It's never been since again since that day. But of course, everyone In Georgia believes it was the Khan who took it; it was so much in his style, the sheer audacity of it. Even down to the bogus tip-off that got the real conservators held up in customs. So even though no-one has seen the icon for twenty years, we all believe it has been returned to Georgia, and feel proud.'

'It sounds like you admire him,' said Friend.

'In a way I do. Yes, I know he was a criminal, but he did everything with style, with panache. Perhaps there is still something in us Georgians that leads us to admire the wild romance of the hills, the bandit even.' She stifled a giggle. 'Perhaps that's why I fell in love with Stephen.'

'Steady!' cautioned her husband, raising a warning finger.

'But he was still a criminal,' said Friend. 'So for all the panache there must have been a darker side too.'

'Oh yes. He was ruthless with his enemies. Even the other warlords were scared of him and tried to stay out of his business. One tried to take over some of his smuggling routes; he disappeared and was never seen again. Then there was the new Chief of Police. This was not long after the theft of the icon, I suppose. Things were getting more stable politically and most of the private armies were disbanded. Lots of foreign aid was coming in for reconstruction and there was more money to be made out of working with the NGO's than by fleecing carpet-baggers from Moscow. This ambitious new Chief of Police was appointed, saying he was going to crack down on banditry and lawlessness once and for all. The whole of the country would come under Tbilisi's writ and there would be law and order everywhere. He put a special task force together and started going after the money, finding out how the Khan's riches were held, laundered or distributed. Then one night his wife went out to the opera leaving him at home working. By the time she got back he had disappeared completely. It was ten years before they found him, high up in the Khevsureti mountains one spring where the melting ice had left him at the bottom of a crevasse. He was still in his pyjamas.'

'So, the Khan was a kidnapper, art thief, smuggler, what sort of things did he smuggle?'

'Oh, pretty much everything, Turkish weapons into Chechnya, Armenian brandy and Russian vodka into Iran, cigarettes, forbidden literature, not drugs though, so people said. Or perhaps they were just being kind to the legend.'

'A fascinating character. What happened to him? I take it he isn't around any more.'

'Well, I don't know. Nothing has been heard of him for some years now. Some say he died fighting the Russians during the war, some say he retired to Switzerland to live off his ill-gotten gains…' She gave a shrug. 'Well, nobody really knows what became of him. But I do know that there is a strongly held belief in the highlands that one day the Khan will return and bring glory to his people.'

'Robin Hood and King Arthur all rolled into one,' said Friend.

'All right, laugh if you must at our Georgian folklore. But if you're not going to take it seriously perhaps you can tell me something interesting instead of boring me with your army tales. How about it? Come on Sebastian, what can you tell me about my husband that I ought to know? Why do they call him 'The Mad Major' for a start?'

'So, you know about that, then?' said Magniac in feigned surprise.

'Of course, my darling. I know more about you than you perhaps realise about yourself. But I don't always know the "why". Perhaps Sebastian can enlighten me?'

'Well, I can try. For a start there's his name.'

'Oh, I understand that already,' Tamara broke in. 'His pet joke, *the G is silent*, so Magniac becomes Maniac. But there must be something else, surely.'

'As a matter of fact, you're probably right,' Friend went on. 'In fact, I'm not altogether sure that the joke wasn't his response to the nickname. I think he had already been dubbed The Mad Major before I met him.'

'So, you don't know why?'

'I can probably guess. If anything, I suspect it's because he has spent much of his life defending a country that he has spent an equal amount of his life criticising, and generally pretty much can't stand.'

'Now, Laddie, I'm not sure that's entirely fair,' boomed Magniac. 'I love my native islands, even the biggest one. I love their landscapes and history, their wildlife, the seas all around them and many of the people who live there. But I loathe much of what its modern culture has become, the consumerism, the vulgarity of its mass entertainment, the smugness of its urban elites, the incompetence of its politicians and, most of all, I hate London. That city is a place where all the things that would have caused outrage fifty years ago are now somehow cited as its greatest virtues: the overcrowding, the fractured transport system, the lack of any feeling of community; you never know who your neighbours are and before you get a chance to try they've moved out and someone else is in. Then there's the litter, the lack of common courtesy – probably the result of people from a hundred different cultures being crowded together without any shared code for how to live together – and the constant undercurrent of petty crime and violence. All this is somehow cited as evidence of its wonderful vibrancy. You know what vibrancy means? It means you can't open your front door without breathing in a fog of marijuana and you've got a significant chance of getting stabbed on your way home from the pub. And if that gives you a thrill, you're welcome to it. And another thing…'

Friend slowly turned his head until his eyes met Tamara's. When they did, his own widened as if to say *well, I think I proved my point.* Tamara burst into a fit of laughter which brought her husband's monologue to a sudden halt.

'Well, anyway,' he said, raising his glass, 'God save the King!'

'That's all right, my love,' said Tamara, 'we won't make fun of you any more. Perhaps we should turn our attention to our guest. Just who is Sebastian Friend? Can you tell me?'

His eyes holding Friend's, Magniac took a long draught from his glass.

'Captain Friend was a good soldier, but in all honesty I could never work out what he was doing in the army. Seb has many gifts. He picks up languages like other men pick up dirt on their shoes. While the other lads were fiddling about trying to find live football on the internet he would be speaking to the interpreters trying to improve his Arabic or Pashtun. A man like that would normally be shunned by his comrades, seen as stand-offish. Joining in is everything in army life. But Sebastian is a kind of social chameleon; he could be just as happy chatting with the men about sport or discussing classical music and politics with a group of journalists. People like him because he listens. He remembers where they're from, asks about their relatives and remembers their names. I don't know whether he's just a good actor or he really can be whatever people need him to be. Either way his men loved him, would have run through brick walls for him. I could talk about bravery too, I could tell you a thing or two about him on that score, only I suspect he wouldn't want me to.'

'Interesting,' said Tamara. 'So why did you join the army, Sebastian?'

'It was cheaper than university.'

'That's quite an evasive answer.'

'Being evasive can be a useful talent when there are bombs and bullets flying around.'

'No bullets here, Sebastian. No bombs.'

'True, although the amount of alcohol on the table is potentially explosive.'

'All right,' Tamara laughed. 'I can see I'm not going to get any further with this line of questioning. Change of tack. Why did you *leave* the army?'

'I didn't leave the army. The army left me.'

'I'm sorry, I don't follow.'

'We had a disagreement over my fitness to continue.'

Tamara felt a sudden chill and pulled her shawl a little tighter around her shoulders. She sensed Friend's awareness of the gesture.

'Are you cold?' he asked.

'No, not at all. Please continue.'

'There's nothing much to say. I got booted out, that's all.'

'But why?'

'Should have got the Victoria Cross if you ask me,' said Magniac.

'Nonsense, I didn't know what I was doing.'

'Bloody brave all the same, Laddie. Saved a lot of lives.'

'Would one of you please tell me what happened?' said Tamara.

The two friends looked at each other for a moment, until Friend gave a resigned shrug.

'All right,' he said, 'you go ahead.'

Magniac refilled their glasses before he began his tale.

'It was in Helmand, Afghanistan. Operation Herrick 11. We were supposed to be keeping the Taliban out of the larger towns like Sangin and the major agricultural areas, giving the local economy space to recover and grow. A lot of it was about winning trust; visiting the elders in local communities to find out about Taliban activity in their areas, establish what help they needed. Seb's job was in what we call HUMINT: gathering human intelligence from local elders and people like that. He was in a convoy of three armoured vehicles heading up the road to a village called Davandur. The area was supposed to be pacified; nothing had happened there for months. Maybe we let our guard down a bit. I don't know. Silly of us because by that stage the Taliban had become a bloody professional operation. They knew how to stage a proper ambush all right, and that's what happened. Seb was in the front truck, one of eight in the back with the driver and local guide up front. It drove over an improvised explosive device which detonated right under the truck. Two things to point out about this. The trucks they gave us were rubbish, any eleven-year-old with a pea-shooter could have pierced the armour, let alone some of the ordnance the Russians left behind and the stuff the CIA were supplying to the Mujahideen. Then the device itself was a nasty one, it wasn't just the blast but the shrapnel it caused. So, this thing went off and blew right through the bottom of the truck ripping everything and everyone to shreds. Of the eight in the back there were five killed outright, two badly wounded. And then there's Seb. Barely a scratch on him. He looks around, the back of the truck's been blown off, he jumps out and sees that the rear truck has been hit by an RPG, the middle one has stalled and the driver is trying to restart it but there's nowhere for him to go even if he does, the road's completely blocked by wreckage ahead and behind. Like I said, it was a bloody professional operation. Over by the roadside half a dozen Taliban are rising out of the dirt with the intention of finishing our boys off. What does Captain Friend do? He charges them. Single handed. Covered in blood, most of it other people's, his uniform hanging off him in tatters, carrying a rifle that he doesn't realise is useless because a bloody great piece of shrapnel has sheared straight through the barrel. He just turns and charges at them, screaming blue murder.

'Sometimes, in battle, surprise is the decisive factor. The Taliban ambush surprised us and they had the initiative. But as soon as Seb comes charging at them from a direction where they think everyone has been neutralised, all of that changes. They're taken by surprise, outflanked. So, what happens? One of them faces him off, but his Kalashnikov jams. Seb smashes him in the head with his rifle butt, picks up a grenade and flings it at the rest. In the heat of the moment, none of them realise he hasn't bothered to pull the pin out. They all dive for cover and by the time their heads come up again the boys from the other trucks have got themselves organised and are raining fire down on the enemy. We got everyone airlifted out an hour or so later. Home in time for tea. Except our hero here is off to hospital with severe shock and something called a non-penetrating traumatic brain injury. Blast wound from the

IED. He must have saved a couple of dozen men's lives that day, the crazy idiot. Charmed life, as I've always said. You'd better tell her the rest yourself.'

There was a distinct silence as Friend wondered how to approach the subject of an incident that for a long time had been a blank in his mind. 'The thing is' he said at last, 'I was a bit of a mess for a while. Nightmares, flashbacks, you can imagine the sort of thing. I'd get these violent panic reactions if I saw the colour red; all the blood from the boys in the truck, I suppose. They shipped me back to England, to a special hospital near Woking. Weeks and weeks of talking therapies for post-traumatic stress disorder, group sessions, cognitive behavioural stuff. None of it seemed to be getting me anywhere, so I decided to take things into my own hands. I read up on the subject and then found a specialist in London who used a method called EMDR.'

'You never mentioned that before,' commented Magniac.

Friend shrugged.

'What's EMDR?' asked Tamara.

'It's a technique that simulates the rapid eye movement experienced in sleep. It helps to bring traumatic memories to the surface in a controlled way, so you can focus on them and on how they make you feel.'

'That sounds like it could make things worse, said Magniac.

'Not at all. The funny thing is, you're in such a relaxed state when it happens, almost semi-hypnotic. You're both more connected to your memories and feelings and at the same time able to view them with detachment. It's really rather an odd experience, but it only took four or five sessions for the flashbacks to disappear completely. I remember pretty much everything about that day now, I can recall and replay the memories like any others, they don't leap out at me from the dark corners of my mind or sabotage my dreams. They don't have the power to make me feel now what I felt then. EMDR helped me control them and put them in the past.'

'So it was a complete cure?' asked Tamara.

'Pretty much.'

'But you still left the army.'

'I didn't want to. I wanted to get back to my unit, back to work, but the army insisted they would have to keep me there for another three months of the therapy that hadn't worked in the first place. They didn't take EMDR seriously or believe in the results I'd had. If I wanted to return to duty, I had to complete their course. And that wasn't all. Even when I did complete the course, I wouldn't be going back to my unit. They were going to pack me off to Regimental HQ and give me a job as a bag carrier for some General or other. Standard procedure for an officer recovering from combat stress or "moral injury", as they put it. That wasn't what I signed up for. I just wanted to carry on with my life and my life was the people I'd been serving with.' Friend halted there for some moments, as if confronting a physical obstacle to his recollections. 'I guess in the end I came to the point where I just had to get out of there and do something, even if that meant something different. I tried to argue my case with the officers in charge, but they just weren't interested. So that was it, I resigned my commission. I didn't want to do it, but it seemed the only choice left to me. That's why I say the army left me, rather than the other way around.'

Tamara turned to her husband.

'Was there nothing you could do?' she asked.

'Nothing. I was still out in Afghanistan and by the time I heard about it, it was already too late. But even if I had been in England, well, you can reason with a human being, but not with a policy.'

'So, what happened then?' Tamara asked Friend, 'what did you do?'

'I found a job. Not a great one, just working in security like lots of ex-servicemen do. And yes, I did find it difficult to adapt to civilian life, but not because of what happened in Helmand. Adjustment disorder, they called it. So, I struggled for two or three years, until my current job came along.'

'Which is?'

'I work for the Foreign Office, for their diplomatic security section. I visit embassies and consulates overseas to inspect their security arrangements, train staff on what to look out for, assess local threat levels, try to spot regional trends, that sort of thing.'

'It sounds interesting, but there must be a lot of travel involved.'

'Yes, but in a way that's what I like about it. There's a constant change of scenery, I get to see new places all the time, meet different people, try different food and drink. I'd much rather do this than be stuck in a dull office somewhere for twice the money.'

'Or be stuck running a winery for half,' said Tamara.

'Oh, I don't know. A winery sounds rather fun. I hope you'll teach me something about it while I'm here.'

'That', said Magniac, as his huge arms reached across the table, 'sounds like a good reason to open another bottle. What do we say? Red?'

* * *

The following day did not begin at an especially early hour, but Friend found it none the less pleasant for all that. He visited the traditional winery and inspected the massive *qvevri*, the giant pottery vessels buried up to their necks in the earth in which the wine matured; he toured the perimeter of his friends' land in the old Land Rover, gazed at the distant green mountains and breathed in some of the cleanest air ever to have touched his lungs. As evening drew on, he sat alone reading on the veranda until the chill night air flowed down from the mountains and spread through the valley, and then over dinner the three of them together formed many plans for the next week spent in this earthly paradise. None of them were destined to reach fruition.

CHAPTER SIX

LIGHTNING ROD

The Karacaahmet cemetery is the largest surviving burial ground in Istanbul. Since the middle of the fourteenth century it has been accommodating the dead of the city's many diverse communities, to the extent that after 700 years of operation it is estimated that well over a million corpses have been interred within its vast 750-acre plot. The cemetery's countless ancient headstones, sitting crooked and askew in the shade of tall cypress trees, continue to draw thousands of tourists each year. And Karacaahmet's tranquil beauty is also matched by its convenient location, for it is situated in Üsküdar, just a few blocks inland from the Asian shoreline and directly across the Bosphorus from the magnificence of the Topkapi Palace and Aya Sofia Mosque.

Elif Çalışkan's family was one of many in the city who retained a plot within Karacaahmet's walls. But the prestige and sanctity of its location was scant consolation to them in burying a beloved daughter, sister and friend so young. Still more worrisome was the delay between death and ceremony. Poor Elif's body had been in the water some hours before it was recovered, and even then it had been retained by the authorities for a considerable time pending formal identification, post-mortem analysis and other formalities.

Despite a century of life as a modern secular republic, the underlying influence of Islamic and pre-Islamic traditions on Turkey's people remains strong. Custom dictates that all funerary rites should be complete and the deceased buried within twenty-four hours of death. The body of a woman should be washed by her female relatives, wrapped in a clean white shroud, her arms either laid straight at her sides or crossed over her belly, and placed in an unsealed coffin. Then, after the appropriate prayers are led by an Imam, the coffin should be carried to the place of burial, whereupon the shrouded body is lifted from the coffin and laid directly in the earth. In certain circumstances the deceased may be buried inside the coffin. This was one of those occasions. The body had been driven directly from the mortuary in a government hearse, leaving the family unable to perform the customary pre-burial rites at home. All of which circumstances led to even greater distress, displayed visibly and without restraint, by parents, sisters, cousins, aunts and other members of the extended family.

Many of Elif's colleagues were also present as her body found its final resting place. Prominent among them was a tall, slender, bespectacled man wearing a drooping moustache and a centuries old baggy tweed suit. Emre Parvan had been Elif's editor at the newspaper *Fünun*, a small-circulation daily whose ten-year existence had been a constant struggle to stay on the right side of both a suspicious government and an inquisitive readership. *Fünun* was a phoenix from the ashes of two previous publications, both of which had failed to achieve the desired balance between these two demands. Even in its latest incarnation, a weary Parvan had spent more time than was ideal on the phone with bankers and advertisers or sweating inside police cells, never sure quite how temporary this latest incarceration might be.

Now he could be seen moving calmly and consolingly among the mourners, dispensing a word of comfort here, a steadying hand upon an arm there, listening with sombre attentiveness as colleagues and friends shared grief and memories with someone who had known the dead woman better than most in her final months.

All this was observed from a discreet distance by a dark-haired young man leaning against the trunk of a cypress tree. Like Parvan he was wearing spectacles, black-framed to match his hair, and behind them his eyes were dark brown and attentive. A dark grey suit and black tie helped him blend into the cypress shadow, where he seemed content to remain, making no move to join the funeral party. Only once fresh earth had been laid over the young journalist's grave and the mourners began to move away did the man step out of his shadow and begin to stride slowly up the slope towards them. Maintaining a bowed head in keeping with the situation, he offered a cautious nod to the one or two mourners who looked towards him as they passed. But no more than that. He was not here to speak with the family or friends; he made straight for Parvan, falling into stride alongside him.

'Mr Parvan? May I speak to you a moment?'

The stranger spoke in English.

'Yes, what is it?'

Parvan kept walking, not wanting to give way to this interruption.

'My name's Hunter. I'm a journalist from London, doing a story about your colleague's life and work. I wondered if I could speak with you about her.'

Hunter pulled a card from his jacket pocket and held it out. Parvan looked annoyed but grabbed the card and stole a quick glance at it before stowing it away in the ticket pocket of his tweed jacket. *Roderick Hunter, Freelance Journalist*, it said, giving only a membership number for the National Union of Journalists and a contact mobile.

'This is hardly an appropriate time.'

'No, I understand that, but I called your office this morning and they were unable to tell me whether you might be free to talk. I have limited time in Istanbul. You know how it is; if I don't file the story quickly it will be old news, no good to anyone. So if you could spare me a few minutes later today or tomorrow I would be very grateful.'

Parvan seemed to consider this for a moment before making up his mind.

'All right. Today won't be possible; I will be busy with her family for the rest of the afternoon. I agreed to help them sort some of her things out. Perhaps you could come to my office at ten thirty tomorrow morning. I have an editorial meeting first thing but should be out of it by then.'

'That would be perfect. Thank you very much Mr Parvan.'

'You're welcome, Mr Hunter.'

Hunter stopped and watched as the mourners moved off down the hill towards one of the roads which bisect the cemetery's acreage. As he watched, he saw a dark grey E-Class Mercedes, parked there as if waiting for the mourners to return, move away from the kerb and drive off, one of its windows sliding shut as it glided away. He had not seen anyone get into it.

* * *

Ninety minutes later, Sebastian Friend was sitting in a small, untidy office above a café in the middle of Istanbul's famous bazaar. The wig and glasses that helped to turn him into the journalist Roderick Hunter lay on the desk in front of him, but the tinted contact lenses remained in his eyes and formed an odd contrast with the shock of blond hair now struggling to regain its shape after its constriction beneath the wig. The office was one of many attached by a single corridor one floor above the bustling marketplace; several flights of steps ran down from the corridor leading to the back rooms of various cafés, spice merchants and carpet sellers. For an operative to disappear into the back of one shop and emerge a few minutes later from another further along the same row was the easiest thing in the world. A quick change of appearance in one of the offices would make pursuit even more difficult. All that was necessary was the co-operation of the merchants themselves, something that Friend's employers in SIS had invested the required time and money in.

'Were you followed?' asked the smartly-dressed woman seated opposite Friend.

'No. There was a Mercedes at the cemetery that probably belonged to the opposition. They may have tried to photograph me, but I doubt they got a useful shot.'

'I wouldn't worry about that too much; they'll have a pretty good idea of Mr Hunter's appearance once you've met with Parvan. Are you quite satisfied of your line of approach?'

'Yes, perfectly. One journalist to another; what could be more natural? When I spoke to him at the funeral he seemed to appreciate the probable interest in the story. My background seems well enough established and the documents are fine, so there should be no reason for him to doubt my bona fides.'

'Good. I'm sorry I couldn't be here to give you a full briefing before the funeral, but I only got in from Saudi two hours ago. I presume London filled you in on everything.'

'Yes. I understand the situation and I'm happy to help. From what they told me my remit extends through Turkey and into Georgia, but if operations should shift to any further location, I need to clear it with you first, if possible, or at least inform you if not.'

'That's correct. I will liaise with you directly in Istanbul. Your field liaison in Georgia is our honorary consul in Telavi. You can contact him through the Embassy; identify yourself as Hunter and ask for Mr Merrick.'

'Merrick? I don't think I know him.'

'Merrick is simply an identifier for the Embassy. His real name is Stephen Magniac. I hope I pronounced that correctly.'

'You did' said Friend with a smile.

'You know him?'

'We've worked together before.'

'And you'll be happy with him as your liaison?'

'I should think so. He knows the territory.'

'Good. After your interview with Parvan, we have to expect that you will be followed back to your hotel. Don't try to shake them. Just go back to your room, type up the interview notes, do whatever our Mr Hunter would naturally do. The best way for a cover to stick is to try and really live it. Far too often we place too much emphasis on tradecraft, on *technique*; nine times out of ten it's behaving like an agent that gets you exposed as one. But if you feel that the attention is getting hostile and you can't shake them, make your way here. There is a good chance of losing them in the Bazaar and the crowds may well deter them from action. I have people in every one of the shops in this row; as soon as you come in there will be more on their way to help you out.'

'I understand.'

'Have you had much experience against this kind of target?'

Friend didn't answer immediately and she saw that he was puzzled.

'I mean organised crime, as opposed to rival intelligence agencies.'

Friend gave a shrug but said nothing. Even with a senior field control, he was instinctively guarded about past missions and past history.

'Don't expect any professional courtesy from these people, whoever they are. I'm an old cold warrior Sebastian; the game was played differently in my day. Once you'd been in it a while the opposition knew who you were and you knew them too. In day-to-day matters we tried to leave each other alone as much as possible. We all understood that we had an important function to serve: we were the lightning rods. We were there to prevent any spark that could turn the cold war into a hot one. Sometimes opposing sides collided and that was too bad, but it happened less often than people think. We mostly treated each other with respect, and tried not to rock the boat if we could avoid it. Today's criminal syndicates are very different beasts. They don't answer to anyone. They're not interested in keeping a lid on international tensions, just in preserving their own business and their own prestige. If you get in their way, they won't be concerned about who might be upset to see you come home in a bodybag. Do you understand me?'

'Yes, of course. And thanks for the tip.'

Alison Holding looked into Friend's eyes.

'You needn't look at me like that. I'm not just some veteran desk jockey. I started my career with your department.'

Friend was taken aback. After a moment he said: 'I had no idea.' Another silence as he recalled the history. 'So, this was when you did the Paris job?'

Paris had made Holding's name. Barely out of university, she had lifted the Stasi files from the East German Embassy safe after spending three months on the cleaning staff.

'My first mission,' she nodded. 'The Embassy safe wasn't the actual objective. But it made for a nice bonus.'

Friend knew better than to ask what the true objective had been. Of course, she had been Alison Willey then, and had it not been for her marriage to a high official in the Foreign & Commonwealth Office and the time lost raising three children, she might even have made it to the very top. Even so, she had carved out an impressive career for herself and her current position, Senior Field Officer: Middle East, based in Riyadh and with a remit stretching from Istanbul to Tehran, from Cairo to Kuwait, was one coveted by many rivals. She had inherited it from another Service legend: Derrick Halsgrove.

'How long were you with the Department?'

'Five years. Eighteen missions, most of them successful.'

'And then you transferred back to the mainstream?'

'I had no choice. The Cold War was over and government took the view that they didn't need such a well-resourced department for operations against an enemy that no longer existed. They merged us with a domestic unit from Five, and it was their man who became the new Director. Funnily enough, his name was Hunter too. Brought his own people with him and cut the rest of the department down to the bone. We used to have up to twenty operatives like yourself, and we didn't have to borrow field liaison from HQ; we had our own team of dedicated specialists familiar with every principal theatre and every kind of mission. Directors in the Field, they were called, because when you were in the field an instruction from them was to be treated as though it came from the Director himself. It was a very different time.'

Her eyes slid away from Friend's and she was silent for a long while.

'Weapons?' she asked, as if the digression had never happened. 'There's a sidearm and ammunition in this desk. Here…' she slid a small brass key across the desktop to him. 'Would you like to take it now?'

'No thank you. It wouldn't fit the cover.'

All the same, Friend reached out and took the key.

'As you wish. Any questions?'

'No. I'm satisfied.'

'Then there's nothing more to say except good luck.'

She stood and held out her hand to him. He gave it a brief shake, then turned and walked quietly out of the door. Alison Holding checked her watch and resumed her seat. For the next few minutes, she did nothing but listen to the distant hum of business from the bazaar, every so often checking her watch. When finally it told her that five minutes had elapsed, she got up once more and walked across the room to where a floor length black garment was hanging from a coat hook. She changed out of her black high-heeled shoes, stowing them in a Bulgari tote, and into a simple pair of red leather slippers. Then she carefully pulled the black fabric over her head until it covered her grey trouser suit down to the ankles. Smoothing it down with her hands, she picked up the tote and walked out of the office, making her way twenty metres along the corridor before descending a flight of steps and walking out into the Bazaar through a small leather workshop four doors down from the café she had entered by an hour before. There she merged invisibly into the crowds, just another modest Muslim wife out for a day's shopping.

* * *

Friend hadn't had much time to absorb the persona of his cover.

Little more than forty-eight hours earlier he had been sipping wine on the Magniacs' terrace in Georgia. But the documentation was good. The passport was genuine; one of a series ready prepared for use in the field. For a year or two after issue these documents would be used for routine travel by low-level operatives, to establish a travel history backed up by genuine entry and exit stamps. There were two rules that governed this: never the same country twice and never a country which required a visa application, as that would involve submitting a photograph of the holder. Once a suitable history was established, the passport entered a pool of documents ready for operational use, where it would remain for a maximum of twelve months. The Hunter passport had been dispatched to Istanbul, in the possession of its original holder, just hours before Friend's arrival, thus giving it the necessary endorsement of a genuine, and recent, Turkish entry stamp. Once at the Consulate, the document was painstakingly unstitched by the resident Passport Officer and a new details page bearing a photograph of Friend substituted for the old. The man who had travelled in on the Hunter passport would meanwhile return to London using different documentation. It was a tried and tested system which had only once given any cause for concern, when a local Immigration Officer in the country destined for use had placed his entry stamp on the other half of the sheet bearing the details page. But since on that occasion the agent had been obliged to leave the country by clandestine means there was, in the end, no real problem.

Roderick Hunter's professional background had been given the same degree of care and attention. Social media profiles backed up his travel history and professional interests; on twitter he followed, and often retweeted, some of the most prominent names in British and American journalism. Some of these people had, out of pure courtesy, decided to follow him back. Articles by Hunter had found their way onto several online news and current affairs platforms, although their editors would have been greatly surprised to find them there. Nevertheless, thanks to some of SIS's more gifted analysts, the articles - on mass migration, wars in far-off countries, corporate corruption and international money laundering – had been written with a reasonable level of skill. Thanks to some of their more inventive technophiles they had been planted onto various moribund webpages belonging to reputable media outlets and seeded with the necessary metadata to ensure that they could be found when they were needed, and not before.

And so Emre Parvan did find the articles, in the hour before he was due to meet with Roderick Hunter at his small office on the Asian side of the Bosphorus. He was suitably impressed. There was a lengthy investigative piece on the *New Yorker*, regular stories on *The Independent* and *Huffington Post*, a couple of shorter opinion pieces on *UnHerd* and one detailed dispatch on the refugee crisis in South Sudan had even made it, in translated form, onto the august pages of *Le Monde*. So, it appeared that Mr Roderick Hunter was exactly who he said he was. Which was a relief in one respect – Parvan knew the sort of questions he could expect; they were exactly those he would have asked himself. But in another way it was a concern. Parvan was not sure what Hunter would do if he managed to uncover all the facts behind the death of Elif Çalışkan; he didn't know all of them himself, but he knew enough to be sure that it would be a poor move on his part to send Hunter on his way with any kind of encouraging leads. And since he knew Hunter to be a most professional investigative journalist, this made him a very worried man. So worried, in fact, that when his secretary announced that a Mr Hunter was here to see him, he had to clasp his hands together across his lap to stop them from shaking.

Friend noticed the subdued atmosphere as he walked across the open-plan floor of the newspaper's offices just before half past ten that morning. Several pairs of eyes slid cautiously towards him, but no heads turned, no questions were asked. Here was the Englishman come to write about Elif's death.

Emre Parvan's office was the only one on the floor with four walls and a lockable door, but the walls were glass and as Friend strode confidently across the room it was a nervous-looking man he observed sitting behind the Editor's desk. Friend gave the transparent door a couple of light taps for form's sake and entered without waiting for a response. Parvan did not get up to greet him, just nodded to the chair opposite his desk, which Friend slid into. He took a small digital recorder from the pocket of his jacket and placed it on the desk between them, asking permission with a raise of the eyebrows. Parvan responded with a shrug and Friend switched the device on. Parvan looked nervous and distracted to Friend's eyes; he kept glancing towards a framed photograph on his desk, a picture of himself, a pretty dark-haired woman and a young girl of about six or seven years. He was a far cry from the smoothly efficient figure who had moved calmly and reassuringly among the mourners at yesterday's funeral. What had changed in the few hours since then? Had something in the Hunter profile not rung true? Had he called contacts in the western media and drawn a disturbing blank? Friend thought not. This was not mistrust he was seeing. It was fear.

Friend opened the conversation.

'Thank you for seeing me so soon after the funeral. It must have been a difficult day for you.'

'Yes, Mr Hunter, a difficult day indeed.'

'Oh please, my friends call me Rock.'

'Rock?' Parvan looked puzzled.

'When I was first learning to talk I couldn't manage Roderick. It came out as Ro-rick or Ro-rock. So, I became Rock to family and friends. Now I'm stuck with it.'

Friend felt pleased with himself as he told the tale. Few things satisfied him more than a successful bit of instantaneous embellishment. It gave life to a legend. The ones that offered no room for improvisation were the ones to avoid. If you couldn't somehow project your personality onto your cover then you couldn't properly live it. And then it would never ring true.

'Rock Hunter. I see. Well then, Rock, if you are here to research a story about poor Elif then I am of course here to help you, although there's not much I can tell you about what she was working on at the time of her death. And please call me Emre.'

'Thank you Emre. Well let's start with the personal side of things. Judging by the turn-out at the funeral she had a lot of friends who were fond of her, as well as her family. What sort of woman was she?'

Parvan drew a deep breath, which he then let out as a soft, lingering sigh before he spoke.

'Elif was a person who was easy to love. You know, in our profession these days there is not a lot of trust for journalists, but Elif you knew you could trust as soon as you met her. Anyone she spoke to off the record knew it would stay off the record. She was the same with her colleagues. If she came across a lead that tied in with something she knew a colleague was working on, she would always pass it on, never keep it for herself. That meant her colleagues treated her in the same way. She was an example to her profession. As for the rest, she was bright, funny, charming, an attractive person and very good company.'

'Did she have boyfriends? Someone special?'

'Not recently that I know of. In love her character possibly worked against her. She could be too trusting at times, unless she was interviewing someone.'

'And what about her work?'

'She had worked with me in Istanbul for a little over ten years. She started out on a local paper in Antalya, on the southern coast, but she had studied journalism in Istanbul and all her family were here so it was only a matter of time before she came back. She started with us around the time we had a lot of Syrian refugees passing through on their way to Europe. It was a big story that covered the whole of Turkey and it became one of our major investigations that year. I got Elif involved by putting her on the personal angle. She was so good with people, I saw that at once. She spoke to them, got to the heart of their stories. It made for wonderful copy, and it changed her as a journalist too. Made her something of a campaigner for the rights of these people. Not in the sense that she thought

Europe should be picking up the mess created by the war in Syria, but she hated the way that the refugees were being exploited by the traffickers, and to a lesser extent by people in power.'

'People in power? You mean the government?'

'Not the national government as such, but certain well-connected individuals who were either involved with the traffickers, turning a blind eye to their activities or exploiting the refugees in some other way.'

'Can you give me some examples?'

'One, for sure. She investigated the Chief of Police in one of the western coastal districts where many of the migrants were boarding their little boats to take them across to the Greek Islands. She found he had been taking bribes from the traffickers to let them carry on their business without his interference. There was solid evidence, so we ran the story.'

'What happened to him?'

'He was brought to trial and acquitted. A very well-connected individual you might say. It caused us some trouble. Elif and some of our other people, including me, found ourselves facing investigations of our own. This was around the time of the coup in 2016. We were accused of complicity with the Gulenists. We all spent time in jail, but none of us were ever charged. It all died down in the end, but it was not a pleasant experience at the time.'

'Interesting. So, let's come up to date. When did you last speak to her? What did she tell you about what she was working on?'

'There's not much I can tell you about that. In the last three weeks or so before she died I didn't see much of her. She had that busyness about her, a kind of suppressed excitement she always got when she was working on something that interested her particularly. I did ask her what it was, but she just winked at me and said she couldn't tell me yet. I let it go because I trusted her. She didn't often go silent about a story but when she did she usually came up with something special. The last time I spoke with her was about a week before they found her body. Maybe ten days, I don't know. She said she was out of town chasing down some angles but was coming back to Istanbul shortly and would come and see me when she arrived.'

'Did she say where she was calling from?'

'No, although she mentioned something about her old colleagues, so I thought it might have been somewhere near Antalya.'

'What did she say about her old colleagues?'

'I'm sorry, I really don't remember.'

'Of course. Never mind. Might it not have been the Black Sea coast she was visiting? Perhaps Trabzon?'

'Trabzon? No, I don't think so. That's where I come from originally so I'm sure she would have mentioned it.'

Friend had sensed Parvan relaxing as the interview progressed, but now as he began to push for details on Elif's final days he felt the tension creeping back into the editor's demeanour. He was hiding something, Friend was sure of it.

'I see. Well, perhaps you're right. Did the police say anything about her movements in the days before her death? Or about how she got into the water?'

'The police? No. They have given away very little about that. Perhaps they know something, or perhaps not. You will need to ask them about that, not me.'

'Do you have a hunch which it is? You must have dealt with them before and have an idea how they operate?'

'No, Mr Hunter.'

'Rock, please.'

'No, Rock. I have no hunches about this. Perhaps I am too close to it. Maybe they don't want to admit that they have no idea. It wouldn't be the first time. But it might not be that at all. I can't say.'

'All right then. What about your own ideas? Do you have a working hypothesis for what she was doing, how she died?'

'A working what?'

'Hypothesis. A theory. What do you think happened?'

'What do I think? I am a journalist, Rock. I deal with facts and try not to think too much without them. In this case the only fact I have is that Elif is dead. Maybe it was an accident, maybe not. I wish I had more but I don't. Anything else would just be speculation.'

'So speculate. You might hit on something important.'

'No, speculation is not my business. It should never be the business of any professional journalist.'

That's me told, thought Friend, who hadn't missed the growing tone of irritation in Parvan's responses.

'All right, I won't push you on that. Just one more question before I leave you. Surely Elif had files, notebooks or something that might tell us what she was working on, who she was investigating?'

'She used her own laptop when she was here and she recorded interviews on her mobile phone. She didn't leave any equipment with us. Of course she had a work email account, but the police came in and downloaded all her files a day or so after her body was found. Everything has been locked since then. Even I can't access it. You will have to ask the police if they found anything, or whether her laptop and phone turned up. Is that all?'

'Yes,' said Friend, 'that's all. Thank you.'

'Then I will say goodbye. I have many things to do today.'

Parvan got to his feet and held out his hand to Friend.

'I'm sure you do,' said Friend, taking the offered hand as he stood. 'Thank you very much for your time. It has been very useful.'

Friend switched off the recorder and returned it to his pocket, acknowledging Parvan one last time with a nod as he left the office. He had made one last observation at the end of the interview: Parvan's hand when he shook it had been damp with sweat.

* * *

Emre Parvan watched as Rock Hunter walked out through the ranks of bent heads, everyone seemingly busy on tomorrow's big story and barely noticing as the dark-haired Englishman with the ridiculous name glided nonchalantly between their desks. He removed a handkerchief from his trouser pocket and wiped his damp hand.

Over the last five minutes he had felt the beads of sweat beginning to form in his hair, but thankfully none had yet started to trickle down his face. His shirt was wet under the armpits and his heart was racing. He took thirty seconds to control his breathing and bring the rate down to normal before he returned to his chair and picked up the phone. The number he dialled he knew by heart. It was answered on the third ring.

'Yes?'

'It's me. Are they safe?'

'Yes, they are safe. Has he been?'

'Yes, he just left.'

'What did you tell him?'

'I told him nothing! I said I knew nothing and didn't want to speculate. He should go to the police if he wants to know about their investigation.'

'How much did he know?'

'Not much, I think. He asked about Trabzon. I said I didn't think Elif had been there. I said my family were from there and she would have told me if she were going there. He seemed to accept it. There was nothing else really, except that he asked questions more like a policeman than a journalist. I recorded the interview as you asked, of course. He recorded it too.'

'You will bring the device with you to the rendezvous this afternoon. I will listen to the recording then. You remember the details.'

'I remember. I will be there as we agreed. Will you bring them too?'

'Your wife and daughter? Yes, they will be there too.'

'And you will let them go?'

'Yes. That's what we promised. You did what we asked with the journalist, so once you bring us the recording all three of you will be free to go home, as we promised. But you remember what you promised as well?'

'Of course. I will say nothing, tell nobody!'

'You know what will happen if you do?'

'Yes. You made that very clear. But what about Hunter?'

'Hunter knows nothing. You said so yourself. Anyway, if he is a problem he is our problem, not yours. You just make sure you are there at the rendezvous as we agreed.'

'Sirkeçi station, five thirty. I'll be there.'

* * *

Within two minutes of leaving the building Friend was certain he had picked up a tail, but it was a sixth sense that told him, rather than anything he had seen or heard. He remembered Holding's instructions to ignore the tail unless it proved hostile, but he knew if would irk him if he couldn't flush them out before he got to his hotel. A little gentle weaving through the streets of Istanbul ought to give him some idea of who was following him. He strolled idly through the busy streets towards the waterside and the ferry terminal that would take him back across to the European shore. There were notably fewer tourists on the eastern side of town. Friend found a likely-looking café with an empty table in the window; he went in and ordered coffee and iced water. He took the recorder out of his pocket and plugged an earpiece into his ear. When the coffee arrived he pretended to be listening to the interview and jotting down notes in a small shorthand pad. But his eyes and his mind were on the street outside, scanning the passers-by for any sign of interest, anyone passing the café more than once. If they were pros there would be around half a dozen of them. Based on the descriptions of the fake gas engineers who had raided Altan Karabeg's apartment, they would probably not quite fit the appearance of locals: paler skinned, more western in dress. But this made it no easier to discern anything unusual on the street. After twenty minutes he had spotted nothing remotely useful. He gathered up his things and moved on.

Friend continued steadily downhill, towards the Harem ferry terminal. Üsküdar would have been a shorter walk from the newspaper offices, but this allowed him more time to try and flush the tail without being obvious about it. It took him fifteen minutes to get there. He purchased a token from the counter and, after ten minutes' wait, joined the queue of locals boarding for the journey back to Sirkeçi. Nobody around him seemed in the least way suspicious. Up on the passenger deck, Friend bought another coffee and took it outside and leaned against the rail and enjoyed the view of the Bosphorus as the ferry bobbed along its choppy twenty-minute route. A few metres away, towards the stern, a group of teenagers stood throwing scraps of bread overboard where several scavenging gulls swooped and dived in a mêlée of beaks and wings to grab the bread before it hit the water. A young woman in European dress with a tiny infant strapped to a papoose across her chest caught Friend's eye as she came up on deck for some air. A pair of locals in dark caps and heavy woollen jackets strolled by, deep in conversation. There was nothing. Perhaps there was a drone up there with the quarrelling gulls, floating on the sea breeze and tracking his every move. Perhaps he was just suffering one of those periodic bouts of paranoia that came with his job. That sixth sense they told you about in training, that only came with experience, wasn't always so reliable. Sometimes it was just there because the situation you were in created an expectation that you *should* be followed. Friend pushed his instincts to the back of his mind. He relaxed and tried to enjoy the scenery until the ferry pulled in to Sirkeçi, and everyone bar the gulls, who had already gone off to pursue an eastbound ferry, disembarked.

* * *

It was at breakfast the following morning that Friend heard the news. An overnight gas explosion had demolished a small apartment block in Üsküdar, just a few minutes north of the newspaper offices Friend had visited the day before. Among the eight confirmed dead was newspaper editor Emre Parvan, together with his wife and family.

PART TWO

NIA

CHAPTER SEVEN

FIELD LIAISON

'Sorry Laddie, bloody appalling traffic.' Magniac was late. 'Six hundred and fifty thousand cars in a city built for fifty thousand people and an equivalent number of horses. Whoever's in charge of transportation around here must have been taking lessons from the Mayor of London. Hell of a bloody rush this morning anyway. It was only two hours after you left our place that they told me you might be working in Georgia and I was to "hold myself in a state of readiness" as they put it. Couldn't they be briefer for Chrissakes? Well, here I am, in a state of readiness. And great thirst, I might add. How can I be of service?'

He had managed to cross the restaurant from door to table, divest himself of his coat and hat, order a bottle of wine and give his little speech before Friend had had a chance to draw breath. Friend greeted his old comrade with a smile and a knowing shake of the head.

The death of Emre Parvan and his young family, coming so soon after the body of one of his colleagues had been found, had caused a frenzy of speculation in the Turkish media, displacing the week's big environmental scandal. A story about dead fish washed up on Turkey's Black Sea coast was no competition for the sudden and violent deaths of two journalists from the same newspaper, however many thousands of them there were. Friend had been called into a crash meeting with Alison Holding, who made it clear that, as one of the last people to see Emre Parvan alive, the non-existent Roderick Hunter would be high on the list of people the police would want to speak to. It was all very well an operative making an appointment to interview a police officer, but being wanted for interview by the police themselves was quite another matter.

Add to this the fact that there were really no leads left to follow in Turkey; Karabeg's files had been stolen, Parvan was dead, there were no other witnesses to what had happened as the May Rose cruised through the Bosphorus. There was no earthly reason for Friend to stay. Friend had breakfasted with the news of the explosion that killed Emre Parvan; by dinner on the same day he was back in Tbilisi. He didn't bother to follow the procedure of calling the Embassy. It would have been ridiculous in the circumstances. Instead he called Major Stephen Magniac's personal mobile and asked him to lunch in town the following day. Magniac suggested a place he knew well: *Dadiani*.

'Why didn't you tell me we were on the same payroll?' Friend asked. 'I thought you'd simply retired and gone into the wine trade.'

'Need to know, Laddie. The old story.'

'Ah, so you knew what I did already.'

'They spoke to me when you were being vetted.'

'Did they now? Is it within the bounds of friendship to ask what you told them?'

'Nothing I haven't said to your face a dozen times.'

'Oh, I see. Reprehensible aspects of my character and so forth.'

Magniac made the familiar booming noise that passed for a laugh among his friends. 'Nothing so dramatic. I just offered a few straight answers to the not-so straight questions these people always ask.'

A waiter arrived with the wine. Magniac ordered food for both of them: *khachapuri*; a Georgian delicacy reminiscent of a calzone pizza or a Cornish pasty, but not quite the same as either.

'You might find it a bit heavy for your taste,' observed Magniac, 'but you can't possibly come to Georgia and not try khachapuri. You won't find anywhere that does it better. They do it in the Mingrelian style here, with egg. If you do find it heavy, just wash it down with a bit more wine.' He took a large sip from his glass, of a size that alerted Friend to the possibility of a two-bottle lunch. 'This is a *pirosmani*; good body with a little underlying sweetness. Very quaffable.'

Friend nodded his understanding. He took a sip from his glass and signified his approval, then he turned the conversation back to serious matters.

'What was he like? The vetting officer, I mean. I assume it was a he.'

'It was. Fiftyish, retired RAF-type. Old tweed, cavalry twill and Hush Puppies. Basically wanted to know what made you tick.'

'I'm not sure I could answer that one myself.'

'Who could? About themselves, I mean. It's not always easy to spot your own motivation for doing things, is it?' Magniac gave a shrug, as if trying to avoid the subject veering towards his own choices. 'Anyway, he didn't ask that in so many words. That's what he was driving at, but the questions he put sort of danced around that area without going into it directly.'

'So, nervous tics, sexual preferences and political inclinations.'

'Oh, he asked about your politics all right, but I don't think he understood the answer. As for sex, the poor devil probably has to submit a formal application to the memsahib in triplicate. The subject would simply have embarrassed him.'

Two steaming khachapuri arrived and Magniac immediately lanced through the crust of his with a single stroke, feeling the rising vapour coat his beard and watching with amusement as Friend inspected this new culinary experience with his usual curiosity, but perhaps less enthusiasm than it deserved. Magniac chewed his first mouthful slowly, thinking back to his conversation with the vetting officer. He spoke again.

'Actually, perhaps I've been a bit unfair to the old boy. He probably did understand what I said about your politics because he asked quite a perceptive question afterwards.'

'Which was?'

'Well, it was after I'd spoken about you being politically homeless, because you can't abide the left's smug moral superiority or the right's blind faith in markets...'

He paused to take another mouthful and Friend continued the train of thought.

'...and how the growing dominance of global business interests whoever's in charge means there isn't a fag paper's width of difference between them.'

'Exactly. Well, he was silent for a moment, obviously giving the matter some consideration, and then he asked: "so if Captain Friend is so critical of his country's politics why on earth does he want to defend it?"'

'And what did you say to that?'

'Oh, I gave him some guff about there being more to a country than its politics. About people and landscape and a thousand years of cultural history that warranted protection...' Magniac spotted the look on Friend's face. 'Yes, you're right. I was speaking about myself there, I expect. I think he noticed that too. So then I gave him a more honest answer.'

'Which was?'

'I told him that you'd wandered into the army more or less by accident, for want of anything else to do, and that it had given you the variety and a sense of belonging and purpose you were looking for. It brought you into contact with many different kinds of people in all sorts of different places. You experienced cultures and languages you never would have done in any other trade, and it had put you in danger too, which you probably became a little addicted to. And then quite suddenly you were wrenched out of that life and, deep down, I think you're still fighting the war you were pulled out of, still attached to the unit you fought with. That's what I told him.'

Friend chewed on a mouthful of warm, gooey stodge while he gave Magniac's words some thought.

'I read a book recently by Aris Roussinos,' he said at last. '*Rebels* it was called. There's a line in it that sticks in my mind: "the hidden awful truth about war is how much fun it is". I'm not sure "fun" was the right word. It wasn't much fun getting shot at, or even shooting back, but it was *exhilarating*, and perhaps that's what he meant. All in all, I enjoyed being in the army. If I had my time over again, I don't think I'd do anything different, despite what happened in Helmand.'

'Me too. It's about belonging. A group of close-knit people with a shared sense of purpose. Like having a family that's always backing you up. You know, I *would* say it was fun at times, but that wasn't the main thing about it. The main thing was that there are a couple of dozen blokes dotted around the world that I'd still lay down my life for, even today.'

'There used to be a few more than that,' mused Friend, almost in an undertone.

'So there did,' agreed Magniac, his voice uncharacteristically sombre. He raised his glass. 'Here's to absent friends.'

'Absent friends,' repeated Friend. He sipped at his wine and was silent for a time, aware of Magniac's quiet eyes watching him. 'Interesting,' he went on. 'Psychological flaw as motivation. It's a wonder they took me on.'

'You think so? Perhaps you were exactly what they were looking for. A young, fit, intelligent man with some experience of the world. A gift for languages, a knack for getting on with people, attracted to danger, but in a controllable way – no death wish – and with a remarkable ability for coming out of hazardous situations unscathed. Napoleon liked nothing better than a lucky general; I daresay they like nothing better than a lucky operative.'

Friend said nothing for a while. He sipped his wine and looked across the table at Stephen Magniac, who was digging into his food with gusto, as if the two of them had been discussing nothing more serious than the prospects for the weekend's football. *A good commanding officer knows his men inside out.*

'Still friends, Laddie?' said Magniac after a few minutes.

'Never anything else, Major. I'm just a little surprised to find us both on the staff.'

'Yes, well it was a condition of resigning my commission to move here. If I hadn't agreed I would have spent years on the reserve list having to report for training all the time. Instead, I got to move out here straight away and gave up much less of my time. It's hardly an onerous task, being Honorary Consul in Telavi and part-time representative of His Majesty's Secret Intelligence Service.'

'What does Tamara think of it?'

'She came around. My remit doesn't involve spying on Georgia, just picking up titbits about Russian or Iranian activity and helping operational agents like yourself as and when required. Which, in point of fact, hasn't been required at all before today. My contract expires in less than two months, so this will probably be my one and only real job.' He grinned. 'Hope I don't muck it up!'

'And what will you do in two months? Resign?'

'I expect so. This isn't really a productive use of my time or the government's money.' He finished off the last of his khachapuri and laid down his knife and fork with an air of finality. 'Besides, this is my home now. When I go back to England it feels like a foreign country. Even Guernsey isn't how I remember it in my youth. It makes me feel that all these years I've been fighting for a memory, for something that no longer exists. And at last I'm ready to admit that I don't want to fight those battles any more.'

'You may still have one more battle to fight, Major.'

'Yes. But this one won't be for England. It'll be for a friend. So, what's the story? What danger can I assist with getting you into, Laddie, and hopefully out of?'

'Before we get into that, let's make sure we both understand your brief correctly.'

There was a subtle but distinct change in tone as Friend switched the subject to the mission.

'Exactly how I'm to help you, you mean?'

'What you understand by the role of field liaison.'

'I was told to make sure you have any support you need locally, whether that's background information, documents, escape routes, back-up called in from London or recruited here. I'm also your signals relay. You debrief to me when you have anything to pass on and I send it to Holding on the Embassy wire. Any supplementary instructions for you will come back through me in the opposite way. How does that sound? Is it what you're used to?'

'I'll let you know if I need any support, but whatever you do don't put anyone on me unless I ask for it. If I spot anyone on my tail, I want to be sure it's the opposition, otherwise it can get confusing. And dangerous. If the opposition spots someone else tailing me it could blow my cover. I don't carry weapons so I've only got three things to protect me: my training, my wits and my cover. I need all three, but cover is the first line of defence. I can't afford to lose it until we get to the end phase of the mission and the gloves are off. As long as that's understood, the rest is fine.'

'Fair enough,' said Magniac. 'So, what's the story?'

Friend took Magniac through the details he had been given.

'The May Rose is on her way back from Piraeus now,' he said. 'She's due in to Batumi in three days. I'd like to get a look at her once she arrives; find out where she's off to next and what she'll be carrying. If her cargo is human they have to get them on board somehow. It's unlikely they bring them on in sealed containers if Çalışkan was able to get up on deck. But before that I need to find out a bit more about the company that owns her. Guria Shipping and Trading. The current listed owner, incidentally, is Nia Dadiani. She took over after her father's death about two years ago. His name was Alexandre. I need to find out whatever I can about them, and whoever else might have any influence in the company. Can you help?'

'Tamara has a cousin who's a journalist. He might be able to help.'

'That could work. I'm using journalist cover.'

'She'll need to make the introduction though.'

Friend felt a brief stab of doubt. For an operative in the field, anonymity is the greatest asset. In an ideal world even field liaison would only know an operative's workname, not his real one. And here he was about to share his true identity not just with field liaison but also his wife. That the Magniacs were friends only made it more of a worry. And worrying about other people during a mission was a dangerous distraction, an irritation. His skin itched with it.

'Will she want to though?' Friend asked, uncertainly. 'I mean, as a former aid worker…'

Magniac greeted this with a dismissive bark of laughter.

'You think that makes her a bleeding-heart liberal? That, Laddie, is precisely why she would help in a job like this. She's seen at first hand the misery these people cause.'

'Well, all right then. But she'll need to understand that I'm operating under cover and not using my own name.'

'What name are you using?'

'Rock Hunter.'

'That is *so* you,' said Magniac with an appreciative smile.

* * *

Friend woke early with a dry mouth and a sore head. After Magniac had called home with Friend's request, Tamara at once offered to call her cousin Niko and make an appointment for the following day. Then, in the morning she would take a taxi into Telavi and journey onward to Tbilisi by one of the minibuses known all over the former Soviet provinces as a *marshrutka*. This left Magniac at a loose end for the evening, with predictable consequences.

Friend pulled open the shutters and took a breath of air. He could hear the distant hum of early morning traffic a block away on Vakhtang Gorgasali street, but his eyes fixed upon the old Narikala fortress, its ancient stones golden in the morning sun, perched upon its promontory above the old town. He felt not the anticipation and adrenalin that was common at the start of a mission, but a curious sense of peace. It could only be explained by the place, and the company.

Magniac had taken the unorthodox step of cancelling the reservation made for Friend by headquarters and booking them both into a small hotel owned by some friends of his. 'It's a quiet place in the old town, handy for the sulphur baths and close to the river. Has its own wine bar and garden. The owners are really nice people. Tamara's known them for years. We often stay here when we're in Tbilisi, unless we're at the in-laws'. You'll find it much more your scene than that soulless international chain they booked you into.'

It crossed Friend's mind to say that oversized, soulless, anonymous hotels were just what an operative needed, not to mention fitting his journalistic cover. But he had buried his professional conceit and given himself up to his friend's local expertise, and if he could have done without the vodka bottle proffered by his hosts at the end of a six-hour crawl through the bars of old Tbilisi, he couldn't fault their hospitality or fail to marvel at the capacity of Stephen Magniac to make friends and connections as though he had lived in the town his entire life.

It was barely time for breakfast and passing Magniac's door Friend heard the rumble of a volcanic snore that vibrated along the hallway. Blessing the fact that he had been sober enough to decline an adjoining room, he crept softly downstairs and stepped outside. The street was peaceful enough, but the morning air was growing thick with the distant thunder of traffic and began to hum in tune with Friend's wine-sodden head. His nose led him towards the warm smell of baking pastry as the morning's khachapuri emerged from a hundred ovens. A pang of hunger struck him and with half his mind Friend wondered why it was only after drinking too much that he craved carbohydrate.

The hundred ovens he had conjured up in his mind turned out to belong to a single café down the hill at the point where the street opened out into a wide gully filled with the sombre domes, like a field of brick molehills, of the sulphur baths. Above the domes, the old fortress sat perched on its rock in Sphinx-like contentment. The only sign of life was a group of feral cats foraging for breakfast in a rubbish skip. He turned back uphill, treading carefully on the rough, uneven cobbles, gazing at buildings of flattish red brick that might have come from Roman ruins, passing under ropes of telegraph wire that hung like tangled vines from ancient, crooked poles. Near the top of the hill another narrow, cobbled street meandered down to the river; the street sign said 'Firdousi'. The same as Ferdowsi? The Persian poet who had given his name to one of Tehran's great boulevards; the boulevard where, just a few months earlier, Friend had run like a startled fox through a crowd of bewildered civilians, as the bullets began to fly.

A sharp rattle behind him dispersed the memory. A tar-haired boy of eleven or twelve, dressed for school, was casting pebbles up at a window. Moments later the shutters opened and the face of a girl appeared; she shouted something plaintive before disappearing behind a slammed casement. The boy shrugged and kicked away a small stone with one sandalled foot. Friend turned and walked back to the hotel and his breakfast.

Away from the old town, Tbilisi was a different city. Magniac's battered old Land Rover eased its way slowly through the thick traffic. Other drivers mostly gave it a clear berth, having eyed the number of dents in its bodywork and drawn the appropriate conclusion. The traffic hadn't been so bad coming out of the old town, but once they had crossed the river via a broad, six-lane bridge, it had closed in and held them tight. Cars sat bumper to bumper, stewing in their own fumes. An occasional long green bus stood out above them, a grassy island amid a sea of multicoloured metal, honking like mechanical geese.

'Is it always like this?' Friend asked. Magniac just shrugged, keeping his eyes on the road as if the wall of traffic might part for an instant like the Red Sea before Moses and allow them passage.

'You get used to it,' he said at last. 'It's not so bad in Telavi.'

There was plenty of time for Friend to gaze out of the window and take in his surroundings. Before arriving on his walking tour his only impressions of Georgia had come from old Soviet-era films like *Mimino*. In modern Tbilisi, the younger people looked like younger people anywhere in Europe: darker skinned, like Greeks or Armenians, but dressed in the same international style in clothes from the same global suppliers. But the appearance of some of the older folk awakened recognition in him: male heads topped with broad, flat caps like stiffened pancakes, bushy, drooping moustaches that bristled like a hedgehog's spines with every smile, tough skin a mosaic of laughter lines like wrinkled paper; stout, jolly-faced *babushki* joking together on benches, their long spring coats flapping in the breeze. He thought of Vakhtang Kikabidze in *Mimino* and his character's faltering Russian: '*Larisoo Ivanovnoo hachoo*', or something like that. The old boys up in Khevsureti had been more fluent.

Tsereteli, the long boulevard heading north on the east side of the river, was lined with evenly-spaced mature trees, separating the lines of parked cars from the pavement and buildings beyond. Friend's gaze met peeling stucco and wrought iron balconies on old Art Nouveau facades, low, plain brick buildings that might have been factories of some kind and the occasional random single-storey shack like an unrenovated *dacha*.

'No speedbumps anyway', he observed. This drew no more than a grunt of acknowledgement from Magniac, which was probably a good thing, Friend decided after a moment of reflection. His head wasn't up to another London rant.

Tamara was waiting patiently on a bench next to a line of bright yellow *Marshrutki* at the Didube bus terminal. She looked fresher than either of the men did, despite two hours sweating in an over-crowded minibus.

'Heavy night, was it boys? Oh dear, how are you feeling?'

'Seb had a hair of the dog with his breakfast, so he's doing better than I am,' said her husband.

'You didn't join him?'

'Driving.'

A silence ensued.

'Well, well. Spies' night out in Old Tbilisi. You should have had t-shirts printed.' She said this to no-one in particular, then turned to Friend. 'Stephen tells me I shouldn't call you Sebastian, Sebastian.'

Friend responded with a weary nod.

'What was the name you're using again? I forget.'

'Roderick Hunter, freelance journalist. Rock to his friends.'

'Rock Hunter…' Tamara mused. 'Pleased to meet you, Rock.'

They crossed the river into the residential district of Dighomi and soon swung back south towards the city centre along the broad Kazbegi Avenue, the main road into the city from the north.

'Tell me about your cousin Niko,' said Friend.

So she did.

* * *

Tamara described Cousin Niko as an 'old gossip', and fate had been kind in granting him responsibility for the society pages at *Kviris Palitra*, Tbilisi's most popular daily newspaper. He was a short, stockily-built man of about thirty boasting a wiry goatee beard to match the stiff brush of black hair that topped his head. *Give him a few years*, thought Friend, *and his face will be just as happily patterned with laughter as some of the old boys out there.*

'So nice to meet you at last, Stephen,' Niko said in faltering but keen English. 'I have heard much about you. And your friend, Rod-er-ick?' He struggled through the syllables.

'My friends call me Rock.'

'Ah yes. That is much easier. Nice to meet you, Rock.'

'And you. It's good of you to spare us some of your time.'

The office was a cramped little space with room just for one guest chair and a small desk just large enough for Niko's desktop computer. Through the thin walls leaked the rattle of keyboards and a babble of telephone conversations. This would not be a place where much could remain private.

Niko poured four glasses of water from a jug on the windowsill and offered the guest seat to Tamara as Friend explained what he wanted. He was a journalist from England, researching a story on trade and traders on the fringes of Europe. There was a vague post-Brexit, global Britain angle, but this was mainly a human story rather than an economic one. He was interested in Nia Dadiani as an example of a young businesswoman, making her own way in the world.

Niko listened with a smile of encouragement on his face.

'Ah yes, the Dadiani name is a famous one in Georgia. Princes of Samgrelia for centuries. They are a clan as much as a family. The chief they always call The Dadiani. Now this Nia Dadiani is a very sad story. An only child. Lost her mother when she was just eight. Looked after by her father who was building an empire while trying to raise her. But they still seem close, yes?'

Friend and Magniac both nodded, keen for him to continue.

'Well, she married, maybe ten years ago. The man is an engineer, a roadbuilder, trying to improve our broken Soviet *infrastructura*, yes? They have a son, he must be about seven years old now. Then two years ago her father dies. Heart attack. Very sudden. Nia is very upset, she says her father is as strong as a horse. Heart of a lion. Still swimming two kilometres every morning. Why should he drop dead from his heart? Poisoned by his enemies, she says. But the police find no poison. And who are his enemies? Nia says nothing.'

'I remember the stories,' said Tamara. 'There were a few people who found it strange at the time.'

'That's right', continued Niko. 'Nia's husband takes her away after funeral. Two months in the south of France, then she comes back and takes over the business. No more talk of poison. Then a few months later, about a year after her father, the husband is on the site of a road project in the north-west, near Abkhazia. He is out inspecting the new road, on his own, when a big earth mover has a brake failure, rolls toward him and both go over the cliff together. He falls two hundred metres down the mountain. Big tragedy. There is an enquiry of course, but the police find only mechanical failure. It's nobody's fault. Just a tragedy. So poor Nia Dadiani loses both father and husband in one year. Now she has only her son left.'

'And now she is in sole charge of the business?' asked Friend.

'Yes. Owner and Chief Executive. Sometimes the work helps to cope with the sorrow, yes?'

'I expect so. Have there been any interviews with her?'

'Interviews? I don't think so. Maybe there is something around the time of her husband's funeral. One moment please, I will check.'

While their host turned to his computer, Friend and Magniac looked at each other. Each could tell what the other was thinking: in their line of business, two deaths of close family members in less than a year was unlikely to be coincidence.

'Ah yes, I have it,' said Niko. 'No interview unfortunately, but this double tragedy is such a big thing we planned to run a photo story around the funeral. *Heart-broken widow struggles on*, you understand?'

'Yes, of course,' said Friend. 'Can we see the story?'

'Well, in the end we didn't run it. We just took photographs at the funeral, but the story, we never wrote it.'

'Why not?'

'I think there was some pressure. I remember the editor talking about it. Her lawyers asked us to leave their client in peace at this difficult time.'

'And that was enough?'

'Yes, this time. In Georgia, sometime somebody owes someone else a favour and… you understand?'

'I understand. Well, what about the photographs. Do you still have those?'

'Yes, they are on my screen now. Come and look.'

Friend and Magniac stood and watched as the journalist clicked through a sequence of stark, monochrome images. A church on a bare hillside with solemn, black cars drawn up outside, three heavily-bearded priests leading a procession of mourners; a tall, expensively dressed woman walking behind, her face and hair obscured by a broad-brimmed hat and veil but for a single blonde lock which had escaped confinement to rest on her shoulder; mourners gathered at the burial ground, the coffin lowered, the head priest genuflecting, guests offering sympathy to the widow, she stops to share a moment with most of them, but there is one she turns away from: a short, very stout man, completely bald, commiseration written all over his face from his thick black eyebrows to his curiously dimpled chin. Two unmistakeable heavies watching his back.

'Do you know who that is?' asked Friend, pointing directly at the bald man's face.

'Of course,' replied Niko at once. 'That is Mikel Qorghanashvili. Lawyer. Very powerful. Many government connections. Used to be adviser to the Ministry of Justice.'

'Might he have been the lawyer who asked your paper not to run the story on Nia Dadiani?'

'Maybe. I could find out. And one thing I tell you for sure. If Mikel Qorghanashvili asks you not to do something, you do not do it!'

Friend felt a familiar tingle creeping up his spine to the base of his skull.

'Do you think I can get a copy of these pictures? I might want to use one or two in my article, appropriately credited of course.'

'Sure. You use We Transfer?'

Friend nodded.

'Then just give me your email and I will share them with you.'

'Thank you,' said Friend.

* * *

'We should have done this before breakfast.' Friend's voice sounded sleepy and was muffled by the towel he lay on as the *mekise's* strong hands scrubbed up and down his back with a rough, exfoliating glove before dousing him with warm, soapy water and starting again. They had spent ten minutes stewing in the pungent, blood-temperature water of the hot bath and another ten in the cold before the masseur had come in and directed them both to the red marble benches. Inside, the sulphur baths were more elaborate than they looked from the street. Their room was vividly decorated with colourful tiles in a variety of mosaic designs, at least one of which detailed an illustration of the type once described by Victorian booksellers as 'curious'. Now, they were all shrouded in a modest veil of steam.

'What do you know about this lawyer? Qorghanashvili?' Friend asked as he turned over and prepared for a chest scrub. The *Mekise* seemed to pause at the mention of the name; he hadn't said a word since entering the room and had given off an air of practised discretion. The two Englishmen had prattled away in their own tongue, giving little thought to the slim possibility that he would understand more than a word or two of their carefully phrased talk. But this he had understood, and where before his movements had been smooth and habitual, now he seemed to hesitate, his gloved hand poised above Friend's chest in uncertainty. A moment later he had recovered himself and was working away at Friend's smooth skin as if nothing had happened. But the hesitation had not gone unnoticed.

'I know the reputation, much like everybody else in this town,' replied Magniac. 'Better call him *Q* in public. It's easier to say, come to that. Well, from what I've heard he's supposed to be one of the most powerful men in Tbilisi. What Niko said about him being a former advisor to the Minister of Justice is true enough. Tamara says he was widely thought to have had the Minister in his pocket, but then there was a change of government and a new man came in.'

'Not powerful enough to influence elections, then.'

'No, but not to be underestimated. I haven't heard anything exactly criminal about him, but he isn't well liked.'

The scrubbing had finished and Friend moved as if to get up, but stopped at a gesture from the *Mekise*, who turned and dipped what looked like a large floral pillowcase into a bucket of water. When he stood up the pillowcase had become a foam-filled balloon.

He gently placed his burden on Friend's stomach and softly began to massage the foam into his skin. Within a couple of minutes, Friend's entire body was swaddled in froth, from his toenails to the crown of his head.

'Funny sort of place to meet a polar bear,' laughed Magniac.

'I'll need to know more about Q,' said Friend through the foam. 'Can you see what you can dig up for me please? Headquarters might have something on him, but local sources are probably better.'

It was an odd feeling, the captain giving orders to the major. Well, perhaps not orders, but all the same, Magniac reflected as he watched the *Mekise* rinse off the foam with hot water.

'I'll do what I can. What's your plan?'

'Christ!'

Friend had seen the bucket of iced water coming, but he still couldn't stop himself from crying out at the impact. The *Mekise* pointed towards the hot tub and Friend climbed down from the marble slab and slid into it, his whole skin tingling. It was as though he could feel each individual blood vessel in his body springing back to life. Blood was flowing properly again, synapses were firing and despite the cloying heat and steam he could feel oxygen refreshing the whole organism. The *Mekise* was bending over Magniac's prone body and scrubbing roughly at his shoulders.

'I need to be in Batumi when the May Rose gets back to port,' he said. 'And before that I'd like to have a look at Nia Dadiani. I'm supposed to be a journalist, so I can always try for an interview.'

'Judging from those photographs you should enjoy having a look at Nia Dadiani,' said Magniac. 'Just your type, I should say. Christ!'

'What's wrong?'

'Laddie, remind me to get my back waxed before doing this again.'

CHAPTER EIGHT

BATUMI EXPRESS

The train pulled out of the station at 08.00. Friend settled back in his comfortable leather first-class seat and began the five-hour journey browsing through documents on his tablet and reviewing what the last twenty-four hours had revealed about Nia Dadiani and Mikel Qorghanashvili.

Magniac had worked quickly. Nia's father Alexandre Dadiani was a direct descendant of the princely family that had ruled the north-western province of Samgrelia for generations. As a young man he had served the Georgian Soviet Socialist Republic as a dockyard administrator, rising to manage the docks along the southern part of Georgia's coastline, from Poti in the centre of the coast down to Batumi, near the border with Turkey. When the Soviet system collapsed and the old republic's assets were, as in so many places, sold off to the fastest bidder, Dadiani emerged as the owner of a small fleet of merchant ships, some eight in number. Within a decade, the size of the Dadiani shipping line had more than trebled, with road haulage and warehousing facilities added to the thriving business now known as Guria Shipping and Trading.

Dadiani had no known criminal associations, but the source of the funding he had used to launch his shipping line was, Friend was not surprised to read, unknown. It was assumed that he had benefitted from the widespread corruption, the routine system of bribes and favours that enabled Soviet citizens to navigate their way around their country's bloated bureaucracy. Certainly, Dadiani and his family had lived a privileged existence; the fine house in the Batumi suburb reserved for senior *apparatchiks*, the country dacha, the private car. Nia herself, Dadiani's only child, had gone to the best school in Batumi, before continuing her education in Russia, studying Business Administration at Moscow State University. SIS sources had little else to say. There was not even a photograph on file.

Like Nia, Mikel Qorghanashvili had been born into a well-established family. But in his case the connections went straight to the heart of the Soviet administration. His father had been a senior official in the Ministry of Justice, a friend of Eduard Shevardnadze; he had been tipped for a government post in Shevardnadze's early post-independence government, but a sudden, fatal heart-attack intervened. There were, Friend reflected, a remarkable number of sudden deaths in the background of this case. Mikel had enjoyed a privileged childhood before studying law at Tbilisi State University, graduating in 1990. There was nothing on file about any siblings and it may have been that, like Nia, he was an only child.

After leaving university, Mikel Qorghanashvili had joined one of the leading law firms in Tbilisi, eventually becoming its sole partner. Specialising in corporate law, he had acted as an advisor to the Ministry of Justice, while at the same time he made a small fortune out of the break-up and sell-off of state institutions, becoming in the process one of the most powerful, and unpopular, figures in Tbilisi. His relationship with some of the more prominent oligarchs to have come out of Georgia in the post-Soviet period had raised plenty of questions about his honesty. There were rumours of connections with various crime syndicates, both locally and as far afield as Russia and Ukraine, but the rumours were not backed up by any kind of fact and may simply have been the result of the kind of opprobrium that attaches itself to successful men who lack the charm to compensate for their riches.

Qorghanashvili was said to dislike being photographed, and

Friend could see why. The photograph submitted for a Schengen visa application showed a high, well-lined forehead beneath an almost completely round, domed skull. A short, stubby nose was compressed between two pudgy cheeks that were joined by a heavy line of fat running underneath the dimpled jawline. Dark, coffee-bean eyes peered out at him to complete the picture. Apart from the snaps taken at the Dadiani funeral there were only two press photographs to add; both showed the same, undeniably fat man shaking hands at public functions. He wore the same dark suit and thin, dark tie. The same two heavies were within comfortable range. The olive-skinned face was unsmiling.

Friend read further that these two bodyguards, unnamed, appeared to accompany Qorghanashvili everywhere in public and even occupied rooms in the extensive Tsarist-era mansion the lawyer lived in; a building similar in style if not scale to the famous Vorontsov Palace, once the home of the Russian governor of Georgia. Qorghanashvili's home was an opulent marvel overlooking Dedaena Park, just a stone's throw from the Ministry of Justice on Zviad Gamsakhurdia Boulevard. It came with its own swimming pool, tennis courts and an established domestic household that included kitchen staff, housemaids and even an English butler by the name of Foulkes. By contrast, Nia Dadiani still lived, alone, in the house where she had grown up with her parents. Friend gazed out of the window as the train sped past a ravine with a thickly wooded hillside beyond and wondered whether he was heading in the right direction.

He must have slept. By the time he was aware of it a man had already slid liquidly into the seat opposite, as if he had been poured from a jug. He was youngish, little more than Friend's own age, but the sleekly combed mid-brown hair was just beginning to recede to a widow's peak and the clothes were those of a man who wishes to emphasise maturity over youth. He wore a well-cut sports coat in a reddish-brown tweed over a bottle-green turtleneck sweater. The silk pocket square sticking up from the breast of his jacket matched the wool of the sweater almost exactly. On his hands he wore, incongruously, a pair of thin driving gloves in a light tan leather, which he slowly peeled off and placed carefully on the table between himself and Friend. He looked up, and the smile beneath the pencil-thin moustache and the long, fine nose was pleasantly ingratiating.

'You are American perhaps? I thought I saw you reading English earlier.'

Instinctively Friend glanced down to where his tablet lay securely on the table in his shoulder bag. He had been careful to switch it off and stow it away as soon as he had finished reading the documents; before reading them he had even checked whether anyone behind him might have had a clear view of his screen. He had thought he was safe from observation. There had been nothing on screen that might have given away the documents' origin, but still he wondered what the man had seen and felt the creeping nausea that comes with every operative's worst fear: being noticed.

'No, I'm from England,' Friend replied.

'London?'

Friend nodded.

'Alas, I have never been to England, but I learned English at school and always tried to keep it up. Allow me to introduce myself, Alexei Kovalchuk. My friends call me Senka.'

He held out a limp, long-fingered hand and Friend took it.

'Roderick Hunter,' he replied.

'Pleased to meet you Roderick. I may call you Roderick? Good. So what brings you to our beautiful Georgia?'

'Partly its beauty, but a little bit of business as well.'

'Really? What sort of business are you in?'

'I'm a journalist.'

'How fascinating! I am sure we have lots of stories to tell, but what interests your English readers in particular?'

'Oh my readers aren't just English. I've written for the *New Yorker*, for papers and magazines across Europe, even South Africa and Australia.'

'Yes, but what are you working on now?'

'Now? Well, I'm working on a series for *The Economist* in London, looking at small, independent businesses, generally in manufacturing or logistics, on the fringes of the old Soviet empire. Looking at how private enterprise has developed over the past thirty years, in essence.'

'What an interesting idea. But why now?'

'Well I suppose it came out of the debate about Brexit really. You're familiar with that?'

'Everyone is familiar with that, Roderick.'

'Of course. Well, if nothing else it made businesses in Britain consider what opportunities might lie in trade elsewhere in the world. That's how it started out, at least. But it's grown beyond that; more than simply opportunities for British business I think there are some fascinating stories to be told purely from the Georgian point of view.'

'I see. So what kind of businesses are you looking at in Georgia? You are going to Batumi, I expect?'

'That's right. I thought I might look at shipping. That has always been important for the countries around the Black Sea but of course it was all heavily state controlled in Soviet times. I would be interested to see how some of the smaller operators have got on since.'

Kovalchuk spread his hands wide and his smile wider still.

'Then it's lucky for you that I came along, Roderick. I am a business consultant. I work all across Georgia and know all of the important people in Batumi. If it's people in shipping you are interested in I can introduce you to everyone who might be useful.'

Kovalchuk proceeded to rattle off a list of names from which Friend noticed one significant absentee: Guria Shipping and Trading. When he finished, Kovalchuk reached into a jacket pocket and pulled out a business card, which he slid across the table to Friend. One side was printed in Georgian, the other in English. They gave Kovalchuk's name and the name of a business: *Caucasian Credit Trust.*

'Alexei Kovalchuk, that isn't a very Georgian name, is it?'

'No. My father was Russian. He was a military man, but he was stationed here in Georgia and met my mother here. When the Soviet Union collapsed, he left the army and we settled in Tbilisi. Of course I still have relatives in Russia and I went to University in Moscow, but in my heart,' he brought his hand across his chest in an expressive gesture, 'I am Georgian and this is my country. So, perhaps I can be of some help to you, my friend? If you want introductions to some business-people, or if you want to see some of the sights of Batumi. I know all the best restaurants. Or night clubs, if that is your pleasure. Where are you staying?'

'The Wyndham.'

'An excellent choice. Very handy for the port and just a short walk from the beach as well. Perhaps I could pick you up there one evening?'

'Perhaps. I see your number is on the card. Tell me one thing. You know most of the shipping people in Batumi; what do you know about Guria Shipping and Trading?'

'Guria? Oh, that's the Dadiani line.' There was no change in Kovalchuk's face. 'They don't amount to much these days. They used to be important when the old man was around, but since he died his daughter took over and, to be frank, she hasn't done much of a job. Most of their ships are leased out to other companies now. I don't think they would be a very interesting story to tell.'

'That's a shame. What's she like, this daughter?'

'Nia Dadiani? Oh, I don't know her so well. I used to know her father and I met her a few times when she was with him. A very beautiful young woman, I thought at the time. And she seemed gifted too. This would be just after she finished university. But she took her father's death very badly. If he had only lived a few more years she might have had enough experience to take the business over and do well with it, but instead she was thrown in at the deep end, as you say, and she struggled to keep her head above water. Then her husband died too, he worked in construction and had an accident on site, and I'm afraid that was the end for her. Mentally, I mean. She couldn't cope. Went to pieces, more or less. She is still head of the business, legally speaking, but she simply doesn't have the focus on detail that you need to run a business of that kind these days. There are people working with her who could help, but from what I hear she doesn't listen to them enough. So the business suffers. It's a shame. I think if you want to meet her you don't go to her office, you go to the roulette table at the Riviera Casino.' Kovalchuk smiled. 'That's just down the road from your hotel, by the way.'

Friend said nothing. He looked out of the window again, unsure what to make of this uninvited stranger. Much of what he had said about Nia Dadiani was plausible; it tied in with what he had heard from the journalist in Tbilisi. But he had the feeling he was being warned off, that the woman's instability was being exaggerated and the status of her business underplayed. If she were so insignificant, why would a man like Qorghanashvili take an interest in her? What motive would this man have for persuading Friend not to speak to her? He decided to speculate a little.

'Well, you certainly seem to know your business,' he said. 'I must say I'm enjoying finding out about the modern Georgia. It's a far cry from the legends of bandits and warlords one gets told in the west. Although I did hear that it isn't so long since you had some pretty fierce warrior kings up in the northern hills.'

Kovalchuk shook his head sadly.

'Such things are ancient history, Roderick. Fairy-tales for romantic minds. Hardly suitable material for readers of your business journals.'

'I suppose you're right. But there was one legend that might have an appeal for readers in the west. Did you ever hear of a bandit they called The Khan? Tengiz Khan?'

Kovalchuk laughed.

'The Khan! He is the biggest fairy-tale of all. The Khan never existed, Roderick. He was a bogeyman invented for the post-Soviet era. Those were uncertain times; it was difficult for many people to know who was in authority, so they created an anti-authority hero figure for themselves. Every time a prominent person they didn't like suffered a reversal of fortune, it was the Khan's doing. But no such person existed. You can believe me on this Roderick, I have good connections at the Ministry of Justice; if there were, or ever had been such a person as Tengiz Khan I would know about it.'

'The Ministry of Justice? That must be useful. Perhaps you know a lawyer called Mikel Qorghanashvili?'

The change in Kovalchuk's manner was abrupt. The smile left his face as if Friend had slapped it off.

'Qorghanashvili? What about him? Do you know him?'

'No, not at all. Somebody in Tbilisi mentioned he was an influential lawyer with connections to the Ministry of Justice, that's all. I thought he might be a good person to talk to about the legal framework for businesses in Georgia, that's all.'

'I don't think he gives interviews.'

Now it was Kovalchuk's turn to look out of the window. The train had passed through the lush, wooded hillsides of central Georgia and the landscape had flattened as they approached the Black Sea coast, about fifty kilometres north of Batumi. Now they felt it braking as they passed by low, wooden houses on the approach to Ureki. Kovalchuk began to pull on his gloves.

'Excuse me,' he said. 'I need to go for a cigarette.'

A few minutes later, as the train stood idling at Ureki station, Friend watched as Kovalchuk joined the dozen or so smokers taking advantage of the brief halt. Kovalchuk was smoking too, but rather than enjoying the taste of the tobacco in the warm midday sun, he waved his cigarette around frantically in one gloved hand while with the other he held a phone to his ear and spoke urgently into the mouthpiece. When the train started off again for the short ride down the coast to Batumi, Kovalchuk did not return to Friend's carriage.

CHAPTER NINE

FRAGMENT

Senka Kovalchuk had told the truth about one thing at least: the roulette table of the Riviera Casino was a likely place to find Nia Dadiani. Friend strolled casually among the gaming tables for fifteen minutes, passing her three or four times before deciding that the bar next door was a better place to make contact. Gambling held no interest for him, but the Riviera to its credit was more restrained in style than its competitors elsewhere in Batumi. Most of them had taken as their model the garishness of Las Vegas rather than the belle epoque elegance of Deauville or Monte Carlo.

Mercifully little of the Riviera's generously proportioned gaming room was taken up by the mechanical rattle of slot machines. Instead, there were several widely-spaced card tables for blackjack or poker and the single roulette table where Nia Dadiani was sitting, perched sedately on a beige leather stool. And to look at her, Nia Dadiani didn't seem any more interested in gambling than Friend was. She played, it seemed, with barely half of her mind on what she was doing, staking a few chips each time on outside bets without any kind of consistency; winning a little, losing more, and greeting each turn of fortune with the same impassive expression. She looked so bored that Friend found it difficult to imagine what she was doing there.

And yet she was dressed for an occasion. The dress code at the Riviera was no stricter than smart casual. Friend had arrived in the navy-blue suit and polished black shoes that headquarters had sent over from his flat to supplement his casual holiday wardrobe. But not wishing to overdo it, he had worn the suit over an open-necked shirt and allowed the stubble left over from his early morning departure from Tbilisi to remain on his chin. But Dadiani was wearing a figure-hugging black cocktail dress with matching court shoes, her blonde hair swept over her left shoulder, revealing a single, square–cut diamond sparkling brilliantly in her right ear. It was an outfit a woman would wear for a special occasion. But Nia Dadiani didn't look as if she were celebrating anything, nor did it seem that she expected to find herself with any friends in the room either. The friendly hubbub of the gaming tables passed her by, and no-one sought to draw her into it. As much as she looked bored, and more, she looked lonely. As little as she reacted to the spinning of the wheel, and less, she reacted to her fellow gamblers. She might have been staring at a computer screen in her own home, spinning a virtual roulette wheel in a virtual, solitary life.

She had dressed far more casually for the office earlier that day, although it had taken Friend some time and patience to catch sight of her. Guria Shipping and Trading occupied a small suite on the second floor of one of Batumi's many new tower blocks of glittering glass and steel. After some persuasion at the reception desk Friend had finally managed to see Ms Dadiani's personal assistant, a friendly young man who said with visible regret that his employer was in a meeting which would be likely to last the rest of the afternoon. But if he would leave his details Ms Dadiani might be able to spare him a few minutes tomorrow, or possibly the day after. Friend had given the name of Hunter and said he could be reached at the Wyndham Hotel, and then he had retreated to a bench in the shade of a palm tree across the street and waited.

He had waited for almost an hour – it was now just after five o'clock – when the building's double doors swung open and down the steps came bounding the familiar lithe figure of Senka Kovalchuk. He was wearing the same outfit he had worn on the morning train from Tbilisi, but looked as fresh as if he had just emerged from a sulphur bath and had his clothes valeted while he was in it. He trotted gaily down the steps, slipping a pair of aviator sunglasses over his eyes while a large, black S-Class Mercedes with tinted windows drew up by the kerb. Kovalchuk walked over to it and climbed into the back seat. Judging by the expression on his face, he was highly satisfied by his day's work.

It was just possible that Kovalchuk's appointment had been with some other business in the same block, but Friend wasn't about to give that possibility much credence. He had to wait another fifteen minutes to catch a glimpse of Nia Dadiani. She came out at the same time as her assistant; perhaps together they formed the company's entire office staff. She was wearing jeans and a jacket of light brown suede; her hair was tied back and her face half covered by a large pair of dark glasses, but Friend had no difficulty recognising the grief-stricken young woman from the funeral photographs. The sadness in her eyes was hidden behind the sunglasses, but even from across the street Friend could sense the tension in her facial muscles, see the stiffness in her gait. Together the couple walked over to a small Japanese hatchback, parked thirty metres or so up the road from the office block. It was a nondescript car with ugly, angular bodywork. It offended Friend's sensibilities to watch Nia Dadiani fold her elegant legs into its cramped, passenger-side footwell. Japanese designers seemed to him to have grown up watching too many cartoons about robots and taken the same futuristic sensibilities into their work. Beauty had no place in their world. Friend gave the car a disapproving glare as it swung out across the road in a wide u-turn, passing his position, before disappearing up the street.

Friend didn't bother to follow them. He would play the part of the inquisitive journalist and chase up his request for an interview if they failed to contact him as the assistant had promised. In the meantime he would focus on Kovalchuk. And, anyway, Batumi was a small town. Perhaps he might run into Nia Dadiani somewhere quite by chance.

Which is more or less what had happened, reflected Friend, as he sat quietly on his own in the Riviera's comfortably appointed bar, sipping a double whisky on the rocks. He hadn't made 'contact', but he had observed her at close quarters and was getting a feel for her character that would only help when the final approach came. And that might well be sooner than he planned, since the only way out of the Casino was directly through the bar he was sitting in.

Friend had almost finished his drink and was considering whether to order another when Nia Dadiani strode into the bar. He thought he detected a sideways glance at him as she passed his table, a movement of the eye rather than the head, but she did not pause. She walked straight to the bar and spoke to the barman. A few moments later she turned around and marched across the room towards Friend's table, a tumbler of whisky in each hand. She placed one of them down in front of Friend before sitting down in the chair opposite his. He watched in silence as she took a slow sip from her glass, rolling it around her tongue as her eyes met his across the table. Finally she swallowed and put down her glass.

'The barman said you were drinking Dimple Haig,' she said in Russian. 'I've never tried it before. I'm impressed. It's rather good.'

'Yes, it is,' replied Friend. 'You don't see it very often these days. Perhaps they're phasing it out. Aren't you going to introduce yourself?'

'Why bother? You already know who I am. You came into the casino but showed no interest in playing. You tried not to look as though you were watching me, but still you watched. I am used to being watched. I don't like it. It makes me uncomfortable.'

'So why buy me a drink?'

'I don't like to waste time either. Especially not my own. You are Mr Roderick Hunter, a journalist, apparently. You came to my office this afternoon to request an interview. My associate spoke about you. He seemed to like you. He has a strange taste in men. When we left the office you were waiting across the road. He pointed you out to me. And now here you are again.'

'Here *we* are again,' Friend corrected her, finishing off his first glass. 'And?'

'And I think you don't look much like a journalist Mr Hunter.'

'So what do I look like, Ms Dadiani?'

'Trouble, Mr Hunter. That's what you look like.'

'I think plenty of people would say that trouble is exactly what a journalist usually looks like.'

A faint smile played around the edges of Nia Dadiani's mouth.

'True,' she said.

Friend gave her the grin he always gave people when he wanted to win them over, or to challenge them.

He said: 'you know, my grandmother used to say that trouble comes along often enough in this world without you needing to put on your hat and coat to go out and meet it.'

'She sounds like a wise woman.'

'Oh, she was. Which makes me wonder again why you put on that wonderful dress, ordered two glasses of expensive whisky and came over here to meet me.'

'My choice of dress was nothing to do with you, Mr Hunter.'

'So who was it to do with? Or what, if you prefer?'

She paused for a moment, as if considering what sort of answer to give, before deciding to give none at all.

'I wonder what your real interest in me is, Mr Hunter. I'll hazard a guess it has nothing to do with my taste in clothes.'

Friend smiled. He didn't know whether this verbal fencing was getting him anywhere, but it was fun.

'Not directly, no. But perhaps it can help me to understand your character a little better.'

'Really? Do go on.'

'You came here alone this evening. Not to meet anyone, although I'd guess you know more than half the people in here. But you still took the trouble to look, well, magnificent.'

'Thank you.'

'Unlike me you did gamble in the casino, and you didn't much care if you won or lost. Then you walked into this bar, sat down and stared trouble in the face and even shared a glass of whisky with it.'

'And what does that tell you about my character?'

'It tells me you're putting on a show. You want everyone here to know that despite everything that's been thrown at you, you're not going to lie down and be defeated. You want them to see your strength, not the vulnerability they expect. You want them to know that you will be vindicated, and that when you are you will be stronger than ever.'

'Vindicated from what?'

'Whatever is causing them to shun you, instead of rallying round you as a friend in trouble might expect.'

'And what do you think that is?'

'The same thing that caused the deaths of your father and your husband.'

He saw her stiffen at once and knew he would have to choose his next words carefully. He took a sip from his whisky as he considered them.

'What makes you think there is a connection between the heart attack that killed my father and the accident that killed my husband?'

'You said so yourself at the time.'

Nia Dadiani sighed, and as she did so all the stiffness, the pride, the sense of challenge and confrontation left her. For a moment, Friend saw her other self: a damaged and vulnerable young woman, who had been putting on a brave face for longer than she could stand. A woman who needed a friend.

'Have you ever lost someone close to you, Mr Hunter?' she asked.

Friend's thoughts travelled back to Helmand, to an instant of profound silence and confusion, to the knowledge that something terrible had just happened without him being sure quite what, to the men who had been with him in the back of the vehicle: Dodds, Higgins, Hindson, Parnaby, Jobling. To the ringing in his ears and the red mist clouding his vision, to the broken shafts of light pouring in through the buckled doors at the back and the shrapnel holes peppering every wall, to the strange object that seemed have got trapped in the collar of his tunic, that he didn't recognise at first when he pulled it free: a human thumb.

He shrugged, in as off-hand a manner as he could.

'My grandfather, the year before last,' he said.

Nia Dadiani leaned forward.

'Then let me tell you what it's like. I lost my mother when I was eight. Cancer. I was old enough to understand that I would never see her again but too young to understand why. Then some time later my father, then my husband. Very bad luck, you might say. But each time you lose someone close to you like that, a part of you travels with them to the next world. The next time a little bit more of you goes, then a little bit more, until eventually there is hardly enough of you left in this world to keep you whole. So here I am, just a fragment of a human soul, trapped between two worlds; part of my mind, my soul, permanently elsewhere. Those things I said after their deaths, they were the product of that mind. Please remember that.'

'You still have your son.'

'Yes, my son. I sent him away to school in England. Summer Fields. Perhaps you know it?'

'I've heard of it. Near Oxford, I think. It's a good school.'

'I'm glad you think so. The name makes it sound like a good place. So you wonder why I come here to this casino so often? My house is the home I grew up in. Not long ago there were three generations of us living there. It was full of joy, laughter, arguments, crises, emotions and mess. Now there is just silence. Just me. Maybe you can see why I choose to come here instead of staying at home in the evenings.'

'I understand. But why stay there? Why not leave?'

'It is still my home. It belonged to my father, one day it will belong to my son. Hopefully he will have a family and it will be filled with laughter and joy once more. So there you have it. The story of Nia Dadiani. Nothing more to tell. Nothing there worth printing.'

'I disagree, it's a fascinating story and I'm sure there's more to tell, if you give me the chance to hear it.'

No sooner had Friend said the words then he knew there would be nothing more to hear from Nia Dadiani that night. Out of the corner of his eye he spotted a pair of highly polished English brogues that supported the slinky frame of Alexei Kovalchuk.

'Good evening, Mr Hunter. So you found our dear Nia after all?' He turned to the woman and gave a formal little bow. 'Good evening to you too, Nia. Our friend Mr Hunter is staying just across the road at the Wyndham. Very convenient!'

Nia Dadiani acknowledged Kovalchuk's greeting with a nod and sat stiffly in her chair. Kovalchuk turned back to Friend.

'Mr Hunter, I think this unexpected meeting is perhaps a sign that I should renew the offer I made to you earlier today. If you are free tomorrow I can introduce you to some most interesting people who should be very useful to you in your research. I will even buy you lunch. I could pick you up at nine thirty. What do you say?'

Friend looked across the table at Nia and saw at once that Kovalchuk's appearance had put to bed any hopes he had of further confidences from her. But if she wouldn't talk more, perhaps he might get something out of Kovalchuk.

'All right,' he said. 'Nine thirty tomorrow morning.'

'Excellent. I will now leave you two alone to enjoy your drinks. Good night.'

He flashed them a broad smile that showed glistening white teeth, then turned smartly on his heel and walked out. Nia Dadiani gave him a few moments to get clear, then got to her feet.

'It is time for me to leave as well. Thank you for the drink Mr Hunter.'

'You haven't finished it yet. Please stay a little longer.'

'No thank you. I have no desire to spend any more time than is necessary with associates of Senka Kovalchuk.'

'I'm hardly that. I never heard of him before today. We met on the train from Tbilisi.'

'Really? I don't know whether to believe you or not. Perhaps my first instinct about you was right. You bring trouble.'

'If I do, it won't be for you. I promise.'

'Only fools believe promises from strangers, Mr Hunter. Good night.'

Friend stood as she turned to go, and watched in silence as she strode, proudly but elegantly, from the room. He bent down to pick up her glass, noticing the faint red stain of lip gloss at its edge and the dying hint of expensive perfume where she had sat with him. It had been quite a performance, from the careless gambling to the confident challenge she offered to his inquisitiveness, to the dramatic exit which, without even the slightest wobble of a stiletto heel, had drawn the furtive glances of every man in the room. But her reaction to Senka Kovalchuk had been interesting. It was clear that she despised him, yet he had no qualms about coming up to her in public and treating her like an old friend.

Friend tipped the contents of Nia Dadiani's glass into his own and took one large mouthful, rolling the spirit around his tongue and savouring its honeyish warmth. Then, after letting that first taste slide gently down his throat, he raised the glass and downed the rest of it in a single gulp.

CHAPTER TEN

SILVER MOUNTAIN

By one o'clock the following day Sebastian Friend was already beginning to regret his commitment to learn more about Senka Kovalchuk. He had been collected outside the Wyndham at nine-thirty on the dot by the same black, S-Class Mercedes he had observed outside Nia Dadiani's office. From there, the unctuous Kovalchuk, together with his silent chauffeur Josef, who seemed to be leading a one-man campaign to restore the Georgian man's traditional bushy moustache, had taken him on a whirlwind tour of Batumi's business elite. He had interviewed a shipping magnate, an import-export merchant, a hotelier and even the property developers behind the hideous Twin Towers project that would soon turn Batumi's charming seafront of boulevards and gardens into something resembling a giants' graveyard. He had gone through two sets of batteries and three memory cards in his voice recorder and almost convinced himself that he was a bona fide journalist researching a story that would bore readers from Tunbridge Wells to Tokyo. All the while Senka Kovalchuk had simpered at his shoulder, complimenting him on the incisiveness of his questions and his ability to get the most taciturn of businessmen talking freely.

At last he called a halt. It was time for lunch, he said, leading a jaded Friend towards the waiting Mercedes.

'After all, if the Good Lord had meant us to work without rest he wouldn't have given us stomachs that need feeding or heads that need to lay down and sleep.'

'Or tongues that need moistening with drink,' commented Friend acidly.

'Exactly!' said Kovalchuk, pulling a cold beer from an ice box hidden in the arm-rest between their two seats. Friend was only too pleased to accept it.

Summer comes early in Batumi, tucked away as it is in the south-western corner of Georgia, just a short ride from the Turkish border. By early afternoon the humidity in the city had become nearly unbearable, and Friend began to think more kindly of the northern winds that had assailed him up in the mountains just a week or so before. So when Kovalchuk suggested they drive out of town for lunch at a place he knew up in the hills, Friend was happy to go along with the suggestion, uncomfortable as he felt in the man's company.

There was something about Senka Kovalchuk that irked him. He had charm all right, and style and a touch of humour. But Friend was wary of his intense curiosity about the finer details of Roderick Hunter's background, coupled with his reluctance to offer anything more than vague generalities about his own; a combination that made Friend think of an agent with a half-learned cover. Kovalchuk would wave away personal questions as if his own life experiences were not worthy of conversation. Such false humility did not sit well with his evident self-satisfaction and confidence. The businessmen he had introduced Friend to, each a powerful and influential man in his own right, had treated Kovalchuk not as a friend or business contact, but with a kind of deference that suggested an unspoken power dynamic between the two. Some of that deference had translated into an acceptance of Friend's line of questioning; they had behaved to him with greater openness than any journalist would normally have a right to expect. Friend had learned nothing from them that was pertinent to his real enquiry, but he had learned something about Kovalchuk. People were wary of him.

He wondered why he was being shown this VIP treatment. Was it just to keep him away from any further contact with Nia Dadiani? Or was there also an attempt to show Friend the calibre of man he would be up against if they found themselves on opposite sides? Kovalchuk was smart enough to know that Friend's real interest in Batumi was the link between Nia Dadiani and Mikel Qorghanashvili. If there was a further link between this and the murder of Emre Parvan, he would also surely know that this was the same 'Rock Hunter' who had spoken with Parvan in Istanbul. Surely the easiest way to prevent further investigation would be to make Mr Hunter quietly disappear. But if that was the plan, surely Kovalchuk would not have spent the whole morning publicly connecting himself with the soon-to-be victim.

Friend was to be the victim of nothing more than an excellent lunch that day. They drove east out of the city on the main road towards Akhaltsikhe before turning off onto a minor road just after the river Chorokhi turns south towards Turkey. The road tracked the river for a few miles, passing the spectacular Mrveti waterfalls, before they turned east again along the steep, wooded Machakhlistskali river valley on the northern fringes of the Machakela National Park. The landscape seemed impossibly remote compared with urban, westernised Batumi; they passed the odd isolated farmstead, and at one point approached a charming-looking restaurant with a terrace overlooking the river and the wooded bank beyond. But Josef kept his foot down and the car sped past without even a pause. Kovalchuk had been silent and thoughtful for a few minutes and Friend began to wonder whether the bulge under the driver's left armpit had a significance for him after all.

But after another fifteen minutes they turned off the road and made their way through a scattered hillside village.

'We are almost there,' said Kovalchuk. 'It's more of a hotel really, for tourists visiting the national park, but they have a small restaurant too. The food is excellent and the manager, he is quite a character! I think you call them in England "grumpy old men"?'

Friend nodded.

'Well, our friend Dimitri is a grumpy old man to rival any you will have met before. He has had an interesting life and knows more about Georgia and its history than I will ever learn, but he probably won't tell you about it. He doesn't communicate much with strangers.'

'Unusual attitude for a hotel manager.'

'Dimitri is a very unusual hotel manager. Anyway, we might not be lucky enough to meet him today. In this weather he may be off taking some tourists hiking in the mountains. In complete silence of course. But he is an excellent guide. He knows these hills like the back of his hand. I think he is probably more at home in them than he is in the comfort of his hotel.'

'Does he own the hotel?'

'No, he is just the manager.'

'So who owns it?'

'I'm really not sure. Oh look, here we are.'

They had almost climbed to the end of the village. Josef had turned down a short drive towards what looked for all the world like an alpine chalet. A steeply-pitched wooden roof swept down across clean, whitewashed walls. The windows were shuttered and decorated with flower boxes and behind the building Friend could see a small meadow of wildflowers, beyond which stood the thick fringe of pine trees that marked the end of this small riverside community and the beginnings of the mountains beyond. To the side of the hotel building stood a single-storey flat-roofed extension that housed the restaurant.

'Welcome to the Silver Mountain Hotel,' said Kovalchuk.

Friend looked up at the hills as he climbed out of the car.

'Silver?' he said. 'They look pretty green to me.'

Kovalchuk laughed. 'You're right. But I believe there was a silver mine hereabouts many years ago.'

The restaurant was all rustic pinewood, the tables roughly hewn to resemble as closely as possible the trees they had once been, their coverings of red and white linen in traditional Georgian designs. Shelves along each walls bore empty bottles from thirty years of Georgian vintages. But at the front of the building a huge picture window offered a spectacular view back down the hillside over the pitched clay rooves of the little houses to the foaming rapids of the river below. There were only two customers, a pair of stern-looking young businessmen who greeted Kovalchuk with brief nods and went back to demolishing their bowls of fish soup.

A small, pretty, dark-haired waitress greeted Kovalchuk with the same degree of deference Friend had witnessed that morning and ushered them to a table by the window. Kovalchuk didn't bother to ask for a menu; he said a few words to the waitress in Georgian to which she smiled and nodded before scuttling off to the kitchens. Friend noticed that Josef had gone over to sit with the two businessmen, who let him join their table without a murmur, as if it happened every day.

'I hope you don't mind adding wine on top of your beer,' said Kovalchuk, 'but the local Ajarian wine is excellent. I ordered us a bottle of white, plus some local fish and a light salad. I hope that's all right.'

'Perfect. Just the sort of thing I like.'

'I'm so glad.'

Kovalchuk continued with the pleasantries, revealing a knowledge of the local landscape that was impressive in such an apparently urban operator. Friend engaged with the display. He knew they were both playing at being charmed with each other, but at the same time there was much about Kovalchuk that made him good company. He was a gifted conversationalist, with that knack of making whoever he was speaking to feel like the most interesting person in the room. All the same, Friend knew he must be on his guard. Kovalchuk was digging further into Roderick Hunter's background. He asked how he had got involved in business journalism, and Friend replied that it had been a fairly recent change in emphasis for him. Once again, his story was pure improvisation.

'I started out in sport, actually. I did occasional pieces for the national newspapers and magazines, but that's quite a difficult world to establish yourself in and earn a proper living. Too many writers chasing too few bylines. And I'm not sure I wanted to spend the rest of my life writing about sport anyway. So I moved into general news, did some foreign correspondent work. Spent a couple of years in Moscow, which is where I learned my Russian. Then somehow I ended up doing a lot of stories on refugee crises in the middle east and Africa, which really started by accident. The agency I was with needed someone to go to Sudan and their usual man was ill. I was stupid enough to volunteer. After that I spent a couple of years in some pretty hairy war zones, before deciding I'd had enough of that. I got in on an investigation into international money-laundering and it was that really which led me more into the area of business and finance.'

'So you don't do stories about refugees any more?'

'I try not to. But as a matter of fact just last week I was asked to work on a piece in Turkey. It was a waste of time really; I only got called in because a local journalist had died and I had met her once or twice in the past. I spoke to her editor but there was nothing much he could tell me. All her files were in the hands of the Turkish police, and they aren't too cooperative at the best of times. So I told the office there was nothing doing and came back to this. Hopefully I can stick to business and economics from now on.'

'I see. You enjoy it?'

'Very much. I've always had an interest in how the world works. And my mother was a lecturer in economics, so I had a good grounding in that from childhood.'

'What a fascinating life you must have had. So many journeys, so many experiences. And in one so young. I think you are perhaps one or two years younger than me? But I don't suppose it leaves you much time for a home life, or relationships.'

'That's true. I live in a small flat in London that's barely big enough for me. I'm not there often enough to look after it properly, or to find someone to look after it with me. What about you?'

Kovalchuk offered a wan smile and gestured with his hand as if to say: alas, it has not been my lot to be favoured with the good Lord's fortune in that way.

'But speaking of women, how did you find our lovely Nia?'

'Not very welcoming, to be frank. I think she views any approach by a journalist as a hostile intrusion. Not at all like those you introduced me to this morning.'

'Yes, it was as I thought. Nia Dadiani is a rather damaged young woman. Perhaps one day she will recover and become the woman we all know she can be, but…'

He left the thought hanging in the air.

'She didn't seem at all pleased to see you last night,' said Friend.

'No, I'm afraid you are right. As I said to you before, many people have tried to give Nia Dadiani helpful advice since her father died, and I am one of them. She hasn't always taken it well.'

'What advice did you offer her?'

'If you will forgive me, that is her business, not ours. Ah, but I see our food is arriving!'

The fish had been oven baked in foil with garlic and herbs; the salad was of green leaves and peppers decorated with pieces of walnut and pomegranate seeds. It was delicious, as was the wine that accompanied it, which even Tamara Magniac would have been proud to have produced. Friend complimented his host on his good taste.

'Please, Mr Hunter, it is my pleasure. I come here frequently and usually order the same thing, only it is nice to have someone to share a bottle with. It is too much for one at lunchtime, don't you agree?'

'Personally yes, but there are some old journalists in London who would view one bottle each as the bare minimum.'

'Really? By the way, can I ask a favour of you? I would be most honoured if you would call me Senka, or Alexei, rather than Mr

Kovalchuk. I think we know each other well enough know, don't you?'

'Yes, all right. My friends call me Rock.'

'Did you say Rock?'

'Yes. A stupid childhood nickname.'

'How interesting. Oh, wait a moment!'

Kovalchuk looked over Friend's shoulder and grinned.

'Our host is here after all,' he said.

Friend turned to see a small, dark-haired man shuffling slowly towards them, a sombre expression on his face. He wore a rather shapeless black suit with trousers that were too baggy for his stocky legs. To judge from the face, he was about sixty years old but the hair was still jet black with no flecks of grey. He wore it as a thick mop, brushed straight back from a square forehead. He was clean shaven but his upper lip looked as though it were missing a moustache; the thin lips protruded slightly. As he came closer, he slipped off the small pair of rectangular reading glasses he was wearing and placed them in his breast pocket. Friend noticed that the face was slightly pockmarked. The effect was, he thought, rather like a clean-shaven Stalin come to life.

Kovalchuk broke the silence.

'Ah, my friend Dimitri, how nice to see you!' he said, rising from his chair.

The other man held up his hand. 'Don't get up,' he said. 'You are enjoying your lunch?'

The voice rasped harshly, like exhaust fumes over gravel.

'Yes, thank you. As delicious as always.'

Dmitri acknowledged the compliment with a grunt.

'Was there something you wanted to see me about?'

'No, not at all. But since you're here I would like to introduce my friend, Mr Roderick Hunter, a journalist from England.'

A pair of small, black eyes hooded by heavy lids turned to meet Friend's welcoming smile. His expression did not change.

'Mr Hunter,' he acknowledged.

'Dimitri.'

Kovalchuk continued: 'Mr Hunter is researching a story about business in Batumi and I have been making some introductions for him.'

'Is that so?' Dimitri's voice gave little indication of interest.

'But he is also interested in our Georgian culture and history, that's right isn't it, Rock?'

'Yes, certainly.'

Kovalchuk gave Dimitri his most effusive smile. 'Somebody was telling him the legend of Tengiz Khan. But of course, I told him that was just a fairy tale. That's right, isn't it?'

Dimitri's eyes turned on Friend once more. He seemed to be breathing a little more heavily, as if the question annoyed him.

'Right. A fairy tale. Nothing more.'

'I mean, a man with your background and knowledge, you would know if The Khan really existed, or ever had done.'

'I would.'

Kovalchuk sat back in triumph. 'Well, there you are then!' he said.

Dimitri looked irritated. He turned back to Kovalchuk.

'Was there anything else you wanted?'

'No, my friend. Your waitress is looking after our needs perfectly.'

'In that case I will leave you. Enjoy the rest of your day.'

He gave one courteous nod which took in them both, then turned to leave. Friend felt Dimitri's eyes pass over him once more and knew that his face was being committed to memory. He watched curiously as Dimitri plodded slowly away.

'What was all that about?' he asked.

Kovalchuk laughed.

'You must forgive me Rock, I cannot resist teasing him. You see as well as being one of life's grumpy old men, my friend Dimitri is something of a modernist. He is just about the proudest Georgian you will ever meet and he considers legends of banditry and such like to be a stain on our national character. Even if The Khan did exist I believe Dimitri would deny him, although I can assure you he does not.'

Friend did not know what to think, except in one respect. The black-haired Dimitri was another who was no friend of Senka Kovalchuk.

CHAPTER ELEVEN

GEORGIAN ROULETTE

'Your new friend Kovalchuk is a shady little bastard, for starters.' Magniac looked washed out. Nobody looks their best on a video screen, but his skin was grey and his eyes were puffy. He must have been up most of the night chasing down the information Friend had requested on Senka Kovalchuk, the Silver Mountain Hotel and the Caucasian Credit Trust. 'Some of what he said was true. Russian father and Georgian mother. He did go to university in Moscow – business and international relations – he might have had a decent career ahead of him. But he chose another path. According to our sources, the FSB have a pretty hefty file on him. Apparently, not long after he left university, he put together one of the largest-scale bogus dating sites to have operated out of the former Soviet Union, scamming hundreds of thousands of dollars out of gullible American and European men. That one he operated alone, with the help of a couple of girlfriends. The authorities never had enough to press charges against him, but it does seem to have brought him to the attention of one of the most significant crime syndicates in Russia.

'They're known as the *Presnenskaya Bratva*, after the area of Moscow they sprang from. Kovalchuk may have called on their help in dealing with some of his angrier customers. No-one died, but there were a few nasty beatings. Since then, Kovalchuk is thought to have acted as a kind of international fixer for Presnenskaya Bratva: liaising with overseas partners, arranging transportation, transfers of funds and scoping out new opportunities that fit with their extensive portfolio of activities; trafficking of illegal goods and human beings, money laundering, loan sharking, extortion, protection rackets, dealing in stolen goods, to name just a few. He travels widely in former Soviet states, Eastern Europe, the Middle East, and occasionally in the west. Nowhere has he ever been convicted, or even charged, with any criminal offence, so he's either a superb professional or he has powerful protection.'

'Charming fellow,' commented Friend.

'Now, as for the Silver Mountain Hotel, it opened about twenty years ago, but it never made much money. The bank foreclosed on the original owners after about five years and then it passed through a few different hands until four years ago. Which is when it was purchased by a private investment bank called – guess what - the Caucasian Credit Trust.'

'So, Senka Kovalchuk shows me a business card with the name of this bank on it but then claims not to know that his employers own the hotel he takes me to lunch in.'

'For what it's worth, I haven't been able to find out much else about the Caucasian Credit Trust. They have a website, but they don't seem very interested in attracting new business. The only information it provides is their registration number with the Ministry of Finance, an office address in Tbilisi, a contact email that hasn't replied and a telephone number that rings without answer. I dare say I'll be able to dig up more given time.'

'What do you think? A front for Presnenskaya Bratva? I can't see any other reason why a private investment bank would purchase a failing hotel and run it as a going concern.'

'What do they get out of it?'

'Well, it's remote for one thing, and close to the Turkish border. Handy for a smuggling operation. Or they could use it for clandestine meetings. Perhaps it's just a useful place to have on the balance sheet when they have a few million to launder.' Friend thought for a moment. 'What about the manager, Dimitri? Anything on him?'

'Do you know how many Dimitris there are between here and Corfu, Laddie? He's not listed on any documentation relating to the hotel. If he takes a salary the tax office must have a record of him but don't ask me how I'm going to get access to that. Find me a surname and I might get something for you.'

Friend was silent.

'So, that's all I have for now,' Magniac concluded. 'What's your next move?'

'I don't think I'll get anything more from Kovalchuk. Not without showing my hand and I don't want to be too close to him when that happens.' He shook his head. 'I can't help feeling that if I'm going to make any progress with this, it will be through Nia Dadiani. One way or another, I have to get her to talk.'

Magniac didn't ask, but he wondered what way Friend had in mind.

* * *

Friend's cover ought to have been holding up well after his day out with Kovalchuk, but he wasn't too surprised to see Josef lurking in the hotel lobby when he came down for breakfast. The man with the drooping moustache quickly ducked behind a pillar as if it would prevent him being seen. *Amateur*.

But the others weren't. He spotted the first of them easily enough: a small, neat fellow who quickly folded his newspaper and got up from his chair as Friend walked out through the lobby an hour or so later. The other two he didn't pick up until he was on the beach. They weren't bad at all, but in their city suits they stood out from the crowds of sunbathers and sightseers. They were too young to be ex-KGB but someone from the *Komitet* might have trained them. The trouble with these criminal organisations was they weren't really set up for surveillance; that wasn't their business. Very few of their people would know how to tail a mark and if he happened to lead them somewhere where they didn't fit with the background they were stuck with it. There was no reserve team to swap in. Friend didn't mind. He wasn't doing anything that required him to flush his tail; so let them watch him and reinforce the cover of a journalist enjoying a morning off.

Friend left the beach just as it was starting to get hot and busy. He strolled down the palm tree-lined Old Boulevard, though the elegantly planted gardens, past a smart looking tennis club and a couple of rather tacky casinos. There was an international air to the sea front; Georgians mixing with Armenians, Iranians, Azeris, Ukrainians and Russians, Turks, even the odd western tourist. Holidaymakers and office workers taking a sun break. Couples strolling arm-in-arm. Mothers out walking with their babies and meeting up with other Mums for coffee and ice cream.

At the end of the boulevard the line of sandy beach ran out and the shore curved round towards the harbour. The start of the port was marked by Batumi's small 19th century lighthouse, now dwarfed by a pair of modern towers and a giant new Ferris wheel. Did everywhere have to have a London Eye now? Friend walked on past the Ottoman-style Chacha clock tower and saw the blue stucco of the Port Authority building and the tall masts of the yachts moored at the adjacent marina. Further on, past the yachts and pleasure cruisers, the promenade ended and marina became seaport. The rest of the harbour road led east, hemmed in beside the port road and the rail freight terminal. Through the fence that blocked his access, Friend could see the railway sidings where containers were lifted on and off the moored vessels by a row of tall cranes. He joined the road and walked further. There was no obvious means of access at this point, save for jumping the fence in full view of the main road, or stowing away on a freight carriage.

The possibilities were better at the ferry port. Both the ferry and container terminals jutted squarely out into the harbour, while a narrow, tree-lined mole offered further moorings in a straight line back towards the marina. An access road led directly into the ferry terminal, and as far as Friend could see there was nothing to prevent him from leaving it and walking into the container port. He passed several people heading down to the terminal where a ferry to Trabzon was waiting to board. Walking further on, he came to the fish market. After wandering through its aisles for a few minutes and making himself thoroughly hungry, he walked out through the back towards the seafront, where several cafés and restaurants lined the harbour wall. There were options here too, depending on where the May Rose might be moored.

'What's good today?'

None of the traders in the fish market seemed to be doing much business and several of them called out in Russian to the blond-haired foreigner as he passed by. Friend picked the one who didn't bother: a rather scruffy, unshaven man of uncertain age, wearing a badly faded blue and white striped shirt beneath an apron that might once have been white before fish guts and blood stained it beyond redemption. The man gave a shrug and pointed to some firm-looking sea trout.

'These aren't bad. They came in on my brother-in-law's boat this morning. But you should have seen this place twenty years ago. Not so many tourists but many more fish. Tuna, swordfish, mackerel, we used to have them every day. Thousands! Not any more. Those damn Turks took them all. They fished the Black Sea out. Then there's pollution from undersea oil drilling. Sunlight can't penetrate to the same depths as before because the water is dirty, so some fish die because of that and others because they live on those fish. Last year our catch dropped by more than half. Can you imagine? All we have left is this sea trout, barabulka and flounder, anchovies and sprats. Small stuff. Even bluefish you hardly ever see now. It's a tragedy!' The old man shrugged and poked at the largest of the sea trout with a not-very-clean finger. 'What about this one? If you want it for lunch, take it out back to the Blue Wave and they'll grill it nicely for you. Tell them Tengiz sent you.'

Friend smiled. It was the first time he had heard the name in use. He handed over a few notes and then watched as Tengiz, with the expertise of decades, trimmed the fins and cleaned out the guts.

* * *

At nine o'clock Friend strode through the Riviera bar towards the gaming room. Nia Dadiani was already in her usual seat at the roulette table; he had watched from across the street as the taxi dropped her at the casino entrance twenty minutes before. She glanced up at him as he took up his station behind the vacant seat opposite, her face expressionless. Then she returned her attention to the game. Today she was wearing a light grey trouser suit over an emerald-green silk blouse with a single string of pearls at her throat; her hair was tied back in an elaborate braid.

None of the other gamblers were dressed with such formality and elegance. The man on his right Friend took to be an Armenian businessman; mid-forties, slightly paunchy with an incipient double chin and a powerful, rather hooked nose. Beneath his tightly-fitted black velvet jacket an open-necked white shirt revealed a forest of chest hair bursting for freedom. On his left sat a powerfully-built, completely bald Russian in a scarlet shirt and black trousers, a dark-haired local beauty at his shoulder. Probably a tourist enjoying what he thought of as the high-life. On Nia's left sat a quiet-looking middle-aged Georgian with a mop of curly grey hair, a drooping grey moustache and thick, black-framed glasses. The seat to Nia's right was occupied by a studious-looking young man, thin and pale and looking like he normally did his gambling in his bedroom and had wandered in here by accident.

Friend had no intention of playing the same game; he was here to make an impression, not a killing. Just as Nia was showing her tenacity, her defiance of fate in being here, so Friend would show that he would not be giving up. He wanted her to see him there, directly opposite her, and wonder what game he was really playing. She was used to being watched. *I don't like it. It makes me uncomfortable.* He wanted her uncomfortable.

The croupier called for bets. The other players quickly selected theirs, but Nia waited, as if she wanted to see whether Friend would move first. Eventually she slid two chips, $50 each, onto the first dozen. The croupier gave Friend a look, as if to say either play or get out. Friend leaned forward, settling his arms on the chair back, and ignored him. The croupier shrugged and called an end to bets, span the wheel with a flick of his wrist and dropped the ball in. For a moment, as the ball whirred around the wheel, Friend was almost captivated by the uncertainty of the outcome, but then the anti-climax as it stuttered, jumped, bobbed and landed in number three, red. Nia glanced up at Friend as she gathered in her winnings. Getting no reaction, she slid her original two chips across the table and left them on evens. She was playing a low-stakes, low-risk game.

The ball span again and dropped into 22, black. The third spin: Nia opted to return to the dozens, this time the third. Once more her luck was in: 33 black. She shared her win with the Russian, who gave a whoop of joy and received a kiss from his lady friend that he barely noticed. Nia raked in her winnings and glanced up at Friend again. He met her gaze but offered no smile, no acknowledgement of her win. It *was* making her uncomfortable. Would she call Security and ask them to remove him? But with what excuse? There was no rule against watching the play.

The red rectangle was empty. Nia Dadiani swept together a large pile of chips between her hands and slid them across to it. She looked at Friend with challenge in her eye. Since he arrived at the table there had been no conversation, just the croupier calling the bets and the few isolated noises of joy and despair made by the players. But now Nia spoke directly to Friend.

'This looks rather like stalking, Mr Hunter. Or are you intending to play this evening?'

'I'm happier watching you win than watching myself lose, thank you, Ms Dadiani.' And watching her win so frequently he was beginning to wonder if this was some kind of pay-off. 'And at least I seem to be bringing you luck.'

The ball span. Six, seven, eight times it described its circle until Friend gave up counting, the metallic whir became a rattle and the ball hopped up, bounced off the bar between 24 and 16 and landed in 24. Black. Nia sat back in her chair drumming her fingers on the table as the croupier raked in her stake. Her winning run was over. No matter, she wouldn't be running out of money any time soon. But she was running out of patience. This was her space; where she came to escape. And Friend was invading it. Nia's fingers continued drumming the table as the croupier set up for the next spin of the wheel. She glanced up once and quickly away again. A moment later came another brief glance. Then she folded her arms and spoke to him directly:

'You're not bringing me luck any more Mr Hunter. So what now?'

'A temporary blip, I hope. Perhaps your luck will turn again.'

'Mr Hunter, if you don't intend to play, I suggest you spend your evening somewhere else. Lurking here like this you're just disturbing everyone.'

Friend put on an apologetic smile.

'I'm sorry, Ms Dadiani, I really did think that I was bringing you luck.'

She glowered back at him.

'But if you prefer not to be observed, perhaps you might join me for a drink in the bar later?'

'I don't think so, Mr Hunter.'

'A pity. In that case, perhaps you'll accept my parting gift.'

He removed an envelope from his jacket pocket and tossed it onto the table in front of her. Her chips scattered. Without pausing for her reaction, Friend turned and walked towards the bar.

* * *

It took less than three minutes. Nia Dadiani stormed into the bar and made straight for Friend. Where before she had been proud, defiant, now she was simply furious. She threw the envelope down in front of him.

'What the hell is all this about?' she demanded.

'I bought you a whisky,' he replied in an even tone, as if unaware of her fury.

'Damn your whisky! Drink it yourself. I want to know why you came here tonight and threw this rubbish at me. What has it to do with me?'

'It's your ship.'

'What do you mean?'

'The ship in these photographs. It's one of yours.'

Friend opened the envelope and spread the contents across the table. He pointed at one of the photographs taken by the Istanbul ship-spotter Altan Karabeg.

'The May Rose, owned and operated by Guria Shipping and Trading. Pictured passing through the Bosphorus on its last voyage out of Batumi.'

'What of it?'

He pointed at another pair of images, grainier, as if they had been blown up from a wider original.

'These were taken a few moments later. They show a man and a dark-haired woman fighting on board the vessel and the woman going overboard. She was a journalist called Elif Çalışkan. Her body washed up at Fenerbahçe Marina thirty-six hours later. She died in the water, but not of drowning; she was already fatally wounded when she fell in. I also included press reports about her death in what I gave you.'

She snorted. 'If all this is true, then why have I not been questioned by the police? Why is it you who brings me this "evidence"?'

'Because the police do not have the photographs. They have nothing to connect you with the death of Elif Çalışkan.'

Nia Dadiani looked away and gave a knowing smile at no-one in particular.

'All right, what do you want, Mr Hunter?'

'I want you to sit down, drink your whisky, and listen to me for a few minutes.'

She sat down, but she did not touch her whisky.

'I knew you looked like trouble Mr Hunter. And now I find you are. Not a journalist, just a blackmailer.'

'I'm not here to blackmail you.'

'Oh really? So what would you call it? A business arrangement? You have evidence implicating the company I own in a murder. The police don't have the evidence and you won't give it to them unless… unless I do what?'

'I don't intend to give the evidence to the police at all. Whether in Georgia or Turkey I don't trust the police to handle the matter in the right way. I am concerned that you would be held responsible for things which are really the fault of others. I will only hand the evidence over to the police if I am convinced that in doing so I can bring these others to justice.'

'What "others" do you mean?'

'Our mutual acquaintance Alexei Kovalchuk, for one.'

'Kovalchuk? Save your efforts Mr Hunter, and don't waste my time. The only way Kovalchuk will get his just desserts is when he double-crosses someone even nastier than himself. I'm sorry for the death of this woman, but I don't see that getting me involved can possibly help her now.'

'All I am asking is that you tell me about your involvement with Kovalchuk, how he acquired a hold over your business and anything else you know about him, his activities and his associates. That might help others and it might even help you.'

'All? You really don't know what you're asking.'

'I believe I do. Kovalchuk, or those he works with, had your father and your husband killed. They now threaten your son to ensure your co-operation. That's why you sent him to school in England. But even there you fear he is not safe, so you co-operate with Kovalchuk, give him what he wants and hope that one day he might go away. But you know he won't. And one day, if nothing changes, your son too will be under the same pressure as you are now and that dream of a happy family home, you, your son, his wife and family, three generations happy under one roof once more, will never come true. That is the future unless somehow you can get rid of Kovalchuk once and for all, by bringing him and his people to justice. I am your chance of doing that. Don't miss it.'

Nia Dadiani stared at Friend. Her bottom lip quivered slightly and he saw her bite it back. She picked up the glass of whisky in front of her and drank slowly, then she put it down and picked up the photographs instead, slowly leafing through them and studying each in detail. Finally, she put them down and took another drink.

'Put those away,' she said. 'I don't want to see them again.'

Carefully, as if by making too much noise he might jeopardise an imminent surrender, Friend collected all the photographs together and returned them to the envelope, slipping it back into the pocket of his jacket.

'All right Mr Hunter. I will talk to you. But not here. And it must not look as if we parted friends. Come to my house for dinner tomorrow evening. Nine o'clock. There is someone I would like you to meet.'

'Thank you. I'll be there. What's your address?'

Nia Dadiani smiled and leaned forward in her chair.

'You're an investigative journalist, Mr Hunter. So investigate.'

And with that, she picked up her glass of whisky and threw the contents in Friend's face.

CHAPTER TWELVE

FAMILY

Friend slept away the heat of the day in his room, then in the cool early evening he wandered idly among the streets in the general direction of the seafront. He had become almost convinced by the confusion of architectural styles Batumi boasted. 'Almost' because he knew that inevitably the old would be outweighed and dominated by the new; that the old city's charm could not survive the giganticism of new developments like the Twin Towers. He wished that the mountains could stay where they had always been, in the distance, a comforting presence on the horizon. Close enough should you wish to climb them, but never so close that their overwhelming size could cast a whole city and its people into their shadows.

He found a restaurant with a terrace bar overlooking the seafront not far from the Port Authority building, and settled there with a beer, watching in silence the sun sink towards the horizon over the Black Sea. By eight-fifteen the sun had set, and the western sky was edged with a dazzling deep blue. Friend paid for his beer and walked out onto the promenade alongside the marina. He had only gone a couple of hundred metres when he spotted a taxi heading in the opposite direction; he dashed across the road and hailed it, stealing a quick glance over his shoulder as he did so. The promenade was quiet; couples out for an evening stroll just as he had been. Instinct told him he wasn't being followed. But still, he asked the driver to take him to the Batumi Arts Centre, the city's major concert venue. The four-kilometre drive north took fifteen minutes.

The arcaded glass roof of the Arts Centre was visible from a distance away; the venue was lit up for a folk-dance performance put on for tourists from visiting cruise liners. Friend's mind registered the scene as he ducked away from the taxi and made his way on foot to the central railway station. Five minutes later he trotted up the front steps of the station and entered the almost empty ticket hall. He studied the departures board and then looked around as if trying to make his mind up about something. Apparently decided, he walked swiftly over to a side entrance and down the steps back to the street. Several taxis were waiting there for the evening's last arrival from Tbilisi, due just after nine. Friend jumped into the first and gave Nia Dadiani's address to the driver. He was still clean; no-one on his tail, no electronic devices on his person that might be tracked in real time, or later.

Nia Dadiani lived, as might be expected, in an exclusive neighbourhood of well-appointed villas that had once been home to most of Batumi's senior communist officials. North of the city centre, just a ten-minute drive for Friend's taxi, it centred on a street that wound up a lightly wooded hillside above the Korilistskali river, the trees occasionally parting to give a view of the lights of Batumi sparkling across the moonlit bay. Friend could well understand Nia's reluctance to give up this place she called home.

The Dadiani house was set back about twenty yards from the street in the shade of a mature cedar tree. It was hardly secure; just a shallow wall and a pair of waist-high iron gates separating it from passers-by, a solid and simple two-storey building, rendered and painted the dark green colour typical of Russian dachas. Friend paid off the driver and stood waiting on the pavement some fifty metres from the house until the car completed a three-point turn and drove off back down the hill. The street was impossibly quiet. Hardly a light seemed to be showing from any of the houses and the only sounds Friend could hear were the chirping of crickets and the distant hum of traffic on the coast road below. He breathed in the warm evening air; even that simple act seemed to break the silence.

Nia Dadiani opened the door to him without a word of welcome and led him through the spacious hallway and down a second corridor.

'Please wait in here Mr Hunter. I am just taking care of dinner and will be with you in a moment.'

Friend smiled his thanks and walked through the door. A man rose to greet him.

'Please come in, Mr Hunter. I am very pleased to meet you at last.'

Dinner, evidently, had already been served. The dining room table was laid with all manner of hot and cold dishes: breads, cheeses, meats, salads, *mtsvadi* kebabs, *khinkali* dumplings the size of a child's fist, sprinkled with black pepper. The furniture was polished mahogany and the room was big enough to sit eight or ten, but only one man was waiting for him, rising to his feet as Friend entered and extending a hand of welcome. It was the grey-haired man who had sat next to Nia at the casino. Friend took the offered hand.

'I think we've already met,' he said.

'But we were not introduced. Allow me to rectify that now. My name is Levan Dadiani. I am Nia's uncle.'

Friend could not help smiling back at the man. The voice was full of warmth and the two dark eyes sparkled with a mischievous humour; the deep wrinkles in the skin at their corners suggested they did so often. At the same moment, Nia Dadiani coolly entered the room, carrying a bottle of wine in each hand.

'I almost forgot the most essential dish. I hope you enjoy a Saperavi,' she said, offering Friend a view of the label. It came from Tamara's vineyard.

'Very much, in fact that's one of my favourite vineyards. But I'm surprised you aren't drinking something more local.'

'Ajarian wine is very pleasant,' replied Nia, 'but tonight's conversation will be serious, and for that we need a serious wine. Uncle Levan, perhaps you will do the honours.'

Levan Dadiani took the bottle and began stripping away the foil cap with a small pocket-knife.

'You did not just come here tonight for dinner and wine, Mr Hunter,' said Nia, 'you also came for information. I have discussed your proposal with Uncle Levan, and I am prepared, as I told you, to give you what information I can. But before I do that I have one condition.'

'All right, go on.'

'You said that you could help me to get rid of my difficulties with Senka Kovalchuk. Tell me how, please.'

'Well for one thing, I can arrange protection for your son in England. Our security services are excellent and I am sure the school will co-operate. He will be quite safe and not even aware that measures are being taken to protect him from danger. If matters become more serious, we can arrange for him to be moved to a secure location. Temporarily, of course. I assume threats against your own person would not concern you, so once you know your son is safe, Kovalchuk will have no further hold on you.'

'Is that the sort of service normally offered by investigative journalists in your country?' asked Levan, casually stuffing the stripped foil into his jacket pocket and plunging a corkscrew into the bottle.

'Probably not.'

'Then perhaps it would not be impolite of us to ask who you really are?'

Friend felt both pairs of eyes boring into him. The atmosphere was somewhere between a family party and a difficult job interview.

'I work for the British government.'

'Oh, a spy?' said Nia, resting her chin on a cupped hand and sounding charmed by the idea.

'Something of the sort.'

Plop! The cork followed the foil into Levan Dadiani's pocket and he began to pour the wine.

'I am getting to be an old man, Mr Hunter,' he said. 'But apparently not so old that there are no new experiences to live through.

This is the first time I have shared a table with a British spy. It's not the sort of thing that would have gone down well in my working days.'

'Oh? What did you do?'

'We will come to that later. For now we will focus on you, if you don't mind. But please help yourself to some food. This is a business dinner, not an interrogation.'

Friend picked up one of the khinkali by its topknot and dipped it in the sauce bowl. He took a mouthful and chewed thoughtfully as he waited for the next question. It came from Nia.

'So Roderick Hunter is not a real journalist. Is he real at all, or is that not your identity?'

'It's not my real name, no.'

'So what is your real name?'

'It will be better for all of us if you don't know that, believe me. For the purposes of our business let me remain Roderick Hunter, Rock to his friends.'

'All right, Rock,' said Levan, sitting down and sipping his wine. 'Tell me this: why does the British government send one of its agents to Georgia to investigate the death of a Turkish journalist in Istanbul, two thousand kilometres from British shores?'

'Our government became aware of a pattern. Large numbers of undocumented migrants had been picked up near European ports shortly after one of your ships had docked there. We believe the ships your company owns are being used to facilitate illegal migration on a massive scale, bypassing the controls on the Turkish-Greek border that have been built up in recent years. Elif Çalışkan, the journalist who was killed, had built her career on stories about migration through Turkey to the west and the people who organise it, so it does fit.'

'But many of these people will be simple refugees will they not? Why worry?'

'Some will be of course, but there are also criminals or terrorists using these routes and if they have found a back door into our country we have to close it. And to prevent the people who get them through that door from finding another one. There's a moral issue here too. I want to find out who in this country is packing human beings like cattle into sealed containers and dumping them on the shores of western Europe. Not all of them survive the journey and I don't suppose their families get a refund. I believe Senka Kovalchuk is one of the people organising this human cargo and if I'm right I intend to stop him. Am I right?'

There was a pause. Levan looked at Nia, who gave a shrug and moved a fork around her plate. Eventually Levan broke the silence.

'You may be right. We cannot be sure.'

'Not sure? How?'

Nia broke in.

'I don't know what cargo my ships are carrying. Kovalchuk gives me the schedules and cargo manifests and I sign them off. I have no choice. But I have no idea whether what is on the manifest is what actually goes on the ship.'

'Could I get a copy of one of those manifests?'

'Yes, I can arrange that.'

'What about the crews?'

'Since my husband died all the crews have been replaced by Kovalchuk's own men. I don't know the people on board any more.'

'What else can you tell me?'

'What do you want to know?'

'Well, how did this start, for example?'

Nia laughed.

'Start? It started before I was born.'

'Not with Kovalchuk, surely?'

'No, of course not, the people were different then. But it started with my father. My father and the Khan.'

'The Khan?'

'You have heard of him? Good, then I won't need to explain. But I should explain about my father. Sorry, Uncle Levan.'

Levan Dadiani gave a sad smile and sat quietly as his niece told the tale.

'My father, Alexandre Dadiani, was a good man, but not a wholly honest one. I don't think there were many wholly honest men or women in Soviet Georgia. The system was too strict and bureaucratic, so people had to find ways around it to get what they needed. There was plenty of corruption, both big and small in scale. Honesty was a relative concept. Some people were fundamentally honest; they might pull off a few tricks and bend the rules a little, give or take a few little bribes along the way, but in big and important matters they could be trusted. Other people were superficially honest; they might make a show of being decent and trustworthy but underneath it all they were fleecing everyone left, right and centre.

'My father was of the fundamentally honest kind. He was a shipping official here in Batumi. Yes, he took bribes, but he never asked for too much and he only did it because that was the way the world worked. It was not his personal inclination. When the Soviet era came to an end, he was able to start up his own shipping line, in a small way. It was a struggle for a few years, but we got by. And then my father received an offer from the Khan. He wanted to use my father's ships to move goods around the Black Sea. Contraband of course. He wanted to take advantage of my father's good reputation and good relationships with customs officials elsewhere.'

'Excuse me for interrupting,' said Friend, 'but how do you know this?'

'My father told me, before he died. He regretted getting involved. But he said that for several years it had gone smoothly. The Khan had paid him well, the money had stabilised the business and allowed him to expand a little. None of the goods had ever been seized and the Khan had not interfered in the running of the business otherwise. But that all changed a few months before my father died.'

'Did your father meet the Khan personally?'

'Yes, frequently at first. He even came to this house once.'

'Really, did you see him?'

'Yes, briefly.'

'What was he like?'

'His appearance? Dark, neat, a big moustache. Kindly eyes. A bit like Uncle Levan. I was just a child at the time. I suppose it must have been around the time of my mother's death. Perhaps he came to offer sympathy.'

'I see, so what happened when the Khan stopped coming?'

'Nothing at first. One of his people came instead, but nothing else changed. Not until Kovalchuk took over as proxy some months before my father's death.'

'Did Kovalchuk definitely represent himself as working on the Khan's behalf?'

'Oh yes, quite definitely.'

'And there were no other changes that you recall before that?'

'Well the bank that they use to pay us changed, but that was only just before Kovalchuk turned up.'

'What bank do they use now?'

'The Caucasian Credit Trust.'

That name again. The only thing he wasn't sure about was why the relationship between the Khan and the Dadianis had become more sinister since Kovalchuk arrived on the scene.

'All right,' he said, 'so for several years this business of fairly innocuous smuggling went on with your father's ships without any trouble, until Kovalchuk appeared. Are you sure it was innocuous?'

'That's the whole point,' said Nia. 'My father told me the Khan had agreed with him at the outset that certain things would be off limits; no drugs, heavy weaponry, poisonous substances or large numbers of human beings. He didn't mind the odd refugee, but never more than two or three per trip. Then when Kovalchuk came along, that agreement was ripped up. My father was to have no knowledge of what was being carried on board his ships, no right of veto. He was to take his money and shut up. When he refused Kovalchuk took an even harder line; he wanted total control of the schedules and cargoes. Nothing would move anywhere without his say so. That's where we are now.'

'Do you have any idea why things changed? Was Kovalchuk

himself responsible for this harder line, or did the order come from the Khan himself?'

'Since Kovalchuk claimed to be acting with the Khan's authority I have to assume it was the Khan's decision.'

Levan Dadiani shook his head.

'It doesn't make sense to me,' he said. 'Why would a mercenary like the Khan, with years of established method behind him, suddenly take to murder and extortion like this? It doesn't seem in character.'

'Are you sure? I understood he kidnapped and murdered the Chief of Police at one point.'

Levan laughed.

'I don't think you heard the full story, Rock. Let me explain. I spent most of my working life as a fairly senior official in the Ministry of the Interior. I started off during the Soviet period, but since I was a pragmatist rather than an ideologue I retained my position after the Soviet Union broke up. My department was well aware of the activities attributed to this man. He was an annoyance, a troublemaker, but we never got the sense of real evil from him. He was too restrained, and he was very popular with his people. All of the other bandits and warlords around at that time were thugs. I could believe virtually any of them might be involved with someone like Kovalchuk in this kind of business. With the Khan, I find it more difficult.

'The story about the Chief of Police, Chavchavadze, is basically true. He was abducted from his home one night; in a similar manner to some of the Khan's other victims. In other cases there was always a ransom demand and the victims were returned unharmed to their families after the money was paid. The victims always said they had been treated well during their captivity. In Chavchavadze's case there was no ransom demand. Instead we received a note from the Khan explaining that Chavchavadze had escaped during his first night in captivity. They had taken him to their stronghold up in Khevsureti and seen no reason to guard him very closely; after all, he was way up in the mountains dressed in no more than his pyjamas. But

Chavchavadze was a fool. He tried to escape when he had no hope of success. If he had sat out his confinement in peace he would still be with his family today. Instead, he got himself killed falling down a crevasse in the darkness. The body was well preserved. It was the fall that killed him, that and the cold. Nothing else. The Khan's men even helped the mountain rescue teams to look for him, under a flag of truce. No, my friend, it does not make sense to me that the Khan would be party to work like that of Kovalchuk.'

'So what explanation can you give?' asked Friend.

'The Khan is dead. He would probably be over fifty years old now, and it is a hard life up in the mountains. No, he is dead, and his business has passed to a new, more brutish generation. Like Claudius giving way to Nero in ancient Rome.'

'And what do you think?' Friend asked Nia.

'Me? I think these people are criminals and will do whatever they have to do to make money outside of the law. Times change, people change. Perhaps the Khan's business became tougher and he became tougher in response.'

'I disagree,' said Levan. 'I'm sorry, Nia, but I just don't think it fits.'

There would be no agreement on that point tonight.

'All right,' said Friend, 'what else do you know about the Khan?'

'Nothing useful,' said Levan. 'Just the legends that everybody has known for more than a quarter of a century. He must be a native of the north to command such loyalty up there. His name probably is Tengiz, which accounts for why be became known as the Khan. Nothing else, apart from a litany of crime and misdemeanour. And what about you, Rock? Can you tell us anything more from your sources?'

'About the Khan?'

'Or anything else to do with this business. Kovalchuk, for example.'

'We have information that Kovalchuk is involved with a criminal syndicate based in Moscow, which operates throughout the Black Sea region and into the Middle East. They are mixed up in just about every kind of illegal enterprise you can imagine.'

'So why would an independent operator like the Khan get involved with people like that?' asked Levan.

'Perhaps he had no choice either,' said Nia.

Friend remembered the photographs he had seen of Nia in Niko's newspaper office.

'One more thing,' he said. 'I believe you know a lawyer in Tbilisi. A man called Mikel Qorghanashvili.'

'My father knew him. I think he did business with him a few times, but I don't know the details. I only met him once or twice. I can't say I liked him much.'

'Was it the same business as your father was involved in with the Khan?'

'Possibly. I can't be sure.'

'Did Kovalchuk ever mention him?'

'No.'

'When did you last see him?'

'At my husband's funeral. Is it important?'

'Maybe.'

'Mikel Qorghanashvili is an extremely influential man,' said Levan. 'I came across him a few times in my work for the Ministry. He was personal adviser to the Minister of Justice. He took a close interest in the efforts to being the Khan to justice. It's probably the only venture he ever failed in. I hope he is not involved in this in any way. If he is, it becomes much more serious. It is difficult to bring a man like that to justice.'

They ate in silence for a few minutes, none of them sure how much further this exchange of information had got them. The second bottle of wine remained unopened. Eventually Friend placed his fork down quietly on his empty plate and turned to Levan.

'Can I ask you a question? Why were you with your niece at the casino last night?'

Levan shrugged. 'Nia told me about you. She said she thought she had not seen the last of you so I decided I should take a look at you myself.'

'I see. And was it your decision to have this meeting tonight, or Nia's?'

'Nia's. I try to help and advise when I can, but it is up to her to decide such matters.'

'You have been a great help, Uncle Levan,' said Nia, placing a hand tenderly on his arm. She turned to Friend and said: 'He has helped me put together a file. I have recorded many of my conversations with Kovalchuk, made copies of the documents. Every week or so Uncle Levan visits me and I give him some more. We hope we will be able to use it one day, when I am sure my son will not be in danger.'

'That time may be sooner than you think,' said Friend.

'So what do we do now?' asked Nia.

'If you can get me some examples of the manifests, I would like to have a look at them. More importantly I need to get on board one of your ships before it departs Batumi. We need to be certain what the cargo is.'

'We have nothing in port at the moment. The next due in is the May Rose. She had some engine trouble, I understand, but should be back in port the day after tomorrow.'

'Could you get me on board?'

'It won't be easy. As I said, all the crew are Kovalchuk's men now.'

'Perhaps I can help,' said Levan. 'I still have one or two connections that might help me with harbour security. But it may take me a couple of days.'

'That should be fine. When does the May Rose leave harbour again?'

'Not until the end of the week,' said Nia.

'So that gives us four days.'

'What will you do in the meantime?'

Friend sat back in his chair and finished his wine.

'Do you know a place called the Silver Mountain Hotel?'

'No. Why?'

'It's up in the hills between here and the Turkish border.

There is a man there who might be able to tell us more about Kovalchuk.'

'I see,' said Nia.

She looked distracted. Her fingers toyed with a loose thread in the tablecloth. Her eyes stared blankly at the wall behind Friend, where there was no picture, nor any other object to look at. Friend met Levan's eye; he noticed it too.

'Are you all right?' he asked.

'What?' Nia's eyes came back into focus and she looked back at Friend, forcing a nervous smile.

'Oh, yes. It's just, it doesn't seem real. Sitting here, the three of us. My best china and crystal glassware. Talking about me escaping from a prison I've been trapped in for years, and when I do, I will sit here with my best china and fine crystal glass and it will all be different. I can't imagine it somehow.'

'It will be real if we make it so,' said Friend. 'And it will be different. You will have your freedom back, and your son.'

'Yes, my son. This is his life we are talking about, not just mine. Mr Hunter I am taking a big risk talking to you. Can you promise me you will keep him safe? And if you do, can I trust that promise?'

'Look me in the eye, Nia. I will keep him safe. I promise. You know you can trust me.'

Nia Dadiani looked Friend in the eye, but her hand reached out for Levan who took it and held it tight.

CHAPTER THIRTEEN

TEN GREEN BOTTLES

The little hired Renault bounced up the steep, rutted tracks of the hillside village much less smoothly than Kovalchuk's Mercedes. Sebastian Friend parked the car outside the restaurant next to a large, modern Range Rover and tramped across the gravel to the hotel reception. Dimitri stood behind the desk, engrossed in paperwork. The light from a small, green-shaded lamp glinted off the frames of the small, rectangular reading glasses that were perched on the end of his nose.

'Good morning,' said Friend, throwing his canvas holdall down in front of him. 'My name is Hunter. I made a reservation last night.'

Dimitri looked up slowly and removed the glasses from his nose. His expression, if it could be called that, did not change.

'Mr Hunter. Oh yes, Kovalchuk's friend.'

The voice was just as gravelly as Friend remembered it.

'Well, I wouldn't say friend, exactly. Just a business contact. I'm a journalist and he helped me to get in touch with some people I needed to interview.'

'Is that so?' Dimitri seemed uninterested. He replaced the reading glasses and turned to the screen in front of him. 'I see you've booked in for just two nights.'

'That's right. So how do you know Kovalchuk?'

'I don't really know him, Mr Hunter. Now I just need to see your passport.'

Friend pulled out the Hunter passport from his jacket and handed it over. Dimitri flicked through the pages like an immigration officer, looking up to compare the photograph with Friend's face.

'Your hair seems rather fairer than it does in this photograph, Mr Hunter.'

'Does it? The bleaching effect of your warm, southern sun, I expect.'

'And you're not wearing your glasses today?'

Friend grinned. 'It's amazing what they can do with laser surgery these days,' he said.

Dimitri grunted. 'All right. I'll need to hang on to this for a few hours to register you with the local authorities. You can pick it up again before dinner. In the meantime, if you could fill out this registration form.'

Dimitri slid the form across the desk along with a ballpoint pen. Friend began to write.

'So is Kovalchuk a friend of yours? Or just a business contact like for me?'

'Something like that. You'll be in Room 18. Here's your key. Just for the room, the front door is always open.'

Dimitri handed over a credit-card sized piece of plastic in a plain cardboard sleeve and took the completed form back from Friend.

'Thanks. Is there much to keep your guests out at night in these parts?'

'Some guests have different interests to others. The stairs are over there to the left. Do you need help with your baggage?'

'No thanks, I can manage.'

Friend picked up his bag and turned to go, but then he paused, half turning back as if considering a question. Dimitri looked up again.

'Was there something else, Mr Hunter?'

'Perhaps. I came here for some fresh air and to do a bit of walking. Kovalchuk mentioned you were also a mountain guide. Perhaps I could hire you to take me walking.'

'I'm sorry Mr Hunter, I'm a busy man and it's difficult for me to arrange something at such short notice.'

'Oh, I'm sure I could make it worth your while. And we could make it tomorrow if not today.'

'Tomorrow would be no easier.'

'Oh, that's a pity! Still, I can always walk by myself. Kovalchuk mentioned there was an old silver mine up in the hills near here. That might be fun to explore. Or perhaps you could recommend another route?'

'I wouldn't recommend the silver mine.'

'Why not?'

'It's dangerous. The place has been abandoned for years. There has been subsidence, and landslides. Especially at this time of year. It may be summer down here in the valley but there is still snow melting on the peaks.'

'Oh don't worry about me. I can look after myself. I've been hillwalking most of my life.'

'All the same, I have to warn you that the silver mine isn't safe.'

'Why so worried? It's just an old mine. Where I come from there are old mining lands over half the landscape. I know how to be careful around them, and they're just the sort of places that fascinate me.'

Dimitri glared at Friend over the top of his reading glasses.

'All right,' he growled. 'I'll take you. But not today. Tomorrow. And we'll need to start early.'

'How early?'

'Daybreak. I'll have breakfast ready for us at five and supplies for the road. It'll be a full day's walk so make sure you have some warm clothing. We'll be going over the peaks.'

* * *

Of all the mundane tasks in daily life, there was none Friend enjoyed more than lacing up his walking boots. Their solidity, their snugness and warmth had been his companions during some long days over the course of many years that the mere act of covering his feet with them seemed to promise a good day ahead. Even memories of strains, bruises and blisters were tinged with nostalgic colour. It was still dark the next morning when Friend tightened the laces, then stood and rocked back and forth on his heels and toes to test stability and fit. He was dressed in khaki walking trousers, a thickish t-shirt of red merino wool and a warm grey fleece, unzipped, over the top. The boots still bore the traces of yesterday's mud. After lunch he had strode out for a practice walk, across the small meadow behind the hotel, into the trees and up to the nearest small peak. It sounded a simple task, but navigation had been tricky. The woods were criss-crossed by an abundance of paths and in among the thickly-grouped trees it was difficult to maintain a sense of direction. Without his compass it would have been impossible. But once he had broken through the treeline and emerged into bright sunlight on the grassy upper slopes it had all been worth it. He could see the green land sweeping down into the valley, with the river snaking away to the east. To the west, he could just make out the towers of Batumi through the haze and a blue line of sea beyond. His eyes followed the line south; it grew more distinct the further it went. Somewhere down there, beyond these rolling hills, was Turkey.

When he reached the summit, he found a soft spot of grass with a comfortable little hollow and not too many stones, threw down his daysack, pulled out his water bottle, some bread, cheese, an apple and a book, and sat down to read. Friend loved the hills. He loved their grandeur, their remoteness, their serene unchangeability, their distance from everything that made urban civilisation so sordid and unpleasant at times. To spend time in the hills was to come back purified. He stayed there, in his private little eyrie, until the sun began to sink towards the sea.

The hotel was clean and quiet. The construction was wooden and all the internal fixtures right down to the bed and table in his room were of the same lightly-varnished pine. The sheets were crisply-ironed white cotton. It all had the feel of a modern gasthof in a small village somewhere in the Alps. Perhaps it was still early season, and it was only a small hotel, but there seemed to be just two other guests. Two burly-looking Russians in their mid-twenties who sat together over dinner and barely spoke. Friend had first seen them a little earlier, just after he got back from his walk and was in his room changing for dinner. His window overlooked the back of the hotel, with a view out over the flower meadow. He heard the voices first.

'I'll be glad to get this lot off my back.'

Friend didn't hear the reply, but glancing out of the window he saw the two men in military-style fatigues approaching the building with heavy-looking rucksacks on their backs. Wherever they had been on their walk, they had left it so late that it was already dark by the time they returned.

* * *

Dimitri was wearing a green military tunic buttoned up to the neck, with black trousers and a battered old pair of black walking boots. Perched on his head was a German-style forage cap in a camouflage pattern. He was sitting alone in the restaurant with a thermos flask of coffee and a pile of bread, meat and cheese in front of him. He looked Friend up and down.

'You'll do,' he said. 'Good boots. English?'

'Italian.'

Dimitri nodded his approval. He poured some coffee into a plain white mug and slid it across to Friend. It was black, strong and piping hot. Friend gulped it down and tucked into the food. He asked Dimitri: 'What are we taking with us?'

'Whatever we don't finish of this, apart from the coffee. Plus some dried fruit, nuts and water.'

Friend was surprised.

'Seems pretty light for a full day in the hills,' he said.

'We'll pick up more supplies on the way.'

'Foraging?'

'Something like that. There are plenty of streams to fill up with water.'

For a few minutes they ate in silence. Then, without a word, Dimitri began to wrap up the remains of the food. He stowed it in a small rucksack which he then lifted onto his shoulders. He nodded at Friend. It was time to go.

Dimitri led the way across the meadow to the woods beyond. He walked quickly without seeming to hurry and Friend was surprised to find himself struggling to keep up. Friend was a fast walker as a rule, but he liked to build up to his optimum pace from a fairly easy start. Jumping straight into top gear left him feeling awkward and uncoordinated. He was glad for the moment that Dimitri seemed disinclined to talk.

Only after an hour or so, when they broke through the treeline, was Friend able to get his bearings properly. They were heading almost due south, away from the gentle foothills of the river valley, across the higher peaks that led towards the Turkish border. He saw them looming ahead, great green folds of earth, rock and grass bounding away into the distance. He paused to glance over his shoulder; he could still see the river far below, a winding streak of silver in the morning light. A thin white line of mist coated the meadows between the water and the woods. He might have stopped to watch it fade, but already Dimitri was striding off ahead of him.

Almost two hours in they paused beside a mountain spring. Dimitri threw off his rucksack and stooped to fill his water bottle. He dug out the packet of food and tossed it over to Friend. They each perched on a rock and ate their way through the remnants of their breakfast. When they had finished Friend asked:

'Are we close to the mine yet?'

'Getting tired?'

'No,' Friend had found his rhythm and had hardly broken sweat. 'Just curious about the route.'

'We're doing a circuit. The mine is on the way back. We'll get there this afternoon.'

'I see. And where do we pick up the supplies you mentioned?'

'There's a place I know. Up ahead.'

Friend was getting used to Dimitri's habit of answering questions with the minimum possible information. It was time to try a more direct approach.

'So how do you know Kovalchuk?' he asked.

'That's my business.'

'I get the impression you don't like him much.'

'Do you.'

In Dimitri's flat tone this came as a comment, rather than a question that might invite further engagement.

'Yes, and that interests me because I don't like him much either.'

Dimitri made a noise that was something between a sigh and a grunt.

'And since you don't seem to like him, I wonder why you make him so welcome at your hotel.'

'He's a customer, like you.'

'Not like me, I think. He seems to have a way of making people kow-tow to him. As if they're afraid of him.'

Dimitri got to his feet and slid his arms through the straps of his rucksack.

'We should get moving,' he said.

'All right,' said Friend, raising himself from his rock. 'Lead on.'

For the next two hours not a word was spoken by either man. Friend kept pace with Dimitri, staying always five or six yards behind him. Twice Friend's age he might be, but the stocky Georgian seemed untiring. He neither paused nor stumbled; he did not check his map or take a sip of water. Not once did he look around to check whether Friend was keeping up or had fallen back. He seemed to know by instinct that Friend was close behind.

Dimitri led the way over countless small peaks. The landscape was like an endless green ocean, high swells capped with bright green grass, depths marked by thick clumps of woodland, almost black in the shadow of the hills. Friend sensed they were following a horseshoe course, starting out towards the south-east before gradually turning back towards the west. If they had gone much further south, he guessed, they might have stumbled across the Turkish border. Once, as they traversed a steep slope above a deep river valley, Friend heard the call of a single shepherd from the slope on the opposite side. Dimitri raised an arm in acknowledgement and called a few words back; his gruff voice carried on the wind without ever being raised. There was no other sign of human activity, not even the meanest hut, and Friend began to wonder what sort of place Dimitri had in mind for resupply.

They had been walking almost five hours when he caught his first glimpse of it, a glint of sunlight on bright metal. As they drew closer, the metal glint resolved into an orthodox cross, perched atop a conical tiled roof above a cylindrical bell tower of stone and brick. Now he could discern two or three further low buildings grouped together with the tower protected by a stone defensive wall. The mountain path of well-tramped grass gave way to a wide dirt track which led down from the monastery and meandered away down into the valley. As Dimitri led the way up the track Friend heard a single bell begin to toll in the tower, its peal echoing along the valley. And then the wooden gate to the monastery swung open and out through it strode a tall priest, all in black, the wooden cross around his neck almost covered by an expanse of grey beard. He held his arms out in welcome and enfolded the much shorter Dimitri in a warm embrace.

* * *

Half an hour later Friend and Dimitri raised themselves from the well-stacked refectory table having barely managed to do justice to the mountain of bread, cold meats, cheeses, fruits and wine that Father Gachechiladze had placed before them. Friend had been a silent observer as the priest and the hotel manager cum mountain guide chatted away in Georgian. Friend learned nothing from their conversation, but he did at least have an opportunity of seeing Dimitri smile for the first time. His face barely seemed to move, but the small wrinkles in the skin at the corner of his eyes became deeper, and the pockmarks on his cheeks were joined by two dimples. There was a curious, unexpected warmth about it.

Friend moved to pick up his rucksack, but Dimitri gestured that he should leave it.

'Later,' he said. 'There's something I want to show you first.'

Dimitri's voice could turn even the most routine utterance into an angry growl. Friend found himself wondering what it would be like to hear him say 'I love you' or 'pass the salt, please'. He nodded his thanks to Father Gachechiladze, who bowed in response, and followed Dimitri outside. Dimitri led him along a path lined with small fruit trees past a tiny garden, where two more priests were busy at work. They called out their greetings and as Dimitri raised a hand in acknowledgement Friend noticed a large old-fashioned iron key in his hand. He walked slowly towards the chapel and then down a set of stone steps cut next to its side wall. Dimitri unlocked the heavy wooden door and walked into the crypt.

As Friend followed him inside Dimitri flicked a switch and the crypt was flooded with light. It was a cramped, low-ceilinged space, filled with stone sarcophagi; the bones of previous residents, Friend supposed. He wondered how they powered the light.

'Diesel generator. Filthy machine. I keep telling them they should switch to wind power. No shortage of that up here. Still, they do pretty well for themselves. Plenty of food and drink. The local shepherds give them a sheep every so often, they grow their own vegetables and get whatever else they need from the town.'

Chatting with the priest seemed to have loosened Dimitri's tongue.

'How many of them live here?' Friend asked.

'Only five now. Used to be twice as many.'

Dimitri led the way through the stone mausoleum, until he stopped by one sarcophagus that looked no different to any other. He grasped the stone lid with his hands.

'Give me some help with this,' he said.

Friend grasped the other end, and slowly through an agony of scraping stone the two moved the heavy lid until it lay diagonally across the open coffin. Inside there was no body, just a plain wooden crate, and a crowbar. Dimitri leaned in to pick up the crowbar and began to lever off the lid of the crate. It gave way with a crash of splinters. Dimitri threw the crowbar aside, then reached into the crate, pulling out the uppermost item.

Friend recognised it immediately: a Remington 700 CDL hunting rifle. He watched, unmoved, as Dimitri raised the rifle up to waist height and levelled the barrel directly at him. The two men eyed each other in silence for a moment, until Dimitri turned the rifle sideways in his hands and tossed it across to Friend. Friend caught it easily, then pulled back the bolt to check the chamber. It was empty. He turned the weapon over in his hands to examine it more closely. It was the seven-millimetre magnum with polished walnut stock, sniper's sight and 26-inch carbon steel barrel; a handsome, well-balanced marksman's rifle, brand new and never fired.

'Seems to me you know what you're looking at,' said Dimitri.

Friend looked up. The Georgian was holding an identical rifle in one hand and two boxes of cartridges in the other.

'Come on,' he said.

Outside the monastery walls, Dimitri and Friend took up position some one hundred metres from a low wooden structure, perhaps a woodshed or hay store. On the roof of the shed, Father Gachechiladze was placing a row of wine bottles.

'Take a closer look,' said Dimitri.

Friend raised the rifle and looked through the sniper's sight as the priest moved away from the target. There were ten bottles, empty, and each of them had a cork perched delicately on the top of its neck.

'Think you can manage?'

'I don't know. I'm no marksman.'

'Is that so? Then I'll go first.'

Dimitri waited for the signal from Father Gachechiladze, who settled himself comfortably on the grass with his back against the wall, then he raised the rifle to his shoulder, took aim and fired.

The bottle furthest to the left was undisturbed. It did not even quiver. But the cork was nowhere to be seen. Father Gachechiladze gave a whoop of triumph and applauded in delight.

'Your turn.'

Friend fed a single cartridge into the chamber and dropped the bolt. He looked through the sight, wondering whether he should try and compensate for the wind, whether the rifle was correctly balanced for his body, then with a mental shrug of his shoulders he pulled the trigger. The bottle exploded, showering the woodshed with shards of glass.

'Not bad,' said Dimitri appreciatively.

'Not in your class, I'm afraid.'

'Don't be too hard on yourself. Unfamiliar weapon, unfamiliar conditions.'

Dimitri fired again, with the same result.

'Why do the priests keep these weapons?' asked Friend. 'It doesn't seem a very Christian thing to do.'

'As a favour to me.'

'So why do you need to keep this armoury up here in the mountains?' Friend fired his second round, clipping the bottle and sending it spinning to the ground.

'I like to keep in practice,' said Dimitri, raising his rifle for the third time.

'Practice for what?'

Dimitri paused and turned to face Friend.

'I have a lot of enemies,' he said.

He took aim at the fifth bottle: the bullet went straight through its neck. The cork plopped down onto the shed roof. Dimitri cursed softly.

'I also owe a lot in taxes,' he added.

'Would one of those enemies be Alexei Kovalchuk?'

'It's not a good idea to mention that man's name when I'm holding a rifle.'

'I'll take that as a yes,' said Friend with a smile. He took aim again, this time striking the cork cleanly and leaving the bottle undisturbed.

'Nice shooting,' said Dimitri. 'Tell me, are all journalists in London this good with a hunting rifle?'

'Let's just say London can be a rough town. And you tell me: do all your hotel guests get the same guided tour?'

Friend saw the wrinkles deepen at the corner of Dimitri's eye, but he couldn't be sure whether it was a smile or he was just taking careful aim. Perhaps the latter, he concluded, as the cork flew away once more to be greeted by another cry of jubilation from the priest.

Dimitri lowered the rifle and turned to Friend once more.

'It depends on the guest,' he said.

'Then I'm honoured,' said Friend. 'But how did you get all these rifles and ammunition up here?'

'Mule train. We're only a few kilometres from the Turkish border. Every so often Father Gachechiladze takes the mules and visits some friends on the other side.'

'Doesn't he get stopped at the border?'

'Where he crosses it only the trees and the wolves are there to see him.'

'So, you're a smuggler Dimitri!' laughed Friend.

'In a small way, my friend, in a small way.' He pointed the unloaded rifle at Friend as if he were waggling a playful finger. 'But don't go printing that in your newspapers! Now, are you going to stand here talking all day, or take your shot?'

Friend fired again and missed completely, drawing a groan of derision from Father Gachechiladze. Dimitri shook his head sadly.

'Lack of concentration,' he said.

When they had finished, Father Gachechiladze gathered up their rifles and unused ammunition and scuttled off to clear up the broken glass. Dimitri led the way back to the refectory.

'You must have known Father Gachechiladze a long time for him to smuggle guns for you like this. And whatever else he brings across the border,' said Friend.

'Yes, I've known him a long time,' said Dimitri, ignoring the second part of Friend's question.

'Has he been in this monastery for many years?'

'Eight or nine.'

'And you met him when he first came here?'

'No, before that.'

'Where?'

'Where he comes from. Khevsureti.'

'Oh, yes. I know the place. Fine country for walking.'

'Fine, but tough.'

'Especially when you feel the wolf's breath on your neck.'

Dimitri stopped and turned to face Friend.

'So you really do know Khevsureti, then?'

They gathered up their belongings, now bulging with fresh supplies of food and water, and strode back out into the hills, the tolling of the chapel bell following them along the ridge above the river valley. As far as Friend could tell they were now heading due west, parallel to the border, closer to the sea. The peaks ahead seemed lower, gentler than the ones they had faced before lunch. Dimitri was still striding on ahead with his usual well-balanced strides. He had a knack of moving quickly without seeing to hurry. Friend thought he would try to capitalise on his guide's more conversational mood.

'This is fine walking country,' he said. 'You can really rack up the miles. But there is something really epic about Khevsureti. You go walking there and you remember it for the rest of your life.'

'Uh-huh,' grunted Dimitri.

'It's the sort of place where legends are made. Like that one we talked about with Kovalchuk, about the Khan.'

'You heard what I said about that.'

'Yes, but I don't know whether to believe you.'

'Don't you.'

'Partly because I think you were only saying what Kovalchuk wanted to hear, and also because I have met someone who says they once met the Khan in person.'

'And who might that be?'

'A woman called Nia Dadiani.'

'Dadiani?'

'Yes. Do you know her?'

'All of Georgia knows the Dadianis. What did she say about the Khan?'

'She told me that he used to be in business with her father, Alexandre, who owned a shipping line running out of Batumi. But then Kovalchuk came along and her father died. She inherited the business from her father and now she has to deal with Kovalchuk herself.'

'Then she has my sympathy. You said she met the Khan in person?'

'Yes, once when she was a child. Just after her mother died.'

'What did you say her name was?'

'Nia.'

'Nia,' Dimitri repeated it quietly to himself. He walked on in silence for a while, only responding once several minutes later when prompted by Friend.

'So, does the Khan exist, or is he just a fairy tale?'

'Even fairy tales have some basis in truth, Mr Hunter.'

For the rest of the day Dimitri pushed on at a greater pace than ever, as if racing against the sun to get back to the hotel. They came to the silver mine less than an hour before reaching home. As Dimitri had said, it wasn't much to look at: a landscape scarred by light industry, dusty tracks and rusting, abandoned vehicles, a deep hole cut into the side of a once green mountain, the entrance barred by huge steel gates. Friend went up to the gates and peered into the blackness while Dimitri sat on a rock and chewed on a piece of bread. Then he turned back to the Georgian with a shrug.

'Let's get back to the hotel. It's almost dark.'

Dimitri nodded and got to his feet. Friend followed on as usual five or six yards behind. He hoped he had looked sufficiently disappointed, but he had found out more than he expected. The mine had been disused for more than twenty years, but the padlock on the gates was brand new and the hinges were freshly oiled.

CHAPTER FOURTEEN

CARGO

Levan Dadiani lived in a sprawling single-storey villa shaded by cypress trees in the south of Batumi, close to where the Mejinistskali river ran through Kachinski Park to the sea. Friend was greeted at the door by Dadiani's wife, a petite, grey-haired woman with sparkling dark eyes who smiled in welcome even as a small child, no more than three years old, tugged at the hem of her skirt. She ushered Friend down a broad corridor to her husband's study, at the back of the house, the child dogging her steps all the way. She showed him into a large room, filled with light from the French windows looking on to a pretty garden at the back. The old man rose to greet him, just as the child darted through the doorway and jumped into his arms.

Dadiani laughed and kissed the child, ruffling its hair fondly before handing it back to his wife, who shook her head in exasperation and carried it off amid more squeals of laughter.

'Forgive me my friend,' said Dadiani, offering Friend his hand. 'You find us looking after my grandson. The next generation of our proud line. My daughter found herself an unexpected appointment this morning, and so we have to do our duty as grandparents.'

'You don't look as if you mind too much,' said Friend.

'We don't. Not at all. In fact that's really why we moved back from Tbilisi after I retired from the Ministry.' He gestured towards the desk, which was cluttered with a variety of silver and wooden frames. 'My wife and I have been very lucky. Three children, two girls and a boy, and eight grandchildren so far. The oldest is fifteen now, the youngest you met just now, almost three.'

'They all live in Batumi?'

'Yes, all within a ten-minute drive of each other. It's a great blessing to us.'

'I'm glad for you.'

'You have family yourself?'

'No, I'm not married.'

'But your parents? Brothers? Sisters?'

'My parents live a long way from London now, and my sister's work takes her away a great deal. Just like mine.'

Dadiani clapped a fatherly hand on Friend's shoulder.

'Take my advice, my boy. Find yourself a wife and build a family together. This business you're in has no future. For myself, I had a successful career, but that was just work. Having a family changes your attitudes completely. No man in Georgia has any greater loyalty than to his family. There is nothing I wouldn't do for my family. Nothing at all, believe me.'

'I believe you. But while I am in this business I might just be able to do some good for your family. For Nia.'

Dadiani nodded in self-reproach.

'Quite right. Quite right. You didn't come here to listen to an old man's foolish advice. Please take a seat and we will talk like serious men.'

Dadiani indicated a pair of armchairs next to the window then walked over to his desk and pulled a large manila envelope out from a drawer. Then he walked over to a wooden cabinet on the far wall and pulled out an already open bottle of red wine, and two small crystal glasses. In Georgia, no serious conversation was possible without wine.

'Nia got this to me last night,' he said, holding out the envelope to Friend. 'The May Rose leaves port the day after tomorrow at six-thirty am. They are loading her up now and this is the latest cargo manifest. It's in Russian so you should have no trouble understanding it.'

Friend took the envelope and began looking through the contents as Dadiani poured two glasses from the bottle. The ship's purported cargo was more varied than Friend had anticipated. There was a quantity of Georgian wine destined for the European market, minerals to feed the continent's industries and some other products Friend had never heard of.

'What's this?' He asked, pointing out an item on the manifest to Dadiani.

'Ah yes, granulated phosphorus. It's produced in central Asia and then shipped across the Caspian to Azerbaijan. Then it comes by train to Batumi. As so often, Georgia is just the middle-man in the trade.'

'What is it used for?'

'It's an agricultural fertiliser. Quite common in Turkey and the Balkans, I believe.'

'What about the minerals? I see you have some gold on board. Does that come from elsewhere too?'

'No, the gold is Georgian. From the south-east. A Russian company called RMG has the concession there. Most of the gold goes to Russia but some is shipped direct to Europe for industrial use. I think you will find there is a rather larger quantity of manganese on the manifest. That's mined in Chiatura, in central Georgia. Our mineral industry collapsed after the fall of the Soviet Union, but it's beginning to pick up now.'

'So there's nothing you would call unusual on this manifest?'

'No. But then that is the whole point of the manifest, isn't it? Whatever Kovalchuk and his friends are putting on board Nia's ships, it isn't going to be listed here. My guess would be the manifest is ninety per cent correct, and the remaining ten per cent is plausible enough fiction that no-one would suspect anything. Probably the quantities of some items are exaggerated to cover the presence of any illicit cargo.'

'So as we discussed the other night, the only way we will find out what she is really carrying is by a personal inspection.'

'Just so. And I may be able to help you.' Dadiani reached into his jacket pocket and pulled out a printed ID card attached to a blue lanyard. 'I called in a few favours. This is a good enough likeness to get you past security at the docks. But it won't get you on board. That you will have to manage yourself. The May Rose isn't a big ship, and the cargo is quite varied, so that suggests to me a larger number of small containers. If the cargo is human, I expect they would be brought on board as late as possible. Whether they come to the ship on foot and get into the containers on board or whether they arrive already sealed in is anybody's guess. Either way they would be certain to leave it late, so I suggest you cover the docks tomorrow night.'

'I'll do that. Anything else?'

'Not from me. Just be careful. Don't let them catch you and whatever you do don't let them get hold of the ID I gave you. It would get my friend into a lot of trouble.'

'Don't worry. I'll be careful.'

'Good.' Dadiani smiled and sat back in his chair. 'So, how did your trip to the mountains go? Did you find out anything useful?'

'My host was quite cagey. But I think he is also being used for smuggling operations by Kovalchuk. There's an abandoned silver mine not far from the hotel he runs. It's all locked up but the gates are kept well oiled. They've been opened recently. I think Kovalchuk is having some sort of contraband carried over the border from Turkey and left for collection in the mine. Drugs, probably. There were two Russian heavies staying at the hotel with me. I think they were there to pick up the stuff and bring it back to Batumi.'

'I see,' said Dadiani. 'These are deep waters, my friend. We should be careful we don't drown in them.'

* * *

There were two possible access points and which one was better depended upon where the May Rose was moored. Further away from the ferry port and coming in from that direction would be a bad move. It would be at odds with the image he was trying to project.

The security guard was dozing over a newspaper in his booth. It was just after ten on a Saturday night, it had been dark for more than two hours and the guard was nearing the end of a seven-hour shift. Many of the dock workers and ship hands were enjoying the nightspots of Batumi. Friend, wearing shapeless dark overalls and carrying a small knapsack over one shoulder waved his lanyard nonchalantly and walked through unchallenged. On the railway line to his right a line of freight carriages sat waiting to be unloaded. The May Rose was three berths from the entrance and the docks were dead quiet, but Friend was certain that the ship would not be left unguarded. Kovalchuk would have made sure of that.

The May Rose was a relatively small vessel of no more than five thousand tons. Friend could see her superstructure clearly in the moonlight; the white bridge tower set towards the stern, rising out of the dark blue hull; the silhouette of the two cargo derricks, one serving a rear hold aft of the bridge, the other between the two forward holds. The hatches leading to the lower hold were already covered by containers. She was fully loaded and ready for her next voyage. Unless, of course, any additional human cargo was waiting to be smuggled on board at the last minute.

Friend could see no-one on deck, but this was just his first pass. He needed to reinforce the image before making his move. He walked on towards the line of stationary cargo wagons, dropped his knapsack beside one of them and made a show of inspecting the wheels. Slowly, he made his way along the line of four wagons, gradually working his way back towards the May Rose, stealing a glance at her decks every few seconds. He pulled a small hammer out of his bag and tapped away at a wheel. The one crew member patrolling the upper decks leaned over the beam at the sound but quickly lost interest. The image was consistent. Friend had calculated correctly; the guard's rounds took him past that point every seven minutes. Up on the bridge there was no sign of life at all.

Six and a half minutes' waiting time.

Friend returned his tools to the bag, slung it over his shoulder and walked slowly back towards the guard post just as the man on the May Rose's deck was close enough to observe him. As soon as the man had disappeared behind the bridge, Friend altered course and darted silently up the gangway. The quickest way to access the hold would be through an inspection hatch adjacent to the midships port hatch, that much Levan Dadiani had told him. The gangway ran out from the main deck on the starboard side just forward of the bridge; Friend had to make it to the port side without being seen by the deck guard. Then he had to hope there were no further guards below deck.

From the end of the gangway he darted into a gap between two rows of containers that ran the ship's width. He stopped and listened. There was no sound but the far-off hum of city traffic, the gentle lap of waves against the side of the ship and the single cry of a sea bird. He gave it a few more seconds then darted the length of the gap, wishing the cloth of his overalls didn't make such an obvious swishing noise as he ran. He was now in sight of the port beam. With any luck the guard would now be somewhere behind the bridge, or if he were on the bridge itself, Friend's next move would be covered by the height of the containers. He stuck his head out of the gap and stole a quick look in each direction. All clear. The inspection hatch was right where Dadiani had said: about twenty metres ahead of him. As the ship was in port, the watertight seal on the hatch might not be closed, but even if it were Friend should be able to release it without raising the alarm. He took a deep breath and made a run for the hatch. Five seconds. As he ducked down beside it he could see that it was sealed – he lay flat and pulled at the lever. He felt the suction on the rubber seals give way and the hatch came free in his hand. He lifted it quickly and slid through.

Pulling the hatch closed over his head he found himself in a half-lit hold that seemed much bigger than he expected. If this were a small cargo vessel, what on earth were the real giants of the sea like? The steel gantry he was standing on seemed to run the length of the ship. There were a pair of connecting gantries running at right angles further aft, with steps leading down to lower gantries at the bottom of the hold. There did not seem to be anyone else around. As Friend walked slowly along the gantry the difficulty of his task began to dawn on him. It was all very well getting on board the May Rose and taking a look at her cargo hold, but what on earth was he supposed to be looking for? One container looked much the same as any other. They were firmly sealed and he had no method of getting them open, short of bashing away with his hammer and bringing the guard down on his head. If any one of them were to contain human cargo then it would surely have some airholes punched in it somewhere, but as he walked along he could see no sign of any such thing. Nor did any sound come from within. Cram twenty to thirty people together in a metal container and as long as they can breathe they will surely talk too, however much you tell them not to. The metal walls of each container were sturdy enough to protect the cargo at sea, but they would do precious little to insulate sound from within.

The only thing that marked out any container as individual was the serial number printed on its side. Friend checked a few of these off against the manifest and found no discrepancies. After eighteen minutes of fruitless searching, he decided it was time to leave. If the guard were on schedule, he would be patrolling the starboard deck about now, which should give Friend enough time to get clear of the hatch on the port side. He headed back the way he had come.

Back up on deck, Friend made for the same gap between containers that he had used on the way in. All was still quiet. In another two minutes' time, he estimated, the guard would have completed his patrol of the starboard side and be safely aft of the bridge once more. Friend flattened his back against a container and counted down the seconds. When he thought it was safe to move, he tried to edge away from the container, but the back of his overall had stuck to it. He pulled away with his shoulders and felt himself come unstuck. Curious, Friend decided to risk using his flashlight. He pulled it out of his bag and ran the pencil-thin stream of light up the side of the container. Something dark was oozing out from near the top and had collected in a little pool at Friend's feet. Friend reached into his bag again and brought out a small plastic jar. He unscrewed the lid and lifted a small sample of the ooze into the jar with his pocket-knife. Then he slipped the jar back into his knapsack and switched on his flashlight again.

The container's serial number was printed just above head height. According to the manifest it was a consignment of granulated phosphorus destined for an agricultural supplier in Romania. Whatever it really contained, it didn't look granulated to Friend's eye.

'Hey there!'

The voice came from his left, from the port side. Realising too late that his curiosity about the ooze had made him lose track of time, Friend picked up his knapsack and ran.

'Hey you! Stop!' The voice pursued him, so did the sound of heavy boots at pace. But no bullets. Friend rounded the end of the row and turned towards the gangway. He kept his head down and raced towards it, but then, out of the darkness came the shape of another man running towards him. Friend hadn't expected a second guard, but he wasn't worried yet. This didn't look like one of Senka Kovalchuk's heavies. He was a short, stockily built man with a bald head and bandy legs that looked like they were used to being braced against a heavy sea. He wore dark jeans and an old blue shirt that was unbuttoned almost to the waist. He looked like nothing more than a hard-living sailor who wouldn't look askance at an opportunity for a bit of a bruise-up. Friend had a strong impression of brandy fumes as the two men came together at the head of the gangway. The sailor caused Friend little trouble;

he was moving so quickly it needed the barest shift of weight and the momentum took him over Friend's shoulder and sent him sprawling along the deck. The other guard had to check his run to avoid the obstacle and Friend was off down the gangway and sprinting along the dock. The guard at the gate post barely looked up as Friend ran past at full speed. By the time he ducked into a nearby bar and changed his clothing in the toilets, there was no sign of pursuit.

* * *

The taxi driver began the journey with an ostentatious genuflection. 'Please do not worry – I am giving thanks, not asking for favours.'

'That's all right,' said Friend. 'Just don't be offended if you see me doing the same thing.'

Friend glanced over his shoulder as they pulled away from the kerb and saw a small black Opel pull out into traffic about fifty metres back. From the window of his room he had spotted two of Kovalchuk's men watching the hotel from across the street; two of the same team that had tailed him to the beach and the fish market. There would be others out of sight. He knew they could have dropped him with a single bullet from a high-powered rifle as soon as he left the cover of the hotel lobby. But there was nothing he could do about that. He couldn't afford to wait until dark when he might be able to slip out through a delivery entrance. So, there was nothing to do but walk out of the front door in the full light of day and brace yourself for it. After all, wasn't the risk supposed to be part of the attraction?

Kovalchuk's people would know that someone had got on board the May Rose and there were no other suspects apart from Rock Hunter, so-called journalist. But they might not guess what he had found. The sample jar and the sticky mess of his overalls were already on their way to London for analysis. Magniac had sent round the courier to pick them up first thing that morning.

Friend was finished in Batumi. His last act in this town would be to meet once more with Levan and Nia Dadiani. Nia had called wanting to know what he had found on board the May Rose. He hadn't yet decided how much to tell her, but agreed to the meeting anyway. Nia was grateful. But she remained worried about being seen with him in public, so the meeting would again be at her home and after dark. Friend was to be as careful as possible to make sure he was not followed.

Friend knew she wasn't insulting his tradecraft. The lady was just scared.

'So, where to boss?'

'I have some time to kill. I have an appointment to keep at eight-thirty tonight, then I have to be at the station for the Tbilisi train at a quarter to midnight. I don't know the town so well, so any recommendations you have would be welcome.'

'What sort of thing did you have in mind, boss? High life or low life?'

'Let's say high life for now.'

'Well, if it's all right with you, boss,' The driver's mouth twitched under his impressive black moustache, 'I know a couple of good museums. Interesting stuff to look at, not so many people around. They should kill two or three hours stone dead for you. Then maybe a good restaurant for dinner between your appointment and the train.'

'That sounds perfect. And on the subject of there being people around, I like my privacy. If you see anyone taking any special interest in us, hanging around outside the museum while I'm inside, that sort of thing, please let me know.'

'Like the little Opel that's following us now, boss?'

'You get the idea pretty quick.'

'You want me to lose him, boss?'

'If you can, but don't break any laws trying to. If we can't shake him, you can drop me off and I'll make my own way. Here.'

Friend reached forward and deposited a wad of bank notes on the passenger seat.

'If I have to get out in a hurry, don't try and lose him. If he spots me, he won't follow you anyway. If he doesn't, pick up another fare for yourself. He'll lose interest. I'll make my way to the railway station. If you can meet me there at eight, we're back in business together. If not, I'll make other arrangements. Okay?'

'Sure, boss.'

'Just one more thing.'

'Yes, boss?'

'Stop calling me boss. My name's Rock.'

'Mine is Davit. Whatever you say, Rock.'

* * *

Whoever was driving the Opel knew his business. After almost half an hour he was still twenty metres behind Davit's taxi and sticking like a limpet. Davit managed to stretch the distance to almost thirty along Pushkin Street and Friend thought this was probably as good as it would get. He told Davit to take a right at the Holy Trinity Church and then the next right immediately after it; he took hold of the handle and prepared to roll out of the side door. He took one last look back through the traffic but couldn't see the Opel. For several seconds more he scanned the street behind until there was no more doubt. He let go of the door handle. The Opel had gone. Pushkin Street ran dead straight for more than half a mile; cars parked bumper to bumper at both kerbs and everything moving at an even speed. Davit might have gained a little more of a lead, but it wasn't possible to have lost the Opel. It must have turned off the road. The tail had been pulled.

Which made no sense at all.

It was eight-fifteen when Davit's grey Toyota pulled up on the quiet street fifty yards from Nia Dadiani's house. He switched off the engine. Friend remained motionless, save for an occasional glance around, for another five minutes. Nothing stirred; not so much as a cat on its nightly rounds. With a last burst of light between the clouds, the sun disappeared and night fell like a theatre curtain over Batumi.

'Nobody here, Rock.'

'You're quite sure about that?'

'No doubt about it.'

'All right then. I'll go in. I doubt I'll be more than half an hour, but if you see anything suspicious before I'm back; anyone poking around the outside of that villa over there, or just parking here without an obvious purpose you give two quick blasts of your horn like you're waiting for an overdue fare and then if I'm not back here within five minutes, drive off and wait for me down on the coast road at the next parking space back towards town. Give me another thirty minutes there and if I don't show I won't be needing you again. OK?'

'Got it Rock. You in some kind of trouble?'

'Not at all. Nothing you need worry about anyway. If I don't make it back to you, I've just made other arrangements, that's all.'

Friend pulled out his wallet and counted another 50 Lari. 'Here you are,' he said, leaving it on his seat as he stepped out of the car, 'and thank you.'

'Thank you, boss,' said Davit, momentarily forgetting his instructions.

* * *

All was quiet at the Dadiani house. The gate had been left open for him and he walked slowly and cautiously up the winding drive, part of his mind still registering the night-time scent of the pine and cypress trees and the chirrup of cicadas. Perhaps it was the cool evening air, but he felt the skin on the back of his neck begin to tingle, a voice somewhere inside his head urging: *trap!* He stopped at the front of the house. There were no lights showing, no movement in the shadows, no sound or smell that was in any way inconsistent with appearances. *Stop worrying. Safe.*

There was no response when he rang the doorbell. He gave it a minute and rang again. Still nothing. He looked around and found a small white envelope propped against a stone urn filled with lavender under one of the windows. He opened it and read:

Mr Hunter,
If there is no answer at the door I am probably in the garden.
Please let yourself in and come to the garden through the
dining room. Uncle Levan will join us later.
N.

The note was folded over a single Yale key. Friend slipped the note into his pocket, fitted the key in the lock and opened the door. There were no lights on in the hall and as he walked along the familiar passage to the dining room it struck him that there were no sounds at all, no indication that the house was occupied. He reached the door to the dining room and walked in.

The only light in the dining room came from outside. The curtains were open and through the deep French windows the fading light of dusk cast a glow of pinkish silver across the room. It made the woman's face even more grotesque. She was hanging by the neck above the grand, polished dining table from a hook that normally supported one of three crystal chandeliers. It was Nia Dadiani, her features horribly distended and her swollen tongue protruding from her mouth like a giant snail trying to escape from its shell. For a moment he was stunned, unable to move, but then a faint movement caught his eye; a twitch of a foot, a flicker of an eyelid. Perhaps his own movement alerted what was left of her senses and as he started towards her both eyes opened and immediately he knew that the message they bore him was not fear or pain or anger, but warning. From the corner of his own eye he detected a shadow moving in the darkness by the wall, but before he could turn his head he felt a great weight come down on his shoulder and neck. In the fraction of a second before the darkness swallowed him two thoughts flashed through his mind:

They called off the tail because they knew where I would be.

And: *Uncle Levan will join us later.*

Then he tumbled down into the endless dark pool below.

CHAPTER FIFTEEN

BAGGAGE

Dodds, Higgins, Hindson, Parnaby, Jobling. Hindson was saying something; one of his usual filthy jokes, Friend presumed. The man had a mind like a sewer. It was how he dealt with the tension. Some wanted to talk, some to listen, some to be alone with their own thoughts. It was Friend's job not to be any of those things but to observe, to know what was going on, what was on his men's minds but not to be so involved in their chatter that he was distracted from his responsibility for their situation. So, he would listen with half his mind to Hindson's scatological narrative and be ready with the quiet word to lead them back to business when the time came.

Those five were a team within a team; always in each other's pockets, always sharing some joke or other. Including Friend there were eight of them in the back of the truck, and the other two, like Friend, were more self-contained: Grigg, the quiet farmer's son from Lancashire and Pugh, the graduate from Hampshire for whom the army had been a just a nose ahead in a two-horse race with the civil service. Friend and Pugh sat opposite each other at the back – first out of the door at journey's end – and Grigg was Friend's neighbour on one of two uncomfortable benches that gave the backside no relief from the punishing roads and non-existent suspension.

And then Friend thought he had missed something. Perhaps for once Hindson had delivered a punchline to shocked silence. There was a noise of some sort, but Friend couldn't place it. There was a fuzziness in his head and a nasty smell in his nostrils; smoke and burned flesh, a confused impression of tangled metal, blood and body parts, Grigg's eyes blinking up at him from the floor where he lay half-in-half-out of the truck. He had an impression of bright light piercing through the smoke and an unholy ringing in his ears like a steam kettle whistling louder and louder until it resolved into something that wasn't a whistle at all but a voice speaking to him with a pounding rhythm ever louder and more insistent: 'get out, get out, GET OUT!!'

He stumbled or fell out of the back of the truck where the doors used to be, pulled himself half upright, and felt somebody slap him hard across the face.

* * *

'Boss! Wake up boss! Come on, we've got to go!' Another slap opened Friend's eyes and he saw Davit crouching above him, a look of desperate concern on his face.

'I told you not to call me Boss,' Friend mumbled drowsily.

'Fine, OK, Rock or whatever you want to call yourself. But come on, it's time to go.'

Davit lifted Friend's left arm across his shoulder and began to lever him off the floor.

'Wait a minute,' said Friend, feeling the back of his head and neck with his free hand. 'Am I bleeding?'

'I don't think so. They slugged you pretty good, those two, but I don't think they broke the skin.'

'Two? You saw them?'

'Sure, they came running out the front door no more than two minutes after you went in. Picked up by a big Range Rover and off they went. I gave two blasts on the horn like you told me then figured you maybe needed some proper help in here.'

'You weren't wrong there.' Friend turned his head painfully and saw Nia's body, her eyes still open but empty of life, swaying gently above the dining table.

'Nothing you can do for her. She's gone. I checked,' said Davit.

'OK. Let's get out of here. Did you touch anything on the way in?'

'No. Those two guys left the door wide open.'

'Thoughtful of them. Make sure you touch nothing on the way out.'

Friend got to his feet and stumbled uneasily towards the dining room door. He pulled a handkerchief from his trouser pocket and dusted the door-knob carefully. He stole a last sorry glance towards Nia Dadiani, then with Davit following on his heels made his way to the front door and gave that too a careful wipe where he had opened and closed it after himself on the way in. He let Davit help him back to the car.

'Thank you, Davit,' said Friend as the other crossed himself twice in gratitude. 'Now get us out of here before more trouble arrives. I don't care where we go.'

The sirens were already audible as Davit manoeuvred the car around and drove slowly back down the hill towards the coast road. They were still less than three hundred metres from the Dadiani house when first two police cars and then one ambulance came tearing past them.

* * *

Davit had only driven them a short distance north along the coast before turning inland and pulling up in the small private car park of a nondescript little restaurant in the back streets. There he had installed a listless, uncomplaining Friend at a quiet corner table with a view of the door, before greeting the hostess like an old friend with formal kisses on each cheek. He returned carrying a half pint of Armenian brandy in each hand and a bottle of local red tucked under his arm. The brandies were quickly disposed of, and Davit turned his attention to uncorking the wine with a small pocket-knife.

'I hope you don't mind, but I ordered some food. If I'm going to drive you later on I will need something to soak up the drink and the *khachapuri* here is the best in Batumi.'

'Fine,' said Friend drowsily.

'I also hope you don't mind my being curious. Maybe this is one of those times when a man shouldn't ask too many questions, but I would like to know why those two guys would do such a thing to such a nice-looking lady.'

Friend accepted a glass of wine and gave a shrug. 'I don't know for sure,' he said. 'Maybe they were finished with her. Maybe they just wanted to find a way of getting rid of me and having me framed for her murder was the best they could think of.'

'So, they string her up, wait for you to come along, then knock you cold and call the police on the way out, making sure to leave all the doors open so they can find you nice and easy.'

'That sounds about right.'

'Except, how did they know you were coming?'

'That, Davit, is probably one of those questions you shouldn't ask,' said Friend.

Davit nodded. 'So, what now?'

'Did anyone see us arrive, or leave?'

'I don't think so. I guess if those two guys had spotted me when they ran out, I wouldn't be talking with you now. Their car didn't drive up until they left the house. Maybe somebody heard my horn when I sounded it, but I didn't spot anyone coming out to look. It's a quiet neighbourhood.'

'So, no blood, no fingerprints, no witnesses.'

'Maybe you left some hair behind, some fibres from your clothing?'

Friend shrugged. 'I've been there before as a guest. There's nothing to say I didn't leave those traces behind then.'

'So now?'

'Now we drink our wine, eat our dinner and then you drive me to the station as we agreed. And then it's probably better if you forget you ever met me.'

'Okay,' agreed Davit. 'But maybe two things I should mention.'

'Yes?'

'First: if I'm going to forget I ever met an English guy called Rock, perhaps I'd better go back to calling you 'Boss'.'

'And the second?'

'I think we'd both be able to forget this evening better if I order more of this cognac.'

* * *

'It wasn't your fault.' Magniac's voice was kind, but Friend was only half listening. In his mind he was back on the train, the thin mattress cushioning his frame from the metal banquette, the woollen blanket stretched across his fully-clothed body. The soft clatter of the wheels outside, the gentle rocking of the carriage, the strip of light seeping under the door from the corridor, the dry, sterile smell of the air-conditioned compartment, the distant murmur of conversation. Normal everyday sensations he might have recalled from any journey since childhood. He was as snug as an infant in its cot, but after crashing into a cognac-induced coma for an hour, he had awoken to an old childhood nightmare: a movement in the shadows at the foot of his bed, an unnamed, unseen presence, a pause pregnant with terror before the thing, still unseen, unidentified, landed of a sudden on his chest, crushing the scream from his lungs. He lay quite still, hearing every sound, feeling every sensation his senses could pick up but all the while feeling the thing perched heavy on his chest, knowing it now for what it was: guilt.

He tried not to see her, her eyes wide and filled with warning, her bare toes stretching down, reaching for the table as if the slightest contact might take the terrible weight from her neck. He tried not to think about her last moments. They had probably used a ligature to strangle her, coldly and professionally, until she blacked out, before slipping the noose over her head and raising her to the ceiling to finish her off. Had one of them carefully removed the chandelier while the other had his hands around her throat? How had they got inside? There was no sign of forced entry. Had she let them in, these two killers with their powerful hands and length of rope? Had they intended to make it look like suicide, but changed the plan to frame Friend when he walked in on them? Or had they known he was coming? And when? He tried not to think about these things now. Later he would have to.

Instead, he tried to think about Davit. Friend hadn't felt much like talking over dinner, so the Georgian had told Friend his life story. He was the younger of two sons born to a fisherman in a small village an hour up the coast. The brothers had squabbled bitterly from an early age and when the elder had taken over the family boat from their ageing father, Davit had been too proud to work for him, so he had joined the merchant navy instead and spent eight years at sea. Then his brother had been injured in an accident and so Davit had come home to take over the family boat after all.

For five years he had fished as generations of his family before him, until falling fish stocks and competition from larger boats began to eat into his livelihood. Davit seemed to have accepted quite calmly this change in his circumstances, a change he attributed to pollution in the Black Sea and overfishing by large commercial vessels from Turkey and Russia. He might have been talking about the rise and fall of the tides.

'I could blame the capitalists,' he said, 'but it was just as bad in my father's time. The industrialisation of everything. Socialism and capitalism are two sides of the same coin.'

So, with his family's blessing, he had sold the boat and bought a taxi with the proceeds.

'Lucky for you I did, right Boss?' he said with a wink. 'I wouldn't have been much use to you tonight with a fishing boat!'

But what allowed Friend to force a smile as the two men clinked glasses was not so much the restorative power of Davit's stoicism and wit as the small light bulb that had begun to glow in the back of his mind after what the Georgian had just said.

Hours later, hours of normal sounds, sights and smells, the train slid quietly into a still sleeping Tbilisi. *Please remember to take all of your personal longings with you when you leave the train.* Friend laced up his shoes, put on his jacket, picked up his bags and walked slowly down the empty platform.

* * *

'Polychlorinated biphenyl,' said Alison Holding. 'Otherwise known as PCB. They used to use it as a coolant in electrical apparatus, but it was outlawed in the west years ago due to its toxic properties. It's still thought to be in widespread use in some of the more remote former Soviet provinces in central Asia, which explains what it was doing on a ship sailing out of Batumi. A proven carcinogen, also linked to endocrine disruption. At least that's what it says here.'

Holding laid her tablet device down on the table. She was sitting with Friend in a small, secure room in the basement of the Tbilisi embassy. There was barely space for the pair of them, squeezed into two squat armchairs set at angles to each other. It was almost impossible to move without banging your shins against the low coffee table which was the room's only other piece of furniture.

Friend was listless and unresponsive. Holding had seen the signs before, had felt them herself: the emotional down at the end of a mission, the sudden withdrawal of adrenalin from the system, the absent stimulus of danger. Made only worse by the feelings of guilt at the death of an innocent.

'Don't worry,' she said. 'A few little smears of PCB on your overalls won't have done you any harm. You've done well. We know now that Guria Shipping and Trading was being used as a front by Presnenskaya Bratva, who were surely responsible for the murders of Nia Dadiani, her father and her husband. Her son is safe. We know how Presnenskaya Bratva funds its operations, through the Caucasian Credit Trust. They may well have been smuggling migrants across the Black Sea to Europe, but we now know they have also been dumping toxic waste illegally in its waters. No doubt Elif Çalışkan sneaked on board the May Rose expecting to find human cargo, but it would appear she found something else instead.' She leaned over and picked up her tablet once more; pulled up a series of images and tilted the screen towards Friend. 'These are the pictures taken by Altan Karabeg showing the May Rose transiting through the Bosphorus on the day Elif Çalışkan was killed. You see how high she's riding in the water? How little cargo is on the upper deck? She must have witnessed them dumping it over the side when they were in deep water. That was the secret her murder was meant to protect.'

Friend seemed to stir from his stupor and looked up.

'That report on PCB; did it say anything about it being toxic to marine life?'

She turned the screen back towards herself and began reading. After a moment, she said: 'yes. Yes, it is toxic. In sufficient quantities.'

'There was a story in the Istanbul papers when I was there. Thousands of fish washed up on the Black Sea shore, dead or dying. A fisherman I met in Batumi said much the same thing. Fish stocks in long-term decline, some species hardly ever caught any more. This must have been going on for years.'

'And with any luck, you've stopped it.'

'They must have a system of separate manifests,' mused Friend. 'The list I got from Levan Dadiani was an export manifest: for the port of departure. I just assumed the import manifest for the other end would be the same, but of course it wouldn't have to be. There's no central registry for these things.' He ended the thought with a shrug and asked: 'So, what happens next?'

'That's not up to me. That's a policy decision for government. Our job is just to source the intelligence. What governments do with it is up to them. In this case, there's probably a good chance something will be done. Much of the Great British Public couldn't care less about criminal organisations smuggling human beings by the thousand but dump a load of toxic chemicals in the sea and they'll march on parliament.'

Perhaps, thought Friend. But more likely the wrong-doings of the Khan or Kovalchuk or whoever was behind all this would be seen as too remote from the comfort of Westminster; too distant from the national security threat he had been sent out to expose. Nothing would happen next bar the closure of a slim file. He had known it as soon as he realised he was meeting with Holding rather than Magniac; control rather than liaison. There was only one reason for this: mission concluded. He would be recalled to London. The connection between Kovalchuk and Mikel Qorghanashvili would go unexplored, the mystery of Dimitri and the hold Kovalchuk held over him would be unresolved and Nia Dadiani, Nia would be unavenged. And so he felt it again as he sat bolt upright in his chair, the thing that was shame and guilt pressing down on his chest, crushing the air out of him slowly like an ever-tightening vice.

'So perhaps I haven't stopped it then, and Nia Dadiani and Elif Çalışkan died in vain.'

'Look, Sebastian. We both work for an organisation which aims at the acquisition of information; it isn't an agency of law enforcement, much less a vehicle for moral retribution if that's what you have in mind. If you want to go off on some kind of crusade then do it on your own time, not your employer's. Better still, stop feeling sorry for yourself and take some pride in a job well done.'

Alison Holding waited a moment for Friend to respond. But when he didn't, she went on, putting what sympathy she could into her voice.

'It wasn't your fault, you know. The people you've been investigating are ruthless and criminal. If they weren't there would be no point investigating them. And since they are, we shouldn't be surprised when they act in a ruthless and criminal fashion. You should know by now that as an operational agent your missions are undertaken on a war footing and, just as in any other war, casualties are inevitable. Civilian ones too, on occasion. Regrets don't do you any good. They're unprofessional. They can be dangerous. They can make you doubt yourself, slow you down, and next time it might be your own death you end up regretting. It was one of the first things they taught me in training: *In this business you need to travel light, and regrets make for heavy baggage.*'

'You're right of course,' said Friend as he turned to meet her stare. And she was. Regrets served no purpose. But there was also a thing called conscience.

PART THREE

MIRA

CHAPTER SIXTEEN

SYNDICATE

The small, silent man in the black tailcoat and spotless white gloves glided smoothly around the room gathering up the discarded dishes, piling them carefully one on top of another until the table was clear enough to leave the three diners to their brandy and cigars. Once that was done, he disappeared through a door in the corner of the room, managing to close it behind him despite his burden in a manner that aroused no curiosity from the three men left behind. They had remained silent while the butler did his work, for their talk was of business and these were not men accustomed to discussing their business in front of prying eyes and ears. The oldest of the three men sucked quietly on a cigar, watching the grey smoke curl up into the air. The smoke was just a shade darker than his whitish-grey hair, the thick, straight fringe of which above his forehead gave his suntanned face an even browner appearance. He was dressed with simple elegance, a discreetly cut navy blue suit above a cream cotton shirt and silver tie, a gold tie clip and a matching signet ring on the little finger of his left hand. This, his appearance seemed to say, is a wealthy man, an important man, but one whose importance is so self-evident that it does not need to be shouted about. Sitting opposite him, dressed with similar simplicity in a tweed jacket and open-necked blue shirt was Alexei Kovalchuk. Between the two, at the head of the table, sat a man of little height but much girth, his vast expanse of belly covered implausibly by a double-breasted smoking jacket of deep red velvet. He too wore an open-necked shirt, in this case white, but if that seemed incongruous in combination with the jacket it was at least understandable given the matter of his chins. To have constrained such an impressive array of terraced blubber with a tie or cravat would have involved unnecessary cruelty. A thin, almost pencil-drawn moustache adorned his upper lip and two dark, coffee-bean eyes gazed out impassively from above his bloated cheeks as he sipped at his brandy. His entirely bald skull seemed permanently covered in a thin film of sweat.

It was the oldest of the three who broke the silence.

'A shame,' he said casually, as if discussing the performance of a horse he owned, 'that this British agent could not be found by the police in the Dadiani house. Do we know how he got away?'

The fat man snorted. 'Kovalchuk's men didn't do their job properly.'

Before Kovalchuk could respond, the other man put in gently: 'I have never had occasion to complain about their professionalism before. I am sure Alexei Semyonovich's people did everything they could be expected to have done.'

Kovalchuk smiled. 'Thank you, Vyacheslav Vladimirovich. To answer your question, we believe he may have been helped by the driver who brought him there. My men reported a taxi parked on the street not far from the house as they left. It is not a common place for a taxi to be; most of the residents of that part of town enjoy their own private transportation. We are endeavouring to find out who the driver of this vehicle is; once we do so he will be questioned.'

'You will do nothing of the sort!' snapped the fat man.

'Mikel is quite right, Senka,' said the older man. 'There may be other witnesses as well, if the police manage to identify this man it would be well for our people not to be anywhere near him. Unless there is any chance he might be able to identify them?'

'Very unlikely,' said Kovalchuk. 'It was dark, he was parked at least one hundred metres from the Dadiani house so he couldn't have seen them clearly as they left. The lights on the car they used were extinguished until well after the point where they passed him. It wasn't one of our own vehicles anyway.'

'Well then, I think we have nothing to worry about. Do you agree Mikel?'

Mikel Qorghanashvili gave an emphatic sigh, the tension escaping with the air from his lungs as he availed himself of a rare opportunity to absolve a man of blame.

'Yes, I would not expect us to have any difficulty with the authorities in the matter of Nia Dadiani's death. And even if we did, it would be nothing we could not take care of in the usual manner.'

'You are not sorry she had to die?' asked the older man.

'Sorry? Why on earth should I be? Why should any of us be? She had outlived her usefulness. After what the British found out about the May Rose we could not use the Dadiani line again, so maintaining our hold on her would have been a waste of resources and letting her live a risk to security. She had to die. There is no other possible conclusion.'

'And the British have not found out too much?'

'More than we would wish, certainly. But not enough to be damaging. They know the Dadiani woman was operating under duress, but not what our object was, or who, beyond our friend Kovalchuk, we really are. We allowed the British agent Hunter to slip on board the May Rose knowing that he would find nothing. Mr Hunter is looking for smuggled migrants. He has been barking up the wrong tree for a while now. Let him keep barking. It will do us no harm.'

Qorghanashvili left it at that. There were some things it was better his colleagues did not know.

The older man smiled in satisfaction. He cast a benevolent look across the table to the two younger men. 'I am very glad to hear it, my friend,' he said. 'I must confess that when I first learned of your methods I thought them rather medieval. But perhaps I simply failed to take into account local sensibilities. They certainly seem to work most efficiently here. Perhaps we should consider extending them beyond Georgia.'

Qorghanashvili shook his head gravely. 'In my view, that would be a mistake. Such things are better done on a small scale. It would take too much manpower to employ the tactic more widely, as the Gestapo and NKVD did in the last century. Perhaps there is also an element of domestic prejudice in my view, but I do feel this is a particularly Georgian way of working. A man I once met said that blood is the best security in this business. He was right, in his way, but blood is also the greatest vulnerability. Family loyalty can be a curse as well as an asset.'

'May I ask whether that is why you have no family of your own?'

'No, that has nothing to do with it.'

'But you never married; a man of such great wealth and position must have had opportunities.'

'It was never important to me.'

'But still,' the older man persisted, 'we work in an unusual field it is true, we have to do many things that are difficult, disagreeable, but we remain human beings, with the same human feelings as anyone else. For my part I would find it difficult to go on without my wife and my daughters. And yet you, you are unmarried, your parents are dead, you have no family.'

'But he did have a brother once, or a half-brother at least,' broke in Kovalchuk, sensing an opportunity to prick his host's pomposity.

'A foster brother,' said Qorghanashvili tautly. 'Not the same thing at all.'

'Oh, a *foster* brother,' said the older man, offering the hint of a wink to his compatriot. 'And whatever happened to him?'

'Who can say?' said Kovalchuk, with an exaggerated shrug.

Qorghanashvili gave an impatient snort and downed the last of his brandy, before removing the napkin from his collar. Their knowledge of his family circumstances was hardly complete, but even so this sort of impertinence was too much. Placing his puffy hands firmly on the arms of his chair, he began the tremendous effort of lifting himself to his feet.

The older man laughed and waved him back down at once.

'Please forgive us Mikel,' he said, 'Senka and I were only teasing. It was very cruel of us, after you invite us here to share this magnificent meal.'

Qorghanashvili eased himself back into his chair, which gave a distinct squeak of protest. 'Well, I was glad to,' he said. 'Too often when I entertain, I have to be someone I am not.'

Kovalchuk had to suppress a chuckle. Where else was Qorghanashvili pretending to be someone he was not more than here, among gangsters like himself? Surely he could be more himself among the rich and respectable, the back-room power brokers, than among the outright criminals. This was a man who never got his mouth dirty, let alone his hands. The way he had spoken about Nia Dadiani's death had been the way a man might speak of removing a piece from a chess board. It was cold and mathematical, with no recognition of what the act itself involved. He had others, like Kovalchuk himself, to speak the threats and others still to carry them out. Kovalchuk had seen them when they came back from the Dadiani house; the smell of sweat and tension still clinging to their clothes, the hands that shook slightly as they poured the vodka from the offered bottle, the empty look in their eyes as they pocketed the cash. Men who would kill their own kind, in revenge or in a struggle for power, were ten a penny; but those who would bare-handedly execute an innocent woman without a qualm were more difficult to find. The first kind often didn't last long before their nerves were shot; the second needed watching. They were rarely to be trusted. And were these the kind of people among whom Mikel Qorghanashvili felt most at home? Kovalchuk felt a nagging disgust at the thought. Qorghanashvili was in truth a perfect Himmler; a man who would calmly plan any number of executions but would turn green at the gills and have to be helped back to his limousine if he ever had to witness one in person.

'And with us you can be yourself? You can relax?'

'Yes, I suppose so.'

'Good. Then let us relax a little more and enjoy another glass of brandy.' The older man filled his glass and passed the decanter to Kovalchuk, who in turn passed it on to their host. When all three were filled, the older man raised his glass to the others in a toast: 'to family ties!'

For a while they chatted idly about less important matters; their holiday plans, the purchase of a new car, the schooling of the older man's daughters in Switzerland, but there was one small business matter still left for them to discuss, and it was Senka Kovalchuk who raised again the question of the British agent known to him as Roderick Hunter.

'I do not think Mr Hunter is likely to be much of a problem to us in future,' said Qorghanashvili dismissively. 'He may have been fortunate enough to escape the Dadiani house before the police arrived, but he has now been involved in too many deaths. The British are a very risk-averse people. It is my opinion that they will call him back to London. With the death of Nia Dadiani and the imminent demise of her shipping line, I think it unlikely that they will send anyone out to replace him.'

'And if they don't recall him? If he persists in his investigations?' asked Kovalchuk.

Qorghanashvili replied with a knowing stare, which the older man put into words.

'In that case Senka, it would be very likely that Mr Hunter might suffer an unfortunate accident.'

'Then I will ask my men to keep a close eye on his hotel.'

With that, the three men rose from the table and prepared to make their farewells. Qorghanashvili picked up a little bell from beside his chair and gave it a ring. Within moments the small man in the black tailcoat glided through the door and began to gather up the brandy glasses and empty the cigar ash from the trays.

* * *

'So, this is inconspicuous surveillance,' Magniac shifted uncomfortably in his seat, 'two men with binoculars sitting in a rented car on a major street. I'm surprised the police haven't been called already.'

Mikel Qorghanashvili was quite right. Within twelve hours of making his report to Alison Holding, Sebastian Friend had received the order from the Director's office instructing him to stand down. Friend had expected no less and was prepared with his response. He had been on holiday when first summoned to meet Holding in Istanbul and it was customary for operatives in his department to be granted a period of leave on completion of a mission. Sometimes this was no less than a medical necessity, but it had come to be expected even when the operative was in perfect health. Some wounds, it was acknowledged, remain invisible.

And so he found himself here, sitting alongside a grumpy and impatient Magniac, in a rented Toyota parked along the street from Qorghanashvili's mansion. Magniac's co-operation was unofficial, offered purely in friendship, but then so was the whole operation now. This was no longer a business of state, it was personal.

'Don't worry,' he said. 'I'm not planning a long-term stake-out. I just want to get a feel for the place.'

The house was a forbidding prospect, set back from the street behind a large expanse of green lawn dotted with rhododendron bushes and a tall fence of wrought iron. They had been sitting there more than an hour already, and Magniac was beginning to get irritable, wanting to know what the plan would be and worrying that he ought to have stayed behind with his vines and his lovely young wife. There was no plan, just a hope that one might emerge, somehow, from the very act of sitting there watching, talking, considering.

'Who else do we think is inside?' Friend asked.

'Kovalchuk for one, plus the other man and the two bodyguards you saw go in with him earlier this evening. Assuming there are no other guests – and there's just the one car parked out front – then there is probably just the domestic establishment inside. Qorghanashvili has no family, but he has a housekeeper, two maids, two permanent bodyguards, three kitchen staff and even an English butler called Foulkes. The maids and kitchen staff come and go as required, but the butler, bodyguards and housekeeper live on site.'

'Foulkes?'

'Well, that's what he calls himself. His real name is Harry Butterworth, born in Streatham in 1965. He actually did train as a butler and served for a while on the Duke of Normanby's staff, but was dismissed in circumstances that didn't exactly enhance his career prospects. I couldn't get to the bottom of it all, but I gather there was a burglary at the Duke's Belgravia residence and some valuable jewellery was taken. Police suspected an inside job and Butterworth was in the frame. No charges were brought, but he left the Duke's service without a reference. That would be about ten years ago. Since then he's buttled for various foreign potentates, ending up here with our friend Qorghanashvili towards the end of last year.'

'How on earth did Qorghanashvili come across him?'

'I've no idea. Do you want me to pop in and ask?' Magniac shifted uneasily in his seat again, as if he would have run almost any errand to get out of it.

'What about the housekeeper?'

'Elderly battleaxe. I haven't been able to find out anything about her. Perhaps she's a relative of his. She doesn't look like the type you'd pick up at an agency. Look, how much longer do we have to sit here?'

'Not long perhaps, take a look.'

From the shadows at the side of the house, two men had emerged, slowly walking towards the car parked at the front. A moment later they saw the headlights come on and heard the distant rumble of a diesel engine. Now a shaft of light came from the middle of the house itself and danced down the stone steps at the front before losing itself in the shadow of the car. Three men followed it, dark silhouettes in the artificial light, one a shorter, rounder shape than the others. Friend peered intently through the binoculars.

'That's Qorghanashvili, no mistake, and one of the others is Kovalchuk, I'm sure of it. Any idea who the other man is?'

Magniac stared through the lenses for a moment, then gave a quiet laugh.

'Oh yes,' he said. 'I know who that is. That, Laddie, is Vyacheslav Vladimirovich Komarov, one of the most powerful criminal bosses in Russia. The man who runs Presnenskaya Bratva, no less. He's a real player that one. So, are you planning on taking him on? You, me, a pair of binoculars and a hired Toyota? No kit, no support, no official status? I like a scrap as much as the next man, but …'

Friend was no longer listening. He was no longer even in the car. The man in the dark coat was about fifty yards down from the Toyota walking towards the gate of the Qorghanashvili mansion. He didn't turn as Friend trotted quietly up behind him and crumpled quickly when the Englishman took him down.

The pistol clattered uselessly to the floor.

CHAPTER SEVENTEEN

SCARECROW

The hotel was little more than a seedy flop-house above a fly-blown restaurant a short walk from the railway station. *Gvino Minda* hadn't exactly been the Ritz, but it was clean and pleasant and reasonably consistent with the cover of Roderick Hunter, freelance journalist. But now Hunter was blown and even though Friend had no other solid cover available he had no intention of letting Kovalchuk's people find him quite so easily. This was the kind of place in the kind of area where people passed through quickly and no questions were asked. The kind of place where you looked over your shoulder and thought twice about going out after dark if you didn't crave the wrong kind of excitement. The owner was a contact of Magniac's and sufficiently discreet. Magniac himself was sitting at the bar downstairs, sulking, and keeping a wary eye on the street. Unlike everywhere else in Georgia, it reminded him of London.

Friend poured himself a shot from the vodka bottle and drank it down. He perched on the end of the bed and gazed at the man slumped half-conscious in the armchair. It was a scarecrow figure; a sunken head obscured by a tangled mop of grey hair, shapeless clothes unkempt and uncared for. When at last the head was raised to answer Friend there was no trace of colour, life or humour in the face.

'They used your grandson, didn't they?'

No man in Georgia has any greater loyalty than to his family.

'Yes,' said Levan Dadiani. 'They knew his school, his mother's schedule, everything. That's how these people work, how they put pressure on. And I had seen with Nia's father and husband that these were no idle threats.'

Friend poured two more shots of vodka and passed one over to Dadiani.

'I suppose they gave you a choice.'

'Oh, yes! I told you once before that there was nothing I wouldn't do to protect my family. So yes, they gave me a choice, between two parts of it: my niece or my grandson. What could I do? What would anyone do? I tried to play a double game. I gave them what they asked for, enough to keep them happy, but not everything. I tried to help her too. I watched her back, I helped her collect information that we could use in court if it ever came to that. I was stuck in the middle, trying to keep both sides apart. When I gave them the information about your meeting with her it was just one more little betrayal after hundreds of others. It didn't seem to have any more significance than the rest. How could I have known it was her death sentence? They didn't share their plans with me. How could I have known, Rock? What else could I have done?'

'You could have told me.'

'Told you what? That they would be waiting for you? I didn't know that. What could I have achieved? You think you could have saved her? You didn't know they would kill her either. We were both unprepared. Once they decided to kill her there was nothing either of us could have done. So what do you want Rock? Why did you bring me here? You want justice? You want to take me to the police? All right, let's go to the police. It won't achieve anything, we can't prove anything. I got my threats anonymously over the phone. But, OK, let's both go to the police if it helps you get this off your conscience. It won't do much for mine.'

Levan Dadiani drained his glass and with the last of his vodka the flow of his anger seemed to ebb away as well.

'You're right, Levan. This is on my conscience too. If I hadn't interfered, Nia might be alive today.'

'Or she might not.' Levan gave a shrug. 'Once your people started to investigate her company she was no longer useful to Kovalchuk and his friends.'

'And leaving her alive would have been a risk to them.'

'Of course.'

'But does that really make us any less responsible?'

Levan Dadiani took a deep breath, pulled himself upright in his chair, the palms of his hands laid flat on its arms and closed his eyes.

'We make our choices and we have to live with them,' Friend said at last. 'And perhaps we're not the best people to judge whether they're right or wrong.'

'And who do you think is right? God?'

Levan's eyes were still squeezed shut.

'Perhaps. And the people who love us. You have plenty of them around you, Levan. Make use of them.'

'Make my confession, you mean.'

'Your wife probably understands you better than any priest.'

'And to whom will you make your confession, Rock?'

To my own conscience. It wasn't confession that Friend sought so much as atonement. To salve his conscience, which made for heavier baggage even than regret.

He pulled Dadiani's pistol out from his jacket pocket.

'Whether you want to confess your sins or bury them I suggest you don't add to them with this.' He tossed the pistol over to Dadiani. 'Go home and look after your family, Levan. You still have a life to live.'

'Life?' Levan Dadiani looked down at the gun in his lap as if he had never seen such a thing before. 'I wouldn't know where to start.'

'Start by not thinking of your own grief. Think of your wife's. Didn't she love Nia too? She needs your help. Your grandson needs your help. So does the rest of your family. You need to realise, Levan, that you're at the heart of who they are. If you go down, you'll take them all with you.'

Dadiani shook his head stiffly and said nothing.

'How's the neck?'

'Sore. What did you do?'

'Nothing much, just enough to stun a nerve. You'll be fine in an hour or two once you've got up and walked around a bit.'

Dadiani got up and walked around a bit. He held the gun loosely in his hand.

'I suppose I should ask what you're still doing here?' he said after a few moments. 'Don't your people want you back in London?'

'A little unfinished business. And looking after you, Levan.'

A faint smile crept into the corner of Dadiani's mouth.

'Unfinished business? I see. Not very good at taking your own advice, are you, Mr Hunter?'

When the door closed behind him the darkness enveloped Dadiani once more. There was no light in the corridor apart from what little was thrown up from the streetlights through the window at the end. The darkness had been his only comfort since Nia died. He wanted to sink further into it. It was all he deserved. He managed to drag his feet towards the elevator and pressed the call button. A great tightness gripped his chest and he felt his breath grow short. Guilt. It pounded inside his head until he could stand it no more. What confession could rid him of this? The gun was still in his hand. He raised it to his temple, his finger poised on the trigger.

But the weariness was too great even for this small gesture. He lowered the gun again and gently released the ammunition clip from its housing. He slipped it into his pocket and went to remove the last bullet from the chamber. Before he could complete the action, the elevator gave a soft 'ping', the doors slid open and Levan Dadiani looked up through the dirty yellow light at the scarecrow staring back at him. Instinctively, he raised his arm, took aim at a point about two centimetres above the left eyebrow and pulled the trigger.

The sound should have been deafening: a roar of gunfire echoing down the narrow corridor, the shattering of glass from the elevator's mirrored back. Instead, it was a sound he recognised from years ago. The empty click of a gun whose firing pin has been removed.

CHAPTER EIGHTEEN

FLASH HARRY

Harry Butterworth sat as patiently as he could and tried to resist the temptation to drum his fingers on the table. He watched as the jeweller meticulously picked up each of the little, uncut stones he had emptied from the unremarkable brown envelope with a pair of tweezers and examined them carefully through the glass screwed into his left eye socket. All the man's facial muscles seemed to have contracted around the single focal point of his left eye, concentrating themselves on the task of keeping the glass in place while his mind turned over the problem of what he was looking at through it.

Butterworth stole an impatient glance at his wristwatch. He had one day off each week and he didn't intend to waste it sitting in a gloomy office while this wrinkled old geezer worked out how much to try and swindle him out of. Harry Butterworth was a busy man, with places to be and things to be doing. Six days a week he was the meek, obedient servant with eyes that did not see and ears that did not hear, except what they needed to in the pursuit of his duties. But on this one day, Monday, this day of all days, he was a maestro, a king among subjects, a man whose every whim was there to be indulged. Of course, for that he needed money, more than his admittedly generous salary could stretch to, which is where those eyes that sometimes did see more than they were supposed to, those ears that could sometimes hear pure gold through solid walls and the keen memory that stored the resulting knowledge away until it might prove useful, this was where those things came in.

Harry Butterworth would be the first to admit - to himself, in private - that he had a tendency towards being light fingered. He always had been, even as a boy. But he was never compulsive; he had learned judgement in his youth, and that was another thing his memory had retained and found useful. Most of the time he was a model of restraint, serving his masters with the utmost diligence and professionalism. In fact, he took his duties and his profession as a whole very seriously. But this did not deter him from occasionally permitting himself to redistribute certain elements of his masters' portion of wealth, acquired, more often than not, in breach of the rules of fair play and equality if not of the law itself, in a more deserving direction. Namely into his own pocket. This had always been done with the greatest care and consideration. He took only a little and only that which would not be likely to be missed. In this respect he was in a fortunate profession: all of his employers had been sufficiently wealthy that the odd little trinket here and there would rarely be noticed. He always did his homework and made sure he knew which possessions the family valued most dearly, and, more importantly, which they did not value much at all. But no cash. He never touched cash. Cash could be counted. Objects were a different matter; antiques, silverware, unwanted jewellery, could easily be overlooked. In this way he had managed to stay out of trouble, for the most part, throughout a long and distinguished career.

The one exception, of course, had been that unfortunate business with Lord Normanby. That had simply been bad luck. His Lordship had been in possession of a particularly fine library which, over the course of his eight-year service in the Duke's household, Butterworth had spent a good deal of time cleaning. During those many long hours of dusting shelves and cleaning books, Butterworth had grown curious about the value of the collection, a collection His Lordship had inherited with his title and taken little interest in since. Butterworth had taken to attending book auctions in the West

End of London, watching the proceedings with increasing interest and taking the catalogues home with him for further study. He frequented the local library and ordered books on rare bibliography. It took him well over a year, but at last he felt he had acquired the requisite expertise to begin deriving a justifiable amount of value from his work in the library.

The main difficulty was establishing provenance. With the help of a talented friend, he designed and produced his own bookplate which he stuck over the top of the Normanby plate on the endpaper of each selected volume. The same friend helped him produce a letter, on impressively headed notepaper, authorising him as the agent of an elderly lady of aristocratic family (the lady could indeed be located on the pages of Debrett's) who, finding herself in reduced circumstances, wished to begin discreetly disposing of her extensive library of rare works. The letter explained that the bulk of this collection had been acquired in the 1920's from the grandfather of the present Duke of Normanby; details of earlier provenance could no doubt be acquired from the Duke. At this point Butterworth was able to further impress the keen-eyed auctioneer he took the first books to by lifting up the edge of his bookplate – which was only stuck down at the top edge – to reveal the Normanby plate beneath. When the auctioneer wrote to the Duke requesting confirmation of these details, Butterworth was easily able to intercept the letter and write back, in the character of the Duke's private secretary, confirming the 1920's sale, but regretting that no details of any earlier provenance could be confirmed as the Duke's collection had never been catalogued.

The auction house, based in a provincial town some distance from London, did not seem to feel this was a great impediment to a sale, and indeed some of the Normanby books bore earlier ownership inscriptions which added colour to the story. The genuine absence of a catalogue was, felt Butterworth, a real blessing to his plans. If his Lordship had no written record of what he had, he was even less likely to notice its absence. Nevertheless, he had proceeded with his customary caution, avoiding those books which he knew were the most valuable in the collection, whose sale might bring unwelcome attention to his scheme. In most cases each volume raised between £3-5,000, sums he found entirely satisfactory and worthy of his efforts. Over the course of three years, he managed to dispose of almost sixty books in this manner, not a large number considering the extent of the collection – more than six thousand volumes; it was a matter of just a few minutes to rearrange the shelves and conceal their absence. Many of the books concerned had been gratifyingly thin.

There had been one unpleasant mistake. A slim 18th century pamphlet, with no binding and still retaining its original wrappers of flimsy buff paper. It was not even on the open shelves, but kept in an envelope in the closed, but unlocked, lower section of one mahogany bookcase. The auctioneer had tutted and said that such an item ought really to have been kept in an acid-free archival box or a Melinex sleeve, whatever that might have been. It was one of the few sporting pamphlets in the Duke's collection, a 1794 edition of Samuel Britcher's *Cricket Scores*, the first cricket annual and a most tedious volume containing page upon page of cricket scores with no commentary or reportage of any kind. Butterworth had gained little knowledge of cricket books during his researches, but thought for its age alone it ought to be worth a thousand or so. And he had been amused by the printer's error on the title page which gave the date as 1974. When the auctioneer told him it was one of perhaps only four copies known to exist – the other three having been identified in a study by the late David Rayvern Allen – and gave it a tentative valuation of £25,000, Butterworth felt his stomach sink through his knees and almost bolted for the door. But a moment of reflection kept him uneasily in his chair. The letter from his supposed employer had claimed she was raising funds to help her through her old age; how then could he justify removing the most valuable book he had presented from sale? Still, such a book might achieve £25,000 at Christie's or Sotheby's, but possibly not in a provincial auction house a hundred miles from London.

Butterworth was mistaken. Only one complete set of Britcher's Scores is known to exist, but for the handful of collectors with an ambition to achieve a second this was an opportunity too rare to pass up. Three of them descended on this small provincial auction and the bidding went wild. When Harry Butterworth received the letter stating that his employer's 1794 edition of Britcher had achieved a hammer price of £82,000 he didn't know whether to laugh or cry. It was one of the highest sale prices for an individual lot the auction house had ever achieved, and the sale of this tiny, precious item – 'the property of a lady' – became something of a local cause celèbre. For weeks afterwards, Butterworth expected the news to go national and for the Normanby connection to be revealed. When the cheque came through, he hardly knew what to do with it.

Then came the burglary. Harry Butterworth, it should be clearly understood, had nothing whatever to do with it. Shocked by his experience with Britcher's, he had suspended his activities for a few months, responding to fawning enquiries from the auctioneer by saying that his employer had, for the present, achieved sufficient funds for her purposes and did not wish to sell anything more. He was just beginning to regain his confidence and make new plans when it happened. It had been an inside job all right; entry had been affected far too easily for it to have been anything else. On balance, Butterworth thought the maids probably to blame. He should never have hired those two Albanian sisters. They almost certainly had Albanian brothers who were up to no good. Not much had been taken; some silverware, a couple of the more portable pictures, a small amount of jewellery, but when the Duke's insurance assessor came round, he brought with him something Butterworth had been certain did not exist: a catalogue of His Lordship's library.

It was not, the assessor explained to an evidently interested Butterworth, a comprehensive listing of every item in the Normanby collection; the last insurance valuation carried out some ten years previously, not long before Butterworth had entered the Duke's service, had given the majority of the library a collective value. However, all books and pamphlets thought to have a value in excess of £2,000 were individually listed and this is where Butterworth's troubles began.

The assessor spent two days compiling an inventory to compare with the itemised listing on the old valuation. At the end of it he had identified eighteen of the sixty or so books Butterworth had disposed of as missing. The police were notified. So was His Lordship. Butterworth was the only man with regular unfettered access to the library; if the items had been missing prior to the burglary why had Butterworth not noticed their absence from the shelves? If they had been taken during the burglary, why had the police found the shelves so tidy when the dining room and study from which other items had been taken showed clear signs of disorder? These were not questions Butterworth could answer convincingly. He spent many uncomfortable hours in sweaty, brightly-lit rooms under police questioning. The brief minutes he spent with His Lordship were, if anything, even more distressing. His rooms were searched, his personal finances investigated. He was fortunate that he had a solid alibi for the night of the burglary and that nothing but his salary had ever been paid into the accounts he held in his own name. Everything had been paid to the account of Foulkes, the persona he had invented as the agent of the aristocratic lady in reduced circumstances. And of that account the police found no trace.

After a week of this he had had enough. They had not charged him, but that did not mean they never would. The friend who had helped him build the persona of Foulkes had also provided identity documents: a passport, driver's licence, national insurance card, to help him bank the funds. He now added one further job to the list: a copy was made of Butterworth's prized certificate from the Harrold International School for Butlers and Valets, this time in the name of Edward Foulkes. Foulkes would now be the personal gentleman for the gentleman of personality and means. Butterworth would buttle no more. Butterworth had bolted.

Since then he had gone from strength to strength. He had left England behind him long before; his south London childhood, the first half of his working life a distant dream. He carried his substantial nest-egg with him, adding to it as the opportunity arose. It wasn't all about saving, he wanted to be comfortable in retirement but he had no family to care for, nor any desire for one. This left him enough to enjoy his life; a few luxurious holidays when he could be the kind of man he spent most of his time serving, a few nice clothes, and some pleasant moments in the restaurants and casinos of the cities he inhabited. He had seen Paris, Florence, Budapest, St Petersburg, Hong Kong and now, by some exotic twist of fate he had no desire to question, Tbilisi. It wasn't exactly Paris, but it beat the hell out of Streatham High Street.

* * *

'I'll give you two thousand five. American.' The jeweller sat back in his chair and eased the glass slowly out of his eye with a smooth, practised twist. His face relaxed into a rather mournful expression, trying to convey the feeling that he would have liked to offer more, really he would, but circumstances beyond his control dictated otherwise. His eyes drooped down at the corners; even the black hairs on his neatly-trimmed goatee beard seemed to wilt a little in response.

'Two thousand five? Are you joking? There must be fifteen stones there.'

'Thirteen, I think, but they all need cutting and I'm afraid some of them won't be worth it. Five of them have a very brown colour indeed and one or two show flaws which will impair their value. There are three here I think which should do us nicely but the rest,' he shrugged dismissively, 'the rest I take as no more than a favour. A gesture of goodwill to someone I hope will become a regular supplier. Perhaps?'

'Perhaps if you raise your prices to a more reasonable level.'

'You are always welcome to go elsewhere if you prefer.'

But that was the thing of course. Where else could he go discreetly to dispose of stones he had acquired so discreetly himself? His employer, whom he always thought of as Mr Q., finding the name itself rather a headful to think of let alone to say, received payments in all sorts of ways, myriad gifts that were strewn about his house with little care or attention. He supposed they were bribes, but he was not yet certain what for. He had only been in Mr Q's service for six months, but it showed every sign of being an interesting and worthwhile appointment.

It had taken him just a few weeks to work out the combination of the safe. Mr Q was a man of either limited imagination or defective memory and the digits he chose were lifted from the licence plates of his own car. The diamonds seemed to arrive every second week in little green velvet bags; he had seen Mr Q time and again coming into the house twirling a little velvet bag in his hand as if he hadn't a care. When Butterworth finally plucked up the courage to open the safe he had found seventeen of the little bags piled haphazardly together. Each appeared to contain the same amount of rough, uncut, untraceable stones. The weight varied slightly from bag to bag. He spent another month watching carefully until he was satisfied that Mr Q was not keeping an account of how many bags were stored in the safe before he risked taking one. It led to a nervous few days, but then he saw Mr Q coming out of his study carrying three of the bags, which he took with him to his car, and Butterworth knew he was in the clear.

That first bag had netted him three thousand dollars, which made the two thousand five he had been offered for the second a disappointment. Perhaps he had made a mistake returning to the same jeweller twice; it made it clear that this was no legitimate transaction, which might have been the case for a one-off. But where else was he to go? Tbilisi was not Amsterdam or London; it was not a major centre for the diamond trade. He might have had better luck in Tehran. He shrugged and took the two thousand five.

Half an hour later he was tucking his passport and the remaining five hundred dollars into his pocket after depositing two thousand dollars cash into his bank. From there he would later make an electronic transfer to his main bank in Jersey, which held the bulk of his nest egg, now a little more than £750,000 sterling. Not all of it ill-gotten gains either; aside from an occasional spree following a success and his few little luxuries, Harry Butterworth lived on the whole a simple life, if not a blameless one, and much of his monthly salary was easily bankable. Another ten years or so and that healthy nest-egg, together with some nicely-timed property investments he had already made, would leave him set for life. And what would that mean? A little villa on the Atlantic coast of Portugal near Cabo da Roca, an open-top Mercedes, an occasional fling in the casino at Estoril, the sort of easy, elegant life he had always dreamed of.

Such a pleasant prospect was it that in walking out of the bank he walked straight into a smartly-dressed blond Russian, almost knocking him to the ground. Despite it clearly not having been his fault, the young man, who had the most vivid blue eyes to match his cornflower blue shirt, apologised profusely to Butterworth in a flurry of Russian which he could barely follow before grinning widely, patting him on both shoulders and walking off with what Butterworth could have sworn was a wink. Butterworth collected his thoughts for a moment before turning his mind to the present. He had the whole day ahead of him, money in his pocket, the sun in his face and a beautiful future to look forward to. He would start with a decent lunch, a pleasant stroll around the town, a couple of drinks in one of the city's more exclusive bars before ending the day by taking his five-hundred-dollar stash to his favourite casino. Win or lose, it would be a wonderful night.

The Biltmore Hotel is one of the oddest pieces of architecture in the whole of Tbilisi. The city's first glass skyscraper, it towers over the modern cityscape much as the Mother of Georgia statue looms above the old town to the south. Created by encasing an old Soviet-era concrete block in a modern cage of steel and glass that gleams either silver or sapphire blue, depending on the quality of the light, it sits facing the river north of Freedom Square on the prestigious Rustaveli Avenue. 'Sits' being a permissible term since, while three of its elevations are flat, that facing the river juts progressively outward in a series of harsh angles towards its base, giving it from certain viewpoints the appearance of a squatting figure. It sometimes reminded Harry Butterworth of a modern equivalent to the Moai of Easter Island, and if that said anything about the gods of modern Tbilisi, he would probably have approved of it.

The Biltmore's Jewel Casino is perhaps the most luxurious in Georgia and manages to keep its luxuriousness just the right side of tacky. As Butterworth ambled down the curved staircase into the well-lit gaming room with its neat lines of tables beneath him and the well-stocked bar to the side, he thought as he always did when coming here that it looked like the foyer of an expensive modern opera house, the new Mariinsky in St Petersburg or that amazing waterside theatre in Oslo. As he walked to the bar he caught the eye of a fair-haired young man in evening dress. Was it the same Russian he had bumped into outside the bank that morning? Yes, there was a grin of recognition, and was that another wink? Perhaps the man fancied him. He turned away. That sort of thing didn't interest Harry Butterworth at all.

Butterworth sat at the bar sipping slowly at a vodka and tonic. He spent twenty minutes watching the tables. Sometimes he made straight for the poker room, but tonight he felt like gambling light. Poker was too stressful; one had to be in the right mood. A little roulette, or blackjack perhaps. Yes, blackjack, the table wasn't too busy and he knew the dealer to be friendly from previous evenings. He ordered another vodka and left it at the bar while he wandered over to the cashier to change his dollars into chips. It was only when he plucked the wad of dollars from his breast pocket that he realised his passport was no longer there.

* * *

Two days later Harry Butterworth was sitting in a basement room in the British Embassy in Tbilisi wondering why he felt like he was about to be interrogated. Perhaps it was just the Spartan nature of the room itself; the cheap veneer table and two mismatched chairs, the overly bright spotlights in the ceiling, the total absence of windows, the walls bare apart from a pair of framed photographs of London landmarks and a large rectangular mirror that looked exactly like the kind of two-way affair you saw in TV police dramas where the suspect was browbeaten into signing a confession. He was only here to get his passport replaced.

He had submitted his application form with a new photograph and a copy of the police document confirming that he had reported it lost or stolen. He had no reason to worry. The Foulkes passport had been genuinely issued from the start and he had already renewed it successfully once, in Paris, five years before. And yet he found sweat seeping up through his skin into the palms of his hands and he could feel his heart racing beneath the folds of his crisply ironed shirt. He had been waiting here, alone, for almost half an hour.

At last the door opened and a man entered the room; a giant of a man, with a mop of unruly brown hair, a messy tweed jacket and a knitted silk tie that was not quite straight. His voice boomed with bonhomie.

'Morning! Sorry to keep you waiting. My name's Merrick, Jeff Merrick. Consular Section. Mr..?'

'Foulkes.'

'Oh yes, Mr Foulkes. Forgive me.' He sat down, placing a thin buff folder on the desk in front of him. 'I have all your documents here. Your application form is fine, as is the photo and, of course,' the man's face broke into a grin, 'the fee.'

'Good. So there's no problem with the reissue then.'

'Oh, I shouldn't think so. Just a few formalities to attend to.'

'I see. Such as?'

'Your old passport, you're quite sure you lost it?'

'Yes. Either that or it was stolen. I had some money in the same pocket in the morning, but when I checked in the evening the money was still there but the passport was gone.'

'I see. Funny sort of pickpocket who would take a passport but leave the cash.'

'That's what I thought.'

'So you didn't lose it at home then.'

'No, I spent the day around central Tbilisi. It must have happened then.' He thought for a moment about the young, blond Russian.

'Are you here on holiday?'

'No, I work here.'

'Really? Who for?'

'I'm employed in a private, domestic capacity by a wealthy individual.'

'Oh, I see. Sort of a gentleman's personal gentleman.'

'Exactly.'

'And your stay was regularised with the Georgian authorities.'

'Oh yes, my employer arranged all that. I had the necessary permit pasted into my passport.'

'Your old passport.'

'Yes, of course. I suppose I will be able to get it reissued for my new one.'

'Oh, no trouble there at all. Your new passport will state it has been issued as a replacement for a previous one bearing a specific document number. The local authorities will have that number on file. It might take a few days, and a little bit of money, but it shouldn't be anything to worry about.'

'Good, I'm glad.' This was all most reassuring, thought Butterworth, feeling the skin on his palms beginning to dry out. 'Was there anything else you needed?'

'Just to confirm a few little details. We have to be very careful when issuing replacement passports overseas.'

'I understand. What do you need to know?'

'First of all, your full name.'

'Edward Peter Foulkes.'

'Your date of birth?

'28 July 1967.'

'And place?'

'Newark-on-Trent.'

'Your parents' names?'

'Arthur Morris Foulkes and Irene Foulkes, nee Peatfield.'

'Dates of death?'

'My father died in 1982 and my mother in 1997.'

'And yours?'

'I don't understand. My what?'

'Your date of death.'

'Excuse me? I'm not dead. Do you get many passport applications from dead people?'

'Oh, from time to time. Take Edward Peter Foulkes for example. Born in Newark-on-Trent on 28 July 1967, young Edward died in a car accident at Retford on 15 November 1972. But you knew that already, didn't you Mr Butterworth?'

Stephen Magniac watched with a growing sense of contentment as realisation dawned upon the smug little features of Harry Butterworth's face. Up to now he had been feeling rather less than sanguine about his part in Friend's plans. At first, he had taken it as a bonus to be working with his old army comrade; since he had accepted the part-time role of SIS's local representative in Georgia he had felt that the position was strictly titular. There seemed to be no realistic prospect of him actually doing anything to deserve his stipend, save for submitting a few routine reports which probably did no more than corroborate what GCHQ had already picked up from the comfort of Cheltenham. Then, with just a few weeks left before he would be free to hand in his notice and devote himself full-time to Tamara and her vineyard, a plum job had landed in his lap, and with Sebastian Friend as part of it too. It seemed like a fitting way to sign off. But now Friend's job was done, officially at least. Magniac could understand why Friend thought the results less satisfactory than his superiors, put in the same position he would probably have regretted the lack of closure too, but that was the nature of the job. Orders were orders and you couldn't just go along making up your own. Especially when that involved taking on one of the most formidable mafias in the former Soviet states without any official sanction.

What was Friend thinking? Did he believe that because he could charge a company of Taliban with nothing more than a broken rifle and a mad, bloodstained grin he was immortal? That seemed to be the level of thinking at the moment. And why had Magniac agreed to help? Perhaps because you don't let your mates down when they need you, or because by keeping an eye on him Magniac thought he might be able to stop the bloody idiot getting himself killed. However much he thought about it, Magniac just couldn't come to any firm conclusion about why he had agreed to help Friend 'burn the butler', and see where that might lead, much less why he was playing his role with such conviction and even enjoying the sight of Harry Butterworth beginning to realise that the game was up. Perhaps he deserved the epithet of the Mad Major after all.

'I don't know what you're talking about,' said Butterworth, trying to cover himself again with the last scraps of his tattered false identity.

'Oh, I think you do Mr Butterworth. Or maybe I should call you Harry. Not such a flash Harry at the moment though, are you? Harry Butterworth, born Streatham in 1965, disappeared off the face of the earth after an investigation into a burglary at his employer's home, Lord Normanby that is, began to get a bit too close. The authorities back home have been looking for you for quite a while, Laddie. And it looks like today's their lucky day.'

Butterworth said nothing. He stared glumly back at Magniac, his arms folded defensively across his chest. To Magniac's eye he looked like he was settling in for a long silence.

'I expect you're wondering how we caught up with you, Harry,' he went on. 'Well, I don't suppose there's any harm in me telling you. Your old friend Jed Wilkins, the one who sorted out your first passport in the name of Foulkes, he went down for forgery six months ago and is currently serving his time in Pentonville. It seems his record keeping was at least on a par with that of the Passport Office; possibly better according to the officers from the Met Police who went through his personal possessions with a fine-tooth comb. Not to put too fine a point on it, he kept scans of your application documents, photographs, the Foulkes birth certificate and the death certificate too and once the Met compared them with the original records and matched your details to the application form, it was only a matter of time before the paint began to flake off Edward Foulkes to reveal one badly tarnished Harry Butterworth underneath. And just in case you're wondering, it's perfectly straightforward for His Majesty's Government to extradite one of its citizens from Georgia. You remember the Shepherd case not long ago? He spent about three months in a Georgian prison while the authorities made the necessary arrangements. I don't suppose he enjoyed it much.'

Butterworth remained silent, but while arms remained firmly folded in a defensive posture, his eyes no longer stared challengingly across the table. Slowly as he listened he had lowered them until their gaze met nothing but the floor.

'Don't be so glum, Harry. All good things come to an end. You didn't really think you could get away with it forever did you? And it's only fair of me to say that, honestly, your situation is not without hope. I might be able to help you.'

'Help me? How?' sneered Butterworth. 'By persuading me to return to the UK "voluntarily" so that I don't have to rot in a jail cell here for three months?'

'Well, yes, that is one option open to you. And if you ask me it would make things much easier for you than if you remained uncooperative. But as a matter of fact I think I can go one better than that.'

'Oh really? How so?'

'My masters in London are practical people and not too proud to cut a deal when it suits them. As it happens you might well be in a position to help them, in return for which they might be able to help you.'

Butterworth slowly leaned forward, placing his hands palm down on the tabletop. His eyes were wide with realisation.

'Consular section my arse! You're a bloody spook!'

'Well, if you want to put it that way. But the important point is that I can help you.'

'Help me how, exactly?'

'By making the Normanby case go away. A signed letter from the Home Office, declaring that Harry Butterworth is not a person of interest in respect of any property stolen from His Lordship. That and a new passport in your real name, allowing you to return to the UK in your proper identity.'

'Are you serious?'

'Perfectly.'

'So, what do I have to do? How come I'm in a position to help them?'

'It so happens that your employer, Mikel Qorghanashvili, is a person of interest to us. Since you have been working for him for some time, there is likely to be a great deal you will be able to tell us about him that could be useful.'

'Mr Q doesn't exactly share his secrets with me.'

'I'm sure he doesn't. But there are other things you could tell us. Habits, routines, the people he sees, the layout of his house…'

'Now just hang on, if you think I'm getting involved in a burglary! I wasn't even involved in the one at the Normanby place.'

'Well, I shouldn't think it would come to that anyway. Let's just start with some information.'

Magniac opened the folder in front of him and took out two A5 sized black and white photographs. He slid them across the table to Butterworth.

'Do you recognise either of these men?'

Butterworth nodded.

'The younger one is Mr Kovalchuk. He's a business associate of Mr Q's. He comes to the house every so often, maybe three or four times a month. But I think the Boss sees him quite often at his office and elsewhere too. I get the impression he's something like Mr Q's fixer.'

Magniac was pleased. It looked like Butterworth would genuinely cooperate.

'What about the other man?'

'I recognise him, but don't know him. He came to dinner last week, him and Mr Kovalchuk together, but that was the first time I saw him. Russian, I think, at least they all spoke Russian together. When Mr Kovalchuk is with Mr Q they usually speak Georgian to each other, but that night it was Russian all the way. Nice polite gent, he was. Beautifully dressed.'

'Did you get his name?'

Butterworth shook his head.

'Afraid not. The Boss just said he had an important guest coming for dinner and I was to ask the cook to prepare her speciality – a kind of lamb stew with tomatoes and rice. But he never told me his name and I didn't hear him mention it during the evening.'

'What do you usually do at dinners like these?'

'I serve each course, uncork and pour the wine, take away dirty dishes and glasses, make sure the kitchen has everything on schedule. I don't sit in the dining room with Mr Q and his guests, if that's what you're thinking. Mr Q keeps a little bell on the table and gives it a tinkle when he wants me.'

'So you never get to overhear anything?'

'Sorry. With most of his guests it's Georgian anyway, and I only speak a word or two of the language. Maybe that's why he hired me rather than a local man.'

'Perhaps it is. What about his other guests? Any regulars?'

Butterworth shrugged.

'Businessmen, politicians, journalists, we've had a bit of everything since I've been with Mr Q. He likes to lay on a spread, to impress people. We've had the Minister for Justice a couple of times but no-one you would really call a regular except for Mr Kovalchuk.'

'No family or friends?'

'I don't think he has any of either. Although….'

'Yes?'

'Well there is one. Perhaps it is a family thing. That would explain a lot. It certainly doesn't have the feel of a business meeting, it's much more personal and low-key than that. She comes once a week, regular as clockwork, and she certainly doesn't treat him like a friend.'

'She?'

'Oh yes,' said Harry Butterworth, 'it's a woman.'

CHAPTER NINETEEN

RENDEZVOUS

Sebastian Friend watched her as she stood leaning against the rail of the Juliette balcony outside her bedroom. Once or twice a day, morning or evening, she would open the double doors and step out into the fresh air, standing motionless for a while, staring off into space. The woman's house was a three-storey villa set amid small but elegantly-sculpted gardens behind a high stone wall on the southern edge of the old town, close to the slopes of Sololaki Hill. It didn't take Friend long to realise that it was the hill itself she was staring at, and the statue of Mother Georgia looming over the city from its peak. What, he wondered, did she see up there? Was there something in this gigantic stone figure that appealed to her; the wine-cup held aloft in one hand for those who came to the city in friendship, in the other a sword braced across her abdomen for those with hostile intentions. There was something in the way this woman faced the world that reminded Friend of the statue. An atmosphere of subdued strength seemed to emanate from her and even from a distance Friend had the feeling that her sword hand would be swift and merciless when provoked.

The walls surrounding the villa were high enough to obscure the view of anyone at street level. But Friend had found a convenient spot out of sight of the cable car among the trees that ran up the flank of the hill from where, with the benefit of Magniac's old army binoculars, he was able to gain a fair view of the villa and its grounds. Over the course of two weeks, he and Magniac managed to work out her routine. On Sunday evenings she was driven to Qorghanashvili's house for dinner, always returning by eleven. The dinners were one of three weekly trips away from the villa. The other two took place on weekday mornings; one a visit to a beauty salon near Vere Park where she saw a hair stylist and had a manicure and pedicure, the other a shopping trip to the city centre, where she browsed the clothes stores in slightly bored fashion and spent little money. Both of these concluded with lunch at the same fashionable restaurant with only her two bodyguards for company.

How she spent her time at the villa was less easily determined. She received no visitors. She exercised once daily in the garden, taking her body through an extensive routine of muscular and cardio-vascular exercises. Twice Friend watched her swim in a covered pool that stood to one side of the villa. She clearly believed in keeping herself fit. The only other persons present at the villa were her bodyguards, three teams of two on regular rotation, all of them straight out of the Senka Kovalchuk catalogue of well-muscled henchmen. The woman paid them as little attention as possible. It occurred to Friend to wonder whether they were bodyguards in fact, or jailers.

It was midway through the second week when Magniac brought the news that the villa was also owned by Mikel Qorghanashvili. 'So, what do you think? Kept woman?' he asked Friend.

'You'd think so, except for the fact that he never visits her, and she never stays overnight when she visits him.'

'True. And I suppose the ever-vigilant Butterworth would have noticed if anything more than dinner was taking place.'

'No doubt he would.'

By the third Tuesday both of them were beginning to wonder what the end result of their surveillance would be. Friend was also aware that his period of leave following the official completion of his mission was coming to an end. Such things were treated lightly in his section; so long as no other job came up for him, his time could be more or less his own. The call could, however, come at almost any minute. He had abandoned his observation post on the hill and joined Magniac at street level in the fifth of a series of cars they had rented to avoid arousing suspicion. Tuesday morning was the woman's regular date at the beautician.

When the sleek, black Mercedes pulled out of the gates and purred off towards the city centre they followed at a discreet distance, more out of habit than expectation. As the traffic became more chaotic around Freedom Square and heading north along Rustaveli Avenue they lost sight of her car for several minutes at a time, but didn't let it concern them. They were certain, after all, where she was going. Sure enough, when they reached the beauty salon, they found the Mercedes double-parked outside, Kovalchuk's men still in the two front seats. It clearly didn't matter where you left your car if your paymaster went by the name of Qorghanashvili. Magniac eased the hire car past the blockage through a blaring of horns and circled round the block to where the beauty salon opened onto an alley at the back. The week before, Friend had strolled in through the back door, unchallenged. The guard on the lady seemed, at best, complacent.

The two men sat quietly together for twenty minutes before Friend got out of the car and walked around to the front of the street, where he pretended to peruse the shelves of a Russian language bookshop while keeping an eye on the street outside. When the woman emerged, he made a quick call to Magniac, then walked out to wait on the pavement until the car arrived. There was no hurry, everything was exactly on schedule. It was 12.23 pm and by 12.45 the woman and her two companions would be settled in their regular quiet corner of one of Tbilisi's more expensive restaurants.

Magniac pulled up to the kerb just as Friend could see the Mercedes turning to the right at the end of the street. It was still in view when they rounded the corner in pursuit, but then things began to change. Instead of carrying straight on towards Freedom Square and crossing the river at the Metekhi bridge, the Mercedes turned right off Rustaveli Avenue just before the Parliament building. Magniac shot a questioning look at Friend, who simply shrugged in response. How should he know what was going on? If they had spotted the tail it would soon be apparent they were trying to lose it. Maybe the routine just wasn't quite as set in stone as they had supposed. Now they entered the maze of narrow streets between Rustaveli and the foot of Mount Mtatsminda and the Mercedes was hard to follow at all, let alone discreetly. It was like turning off the Champs Elysses and finding yourself in the *souk* of Tangiers. A couple of times they turned into alleys so narrow and cramped there barely seemed room for a car to pass along it and Friend half expected to hear the scrape and crash of metal as the Toyota's roof took out the supports from one of the precarious-looking wrought-iron balconies that hung from every wall. It seemed to both of them absurd that the car ahead of them should remain unaware of the little grey hatchback on their tail, and perhaps this was only by virtue of losing sight of their quarry every couple of minutes. But their luck was in, and when at last they thought they had lost the Mercedes for good it turned up once again, stationary and parked outside a modest looking café. Friend caught the name above the door as they drove past. It said: *Café de Paris.*

Magniac found a spot about fifty metres up the road and parked carefully.

'So, what now?' he asked.

'Well, I think one of us should go in to see what's going on.'

'Then it had better be me. They might have clocked you standing outside the beauty salon back there. You don't want to reinforce the impression.'

Magniac, opened the door and walked back down the street. Friend watched him go in the car's side mirror, his powerful, lumbering frame like a prowling leopard's. Then he closed his eyes for a few moments' rest.

The next thing Friend knew, Magniac was climbing back into the car. He checked his watch; he had been gone for twenty minutes.

'Well, that was bloody peculiar,' said Magniac.

Friend looked in the mirror again and saw the Mercedes begin to pull out into the road and head towards them. Magniac started the engine.

'What happened?'

'They just sat there, the three of them, with a pot of tea on the table, not saying a word. She didn't drink a thing, just kept staring across the room at some dark-haired cove in the opposite corner.'

'And what did he do?'

'He just stared right back at her and didn't move. Mean looking devil, I must say. I wouldn't like to meet him in a dark alley.'

'Where is he now?'

'He was still there when I left.'

Magniac was still looking out into the road, checking the traffic before pulling out when Friend sensed a movement behind him. Before he could turn his head, he felt the cold muzzle of a pistol pressed into the base of his skull.

'Hello again, Mr Hunter. Small world, isn't it? I'm sorry for the cliché, but please tell your friend to follow that car.'

The growl was painfully familiar. Friend looked into the rear-view mirror and saw Dimitri's black eyes burning back at him.

'Hello Dimitri. I had no idea you knew English.'

Magniac had turned round in surprise, and Friend placed a restraining hand on his arm, before he could do anything rash.

'You'd better do what he says, Stephen, and follow the Mercedes. Oh, and perhaps I should introduce you to our guest. As you may have gathered, we have met before. This is Dimitri, Manager of the Silver Mountain Hotel near Batumi. Dimitri, say hello to my old friend Stephen Magniac.'

'Pleased to meet you.'

'Likewise,' said Magniac, easing the car out into traffic, his eyes searching the road ahead for the black form of the Mercedes. 'And since we're being introduced, do you go by anything other than Dimitri? A surname, perhaps? Most people seem to have them these days.'

'Chopuradze,' grunted Dimitri.

'Chopuradze? Ha! From *Chopura* meaning 'the pockmarked one'. That was one of Stalin's nicknames when he was nothing more than a Georgian bandit. Can't say I've come across it as an actual surname before.'

'I come from a very small family. And why don't you just concentrate on driving instead of yapping like that? I might get irritated and spread Mr Hunter's brains all over the windscreen.'

'Now that's not very nice, is it Dimitri?' said Friend. 'It's a fine way to treat your loyal customers. Why do you want to know where that car's going anyway?'

'That's my business.'

'Something to do with that small family of yours, perhaps? Things are becoming clear to me at last, Dimitri. I think you and I could do with having a quiet talk, and I don't think you'll need the gun.'

'While we're on the subject,' said Magniac, 'I think lunch is off the menu today. Looks like they're heading home.'

'Home?' said Dimitri. 'You mean you know where they're keeping her?'

'That's right,' said Friend. 'We know where they're keeping her. So we don't need to follow them any more and you can stop pressing that gun into the back of my neck like some FSB heavy. We both know you're not going to pull the trigger.'

'So sure, Mr Hunter?'

Friend felt cold metal press into his neck again. Then, at once, it was withdrawn and he turned his head to see Dimitri lounging easily in the back seat, the small, squat pistol held calmly in his lap.

'All right, gentlemen, I'll buy it. For now. But please remember I can shoot you both just as easily from this range as any other. I'm just as good with a handgun as with a hunting rifle.'

'You're the boss, Dimitri,' said Friend. 'Just tell us where we're going.'

'Back to the Café de Paris. It's as good as any place.'

* * *

'She's your wife, isn't she,' said Friend. The three men were sitting at the same table Dimitri had vacated only a few minutes before, three glasses of brandy on the table in front of them, Dimitri's pistol tucked away out of sight in his jacket. Around them, waiters glided with silent efficiency and the café's patrons enjoyed their lunches, their coffee and pastries, oblivious to the harsh thoughts in the minds of the three sombre-looking men at the corner table facing the door.

Dimitri nodded in response.

'How long have they been holding her?'

'Two years and three months.'

'And why did they take her?'

'Why do you think? It gives them power over me.'

'Seems like a lot of trouble to go to for a bit of leverage. Why not just threaten her life? That seems to be their usual method.'

Dimitri shrugged. 'I guess they thought that I was better able to look after her than the other people they've dealt with. Once I was warned, that is. I hadn't expected anyone to try and kidnap her.'

'All right. And why did they need this leverage over you?'

'I'm a smuggler, Mr Hunter', Dimitri smirked. 'I have my networks, my connections, my safe houses, a lifetime of experience. They wanted all that.'

'So why not just pay you for it? You're a criminal used to working with other criminals after all.'

'Not with them. Not for what they wanted. They couldn't pay me any amount of money for that.'

'For what exactly? What did they want?'

'Drugs, women, children. I'm no saint, Mr Hunter. I've smuggled people across borders before, weapons too. But helping refugees or freedom fighters is one thing, helping rich men get richer out of other people's misery is another. I wasn't prepared to do that for them, however much they paid me.'

'But when they took your wife…'

'Once they had Mira, I had no choice.'

'And where did the Silver Mountain Hotel come into it?'

'They bought it. It was ideal for them, close to the border with Turkey, handy for Batumi. They set me up there and got me to arrange all sorts of shipments over the border.'

'Via the old silver mine.'

'Very observant, Mr Hunter. Yes, it was my job to let Kovalchuk know when there had been a delivery and he would send a couple of his men to the hotel to collect.'

'Excuse me,' broke in Magniac, 'but there's one thing here that doesn't make sense to me. Your wife has been kidnapped by a criminal gang who want to control you. So why were you sitting here in the same café as your wife and her abductors?'

'It was part of the deal. If they wanted my co-operation, they had to give me proof of life. And not just life, but good health. I wouldn't accept just photographs or letters or recorded messages. I wanted to see that she was all right, that even though she didn't have her freedom, she was unharmed. They wouldn't allow video calls in case we found a way of slipping messages into the conversation, so they came up with the idea of this monthly rendezvous. The first Tuesday of every month, the same seats in the same café. I wasn't allowed to speak to her or communicate with her in any way, nor she with me. We just sit there, staring at each other. It's crazy, it's frustrating, but at least I can see she's OK, and she can see I'm OK too.' Dimitri lowered his eyes. 'I've actually started looking forward to it.'

'And they always leave before you?' asked Friend.

'That was the arrangement. I'm supposed to wait ten minutes after they leave before I can go. Otherwise I'm in breach. But today when I saw your friend get up and leave so quickly after them, I had to find out why. I had a feeling he had been watching us, but I wasn't sure until that point. Then when I saw him get into the car with you I figured that was the first chance I'd had to find out where they were keeping her.'

'And what do you plan to do with the information?'

'I don't know yet.'

'Are you planning to try and get her back?'

'The thought had occurred to me. But look, what's your interest in all this? Who are you exactly?'

'You know who I am and what I am. I'm a journalist. Stephen here is ex-British Army. I met him in my days as a war correspondent. He's based here now and helping me find my way around. I was just doing some digging into Mikel Qorghanashvili. I had no idea before today that there was a connection with your wife, or you.'

'Bullshit!'

'Dimitri! You really do know English, don't you!'

'Not as well as I know bullshit. You're no journalist; I knew that up at the monastery. Before that, even. You're intelligence, both of you. I know the type. I can smell it. Journalist!' He spat the word out, like something distasteful. 'You're no more a journalist than…'

'Than your name's Dimitri?'

Dimitri smiled, or tried to; the effect was more like a grimace as his lips slid back from his tightly-set jaw like a wolf baring its teeth.

'Look,' he said, 'it doesn't matter much to me who you are or what you think my name is. For two years I've been running round in circles like a rat in a cage. I've had enough. I want my wife back, my freedom back and I intend to get it. If you can help in some way, then tell me. If not, then just let me know where they're keeping her and get out of my way. But let me tell you this…' he leaned forward, his eyes blazing and even Friend felt almost disconcerted by their intensity, by the power of his animal emotion. 'If you get in my way, or cause her any harm, or cause her to be harmed, I will kill you both. And then maybe I will kill your families too. So you'd better be sure what you're doing, otherwise I suggest you drink your cognac and walk out of that door now. While you still can.'

Friend grinned back at Dimitri, trying to make light of his threat. It would be the easiest thing in the world now to tell Dimitri what he needed to know, to give him the information he needed to try and win his wife's freedom and go back to England and leave the outcome up to him. Part of his brain was telling him that this was the sensible, the rational thing to do. But the other part, the part he always listened to, kept nagging away at him with the thought that it was his responsibility to avenge Nia Dadiani. That he would get no peace until he had done so. That Dimitri on his own, whatever his influence in smuggling circles, was no match for Qorghanashvili's machine.

'I understand, Dimitri,' he said. 'The last thing we want is to cause your wife any harm. These people, Qorghanashvili, Kovalchuk and their whole gang, have caused too much harm to too many people already. But let me ask you this: are Kovalchuk's people watching you? Are you sure your movements are not being observed?'

'Of course they're watching me. If I don't arrive back in Batumi on a particular train this evening I'll have broken my pledge and maybe they'll kill us both. But if you tell me where they're keeping her, by this time next month I can have all the arrangements I need in place. I'll get to her before she even leaves the house with them. After two years of submission they won't be expecting anything. They've started getting careless. They used to have this place staked out hours before the rendezvous, just in case I had some of my men waiting to try and snatch Mira back. As if I'd be so reckless; Kovalchuk made it perfectly clear the first bullet would go straight through Mira's head and the second through mine.'

'And now they've stopped watching this place?'

'I check it out every time. Must be nine months since I saw anyone.'

'That's a good sign. But how can you be sure that these arrangements of yours won't be noticed before you have a chance to put your plan into action? How can you be sure they won't move her to another location in the meantime? We've only been watching her for a week or so; for all we know they might move her every couple of weeks. It would be the secure thing to do. It's what I would do in their place.'

'What are you suggesting, Mr Hunter?'

'We know where they're keeping her and we've had a chance to learn her routine. We're better placed than you are to come up with a plan that will work.'

Friend could feel Magniac's foot beating time under the table.

'And so?'

'And so let us grab your wife back from Qorghanashvili's men and deliver her back to you.'

Magniac's foot began to pound the floor even faster, his irritation growing.

'Really,' said Dimitri. 'But why would you do this? What interest could you possibly have in my wife's freedom?'

'I'm only interested in justice.'

'You think my wife's freedom means some kind of justice?'

'For your wife and for you, yes.'

'And what will you do then? Go back to London thinking the world is a better place?'

'Something like that. But I'm also interested in what you will do.'

'What I will do? I will have my revenge on those men and all who work for them, of course.'

Friend smiled.

'You *want* me to kill him, don't you,' said Dimitri.

'Well, I don't see you testifying against him in court.'

'His kind never come to court.'

'No, they live in the shadows and they meet their end there too. I don't like killing, Dimitri, but sometimes it is necessary. These men are too bad to be allowed to continue their lives as they are, and since there is no other way of doing so, their lives must be ended. For you, your wife, for Nia Dadiani and for all the others whose lives have been ruined by Mikel Qorghanashvili and Senka Kovalchuk.'

'Mr Hunter, you talk like an Englishman but I believe you think like a Georgian. All right, have it your way. I will stay out of this and let you make your plan, but I will need to know when it happens.

As soon as my wife is free and they know they can have no further hold on me they'll try to kill me without delay. I need to be ready for that.'

'Fair enough,' said Friend. 'Once we've set a date, I'll call the hotel and make a reservation for that day in the name of Popov. Then you'll know to be ready. How should we get her to you?'

'Don't try and get her to me. Batumi is Kovalchuk's country. You need to take her north. There's someone there I can trust.' He took a menu from the table and scribbled down an address for Friend. 'I will go to the monastery on the day of Popov's reservation. They can hide me well there. My friend in the north will be able to get word to me once you have her safe. There's another thing. She won't just go with you because you ask her to. You will need to give her a message from me. You don't speak any Georgian?'

'No,' said Friend.

'Russian, then. Tell her "The wolf has returned to the mountain". She will understand. Better still if you give her a single white rose too. That was always my gift.'

'Good. That's settled then.'

Dimitri got to his feet.

'I'm putting my trust in you, Mr Hunter. Don't let me down. What I said about you causing harm to come to her still stands.'

Then Magniac broke his silence.

'There's just one thing.'

'Yes?'

'Qorghanashvili has dinner with your wife, once a week. Regular as clockwork. Why would that be?'

Dimitri seemed entirely unflustered by Magniac's dramatic revelation.

'I can't answer that,' he said. 'You'd have to ask the man himself. Or my wife, when you see her.'

Dimitri turned away and walked steadily between the tables towards the door.

Magniac gave it another minute before he said anything more.

'Are you crazy?'

'What do you mean?'

'I mean I've helped you so far out of friendship. Burning the butler, following the girl. But now you're planning to stage an actual operation against one of the most powerful mafias in the whole former Soviet Union, just you and me. No authority, no back-up. In point of fact, no bloody hope. And what for? So one criminal can get his missus back and another gets his head blown off? But how do you know that the one is any better a man than the other? Your friend Dimitri didn't exactly strike me as a model citizen, the kind we're supposed to defend. It seems to me you're planning to risk our lives for nothing, so I have to ask you what the hell you're playing at?'

'Stephen, I'm very grateful for everything you've done. You don't have to do any more, really. I can handle it myself from now on. Go back to Tamara and your vineyards.'

'Damn right I will!'

Magniac got to his feet and started for the door. Then he paused.

'You can't bring them back you know, Seb,' he said over his shoulder. 'Not one of them. They're all gone.'

Friend said nothing. He drank his brandy and turned his thoughts to the problem at hand.

CHAPTER TWENTY

A ROSE FOR MIRA

The man known as Dimitri Chopuradze arrived back in Batumi on the scheduled train. Two of Kovalchuk's men met him at the station and drove him back to the Silver Mountain Hotel. He sat alone in the back seat, feeling the cold metal of the pistol underneath his armpit and wishing the time to use it had come. It was close now, and perhaps that would make the waiting easier, better than all those months of despair when he had no allies, no plan and no hope.

But then as Wednesday passed with no word and Thursday and Friday too his growing agitation seemed to give the lie to that. He was anxious to be in action, like a soldier who hates only one thing more than battle: waiting for it to begin. At last on Saturday morning as he passed through reception he heard the girl take the call. A reservation for Popov, arriving Tuesday lunchtime. Dimitri waited a few minutes, then double-checked the reservation on the hotel's booking system. Satisfied, he walked calmly through to the boot room and began cleaning the mud off his old army boots. He too had his plans to put in motion.

For Stephen Magniac those days were also troubled and worrisome. There was nothing he hated more than letting an old comrade down. But it was one thing to offer help, quite another to abet sheer madness. He prayed to the heavens that Friend would change his mind; he even considered contacting Dimitri and letting him know where his wife was being kept in the hope that the tough old Georgian could take care of the matter himself. But this would be a step too far, too much like betrayal. Tamara disagreed. What was better, she asked, that Friend should die in a hopeless battle against superior forces, or that he should resent his old friend's interference, perhaps terminate their friendship, but still be alive? To opt for the former course and let things stand was sheer selfishness, she insisted. Magniac demurred. To him it was more complicated than that.

Sebastian Friend was calmer and more certain than either of them. He had questioned his own decision, his motives, his ability to carry out what he proposed and there was no foolish optimism in the answers he gave himself. But against all this was the urging of his conscience. If he were to abandon everything now and quietly go back to London leaving Dimitri to handle matters on his own, the guilt of leaving the job undone would nag away at him. His thoughts during the day would drift back towards Georgia; sleep would come uneasily at night. Whatever the risks, he had to try. Not for justice, not for the sake of Dimitri or his wife, but for his own peace of mind.

The plan was simple enough: grab the woman and get her to the address Dimitri had given him; to the man he called *The Falcon*. His advantage was surprise; his challenge getting the woman to trust him quickly enough to get her away before her guards knew what was happening. The time was never in question. It would have to be Tuesday; the day of her regular trip to the beauty salon and the restaurant afterwards for lunch. The monthly rendezvous with Dimitri having already taken place, surely they would now return to the normal routine.

One complication Friend acknowledged: he had no gun. On the whole he preferred to operate unarmed. Operatives in his section were allowed to use their own judgement in such matters and Friend had always held firmly to the belief that carrying a gun made it more difficult for any cover to hold and added an unacceptable danger to civilian life. Even when an operation reached its critical phase and violent action was likely, he believed guns made you lazy and overconfident. They stopped you relying on your wits and your reactions. Then, if the gun jammed or were taken away from you, that was it. You'd had it.

But there was always the proviso of operational necessity. Friend considered it beyond the scope of probability that the woman's guards would be unarmed and once they worked out that she was gone they would come after her without delay and do everything in their power to get her back. If they couldn't get her back, then the next best thing would be for them to kill her; her and Dimitri and anyone else who got in their way. That was the lesson of Nia Dadiani's death: once you were of no further use to these people you were as good as dead. They would shoot on sight and shoot to kill. If they were in range, his wits and reactions would be useless. So the first phase of his operation, the snatch, was better carried out without a gun, but the second phase, the delivery, might be fatal without one. And without any official status or support, without even the assistance and local connections of Stephen Magniac, there was only one way for him to acquire a gun.

He would have to take one from the opposition.

* * *

Tuesday morning. The salon was almost empty; it was still more than an hour and a half before the woman was due. Friend had dressed in his freshly-pressed navy blue suit, white shirt and burgundy knitted tie; he put on his most winning smile to accompany them. In his hand he carried a neat little bouquet of white roses. The girl behind the desk was young, dark and pretty. He spoke to her in Russian.

'Good morning, I wonder if you can help me.'

The dark eyes flashed back at him.

'Of course, if I can.'

'A friend of mine has an appointment here at 11.45.'

'Oh yes, what name?'

'Mira.'

'What surname?'

'Well, I don't know exactly what surname she is using here.' He leaned in a little closer and turned the smile up a further notch. 'She likes to be discreet, if you know what I mean. But it's a regular appointment. Same time every week. I'm sure you know her.'

The girl smiled in response.

'Yes, I think I do. That would be Mira Qorghanashvili. Was there a problem with the appointment? You need to change it?'

'No, no, not at all,' said Friend, trying to keep his mind from spinning at the name he had just been given. He reached into his jacket pocket and pulled out a small white envelope. 'I was just hoping you might be kind enough to give her this.'

'Oh, I see,' she said, taking the envelope from him and looking puzzled at the absence of any inscription. 'Wouldn't you prefer to wait for her and give her the message yourself?'

Friend shook his head sadly. 'I'm afraid that won't be possible. You see she won't be alone, and the people with her won't like me talking to her, or giving her anything, if you see what I mean.'

'I think I do,' said the girl with a smile.

'So if you could just give her the note please, as discreetly as you can, I would be eternally grateful.'

'Of course, I understand. And the flowers too?'

Friend handed the bouquet across to the girl.

'Just one of them,' he said, 'the rest are for you. As a thank you for your help.'

Friend turned and walked to the door. Bewildered, the girl stared down at the roses, then looked up again to see Friend paused in the doorway, a broad grin across his face. He raised one hand to flick a stray lock of blond hair back from his eyebrow, then he was gone.

* * *

The girl was as good as her word. As soon as Dimitri's wife entered the salon and was comfortably installed in a back room with her feet in a tub of warm water, the girl quietly slipped her the note, wrapped around the stem of a single rose. 'From a friend,' she said in a conspiratorial whisper.

Mira Qorghanashvili ripped open the envelope with a polished fingernail and read:

> *The Wolf has returned to the mountain. I am to deliver you to the Falcon. I will be in the restaurant when you are having lunch; blond hair, blue suit, dark red tie. Pay no attention to me, but when I go to the bathroom you are to follow two minutes later. All is prepared.*

She held the rose up to her nose and smelled its scent. Was it some kind of trick, she wondered? Surely after more than two years they were past all of that. She had behaved just as they wanted her to, had sat quietly month after month across the tables of that blasted café from her husband, week after week silently chewing her food while Mikel talked at her. She had done nothing to justify their distrust, out of fear for her husband's safety. Mira was wise enough to realise that if Mikel and his creature Kovalchuk thought they could no longer control her, she and her husband would quickly become surplus to requirements. And so she had spent more than two years playing their game, never giving up on the hope of release, biding her time and waiting.

Waiting for what? For this? If the note was true and her husband was free, surely they would kill her at once. He would never risk that. So he must still be waiting as well, waiting for her to be free before he could make his move. Was this what he had put in motion? This blond man with the dark red tie who had prepared everything? All right then, true or false, this was the only way the game could be played, so she would have to see it through. She ripped the note and the envelope into shreds and dropped them with the rose into the waste basket beside her chair, soon to be covered by toenail clippings. Then she sat back with her head braced against the top of the chair and waited for the pedicurist to arrive.

* * *

It would be a lie to say that Stephen Magniac had supplied no assistance at all to Friend's plan, although what he had done had been unwitting. He had taken Friend to lunch in the restaurant on a day when they both knew that Mira would be securely confined to the house, giving Friend a chance to spy out the land that Magniac already knew reasonably well.

'It's a popular place and busier in the evenings when it fills up with tourists. Then as well as the food they get about four hours of traditional music and dance shows. Tamara once brought me here with the in-laws when I didn't know them so well; I suppose she thought the atmosphere would make up for any awkward pauses in the conversation. It's not my cup of tea, really, but the evening went off all right. It's a different sort of place in the daytime. Quieter, especially midweek when the woman is brought here. Food's not bad – not the most distinctive in town but good, traditional Georgian – and the view is pretty spectacular.'

The view was indeed spectacular, as Friend appreciated once more, settling into a seat on the covered terrace almost an hour in advance of the woman's expected arrival. The terrace, braced by wooden supports, jutted out over the Mtkvari river atop a narrow perpendicular gorge. The large, plate glass windows afforded a glorious view across to the old town and the hill rising beyond it to the Narikali fortress. His early arrival had two great advantages: it was sound operational practice to be in position well in advance of schedule, and there was no harm in getting some lunch into his stomach before things started to happen. The woman always occupied the same table at the south end of the terrace, from where she could just, perhaps, obtain a view of the Mother of Georgia statue that seemed to hold her in thrall. He had arranged a table for himself at the other end of the terrace, which ought to give her a clear enough view of him without needing to crane her head or look around the restaurant in a way that might arouse the suspicion of her companions.

He was mopping up the remnants of his veal shashlik with some fresh bread when the woman came in. She marched straight to her table, trailing her two bodyguards behind. There was the merest flicker of an eye in his direction; not nearly enough to arouse suspicion, but Friend now knew she had received his note. Had she not, he doubted she would have so much as glanced in his direction; if it had been intercepted she would not have appeared at all. Instead he would have been joined at his table by one of Kovalchuk's men with the prospect of a much less interesting afternoon ahead of him. The only thing that remained to be resolved was whether she would go with him or not. His instinct told him that she would. It was seldom wrong.

Friend gave it fifteen minutes before he made his move. The woman had barely consulted the menu, her companions ordering on her behalf. A small banquet of starters had quickly arrived and the woman had picked absent-mindedly at each plate while sipping at a glass of white wine. The two men with her drank nothing but water. They sat with their backs to Friend and the woman could look straight at him between their shoulders, but never once did she look in his direction. Instead, her eyes moved solely from the plates to her glass to the window. She looked bored. If she was feeling any tension before her escape she hid it well.

Friend called for the bill and left some money on the table. Then he got up and walked, as unsteadily as he could get away with, along the terrace towards the door to the bathrooms. He managed to bump, clumsily, into the table next to the woman's, and she looked slowly up at him as he shuffled past, rubbing his thigh. As soon as he pushed through the door into the corridor beyond, Friend straightened up and walked purposefully past the bathrooms to the fire exit at the back. Outside in the bright sunshine, he looked around. Satisfied that the coast was clear, he checked his watch.

Two minutes and twenty seconds later the woman came through the door. Directly opposite the fire door, where the waste bins were lined up beneath a steep, grassy bank, she saw Friend standing beside a 500cc Kawasaki motorcycle. He had a helmet in each hand and the engine was running. She ran across the patch of open ground towards him, glad she had chosen to wear jeans this morning, but regretting the heels on her leather sandals.

'Put this on,' he said to her, holding out one of the helmets, 'and get on the back.'

She did as she was told and settled herself on the pillion. It was years since she had ridden on the back of a motorcycle, not since the early days of her marriage. But to her surprise the blond young man did not get on the bike in front of her. She turned her head inside the heavy helmet and saw that he was standing next to the open fire door, his own helmet still in his hand.

It was probably no more than a minute that she sat there, the engine throbbing beneath her, wondering what in hell's name was going on. It felt much longer. She had been reassured by the sight of the motorcycle and the running engine ready to go; surely they should have been on their way by now. If they had gone straight away they would be out of sight already, probably even before Yuri and Piotr knew anything was wrong. They would have no chance of catching them. So what was the man playing at? Did he want them to be caught?

The thought was still formulating in her brain when she saw the fire door open wider and the bulky, dark-haired figure of Yuri burst out into the light. For a moment he stood absolutely still, staring at the figure of Mira on the motorcycle. She stared back, frozen in position. Then she watched as Friend took one step forward and swung the helmet round into Yuri's face.

The blow caught him square on the forehead; he sprawled back against the wall. Friend placed the helmet on the ground and began searching Yuri's clothes. He quickly found what he was looking for, picked up the helmet and raced back towards her. Mira saw him place Yuri's pistol in the hip pocket of his jacket. Then he was in front of her, the helmet on his head. The bike sped forward, the rear wheel slewing to one side for a moment as the power kicked in. Perhaps there was the sound of a shout behind them, but through the muffling of her helmet she couldn't be sure. Then they were off around the corner and gone.

Friend sped the bike up Metekhi Street and then steered it around the roundabout before turning down Armazi Street into the tangled alleys of the old town. Less than five minutes after leaving the restaurant, they came to a halt next to a dark blue BMW off-roader in the car park of the Orion Hotel.

Friend slid off the bike seat and strode towards the BMW, leaving the key in the ignition and his helmet dangling on the handlebar.

'Take your helmet off and get in,' he said, turning back towards her and running a hand through his disordered hair.

Mira took off her helmet and walked to the car, but instead of going round to the passenger side door she went straight up to Friend. He turned again to face her, the door held open in his hand.

'You prefer to drive?' he said, smiling, before he saw the arm flash out and felt the whiplash sting of her hand across his cheek.

'What the hell did you think you were doing back there?' she cried at him.

Friend put a hand up to feel his cheek, bewildered.

'What do you mean?' he asked.

'I mean leaving me there on the bike like a sitting target while you waited for Yuri to come out and see us. He could have shot me on the spot. You realise when he comes round he'll know how we got away!'

'He never saw me. And anyway, I needed his gun.'

'You needed his gun? You mean you don't have one of your own?'

'I don't usually need one.'

Aghast, Mira turned away and shouted a curse to the heavens in her own language. Then she strode purposefully around the car.

'Come on then, my knight in stolen armour,' she said, 'and get me out of here before I take that gun off you and shoot you myself.'

Friend jumped into the driver's seat and started the engine. He steered the car back towards the main road and turned north.

It was sheer bad luck that the entire performance had been witnessed by one of the Orion's kitchen staff who had come outside for a cigarette break, and that he had a cousin who was a rising officer in the local police force, who just happened to owe a favour to Mikel Qorghanashvili.

* * *

Friend and Mira travelled north through the centre of Tbilisi in silence. The windows were tinted but Friend had still offered her a large-peaked baseball cap and asked her to wear it pulled low over her eyes. She found a pair of new hiking boots and thick socks waiting for her in the footwell and changed into them out of her heels. They were a good fit. Perhaps the man wasn't such a fool after all. She eased back in her chair and let her anger subside.

But it was still a good twenty minutes before she broke her silence.

'So who are you? You're not one of my husband's men. He doesn't normally use Russians.'

'I'm not Russian. My name's Rock Hunter and I work for the British government.'

'British? Why on earth would the British government want to help the wife of a Georgian smuggler?'

'To help bring the people who kidnapped her to justice.'

'I don't think the kind of justice they will face is the kind western governments usually approve of.'

'Maybe not, but sometimes it's the only option.'

'Which leads me to think that while you may be employed by the British government, you are not acting on their behalf at this moment.'

'What makes you say that?'

'You didn't bring a gun with you, perhaps that's because you had no-one you could ask for one. And you haven't contacted anyone to let them know the pick-up went to plan.'

'I haven't really had the time.'

'You've had almost half an hour since we got into this car. Modern German cars like this are usually well set up for communications.'

'Communications can be tracked. And it doesn't matter whether the pick-up went well or not. We either make the rendezvous or we don't.'

'All right. So where is the rendezvous? Where are you taking me to meet The Falcon?'

The car was picking up speed as they went past Jvari monastery at the entrance to the Tsitsamuri pass, the narrow gap between the mountains that guard the northern approaches to Tbilisi.

'We're going to a village called Dirijan, up in the Khevsureti highlands, close to the border with Chechnya. About as far away from Tbilisi as we could get.'

'Between Barisakho and Shatili. My husband's country.'

'Not your own?'

'No. I was born in Tbilisi.'

'So how did you two meet?'

'When we were children, or I was still a child then. He was almost a man. His parents died when he was very young and he was fostered by my family. We weren't the only ones. He never seemed to last anywhere very long; he was very wild. But we formed a bond in those few months which has never been broken.'

'And the rest of your family?'

'That's not a happy tale.'

'Because of him or just generally?'

'Just generally.'

'Do you want to talk about it?'

'Not particularly.'

They lapsed into silence. Friend looked at his watch; it was just after three pm. It was a good five hours to Dirijan; they would be lucky to make it by nightfall. The roads up there were not much good for driving in the dark.

'What about this man we're going to meet, the man your husband calls The Falcon. Why is he called that?'

'He is my husband's eyes and ears. His chief spy if you like. He sees everything, knows everyone and always seems to know what is going on. There's not much he doesn't see coming.'

'Except your abduction, perhaps.'

'I don't think anyone could have seen that coming. Except Mikel.'

'Mikel? You're on first name terms with Qorghanashvili?'

'Why wouldn't I be?'

'Well, the fact that he had you kidnapped and threatened your life.'

'He's also my brother.'

'Your brother? Your brother had you kidnapped?'

'Why sound so surprised, Mr Hunter? I would have thought it exactly the kind of situation an Englishman would expect to find in the Caucasus.'

Friend's hands gripped the wheel more tightly and he tried to force his eyes and his mind to focus on the road. Mira Qorghanashvili; sister of the villainous Mikel. He was trapped in some dreadful family melodrama. He had nothing left to say.

It was some minutes before Mira broke the silence.

'Mikel never forgave me for falling in love with a bandit. He devoted the first part of his life to trying to bring him to justice, then, when he failed, he decided to go one better and humiliate him, bring him under his own power. To do that he had to become a great criminal himself. Such a hypocrite! All of this, just for revenge. Revenge on the hooligan who stole his little sister away from him. A stupid emotion, don't you think?'

Friend said nothing. His head was still spinning.

'It's been a hard life sometimes, but an exciting one. And he's not a bad man, my husband, not such a bad man as Mikel that is.'

'Somebody' said Friend, 'said to me recently that there were two kinds of honest people in the Soviet Union: those who were fundamentally honest might fiddle a little around the edges, trick and bribe their way around the bureaucracy, but could always be trusted on the important things. The others were the superficially honest, who put on a great show of doing everything properly but underneath were swindling on a massive scale.'

'Yes, I think that's true. Mikel would definitely be the latter, my husband the former.'

'Your husband; I notice you never call him by his name.'

'It's a habit I've got into. Partly for security, partly because it annoys Mikel when I remind him of our relationship. Annoying Mikel is one of the few pleasures I've had over the last couple of years. So I call him my husband, my wolf, and keep his name to myself, something personal to me, just like he is.'

'Won't you tell me his name?'

'You mean you don't know?'

'He goes by the name of Dimitri now. Dimitri Chopuradze.'

'Dimitri? That's one of Mikel's sicker jokes. One of our family servants was called Dimitri, a sickly, sour-tempered fellow who always seemed to be unlucky in everything he did. As for Chopuradze…'

'Yes, I know, it comes from "the pockmarked one". A nickname of Stalin's.'

'Another great Georgian bandit,' smiled Mira.

'So, won't you tell me your husband's name?'

Mira placed her hand on Friend's arm.

'Poor Mr Hunter,' she said. 'Involved so deeply with people he knows nothing about and should have nothing to do with. To his friends, my husband is known as *Mgelis*, the Wolf. Only very few people know his real name: Tengiz Armazishvili. But across the whole of Georgia he is known as Tengiz Khan.'

* * *

They made good time along old military highway and reached the huge reservoir at Zhinvali – shaped on the map like an eagle in flight – just inside two hours. There, they turned off the highway and carried on up the quieter road north-east, skirting along the lower edge of the eagle's wing. Glancing in the rear-view mirror

Friend saw a black Mercedes saloon turn off after them, about sixty metres behind. The same car had kept a steady distance behind them for the last half hour, making no attempt to close up on them. Friend had eased his speed up a notch, then down again. Each time the car had maintained its distance. Friend didn't know quite what to make of it. If they were Kovalchuk's men then why didn't they try to stop him? If they were the Khan's then how did they know which car to follow? Come to that how would anyone know which car to follow? He tried to shrug it off; perhaps it was just an innocent driver trying to maintain a safe distance behind the vehicle in front. Only he wasn't sure whether he believed it or not.

The road had become impossibly scenic. All along the reservoir's eastern bank it had hugged the side of winding green cliffs. Now, as they left the water behind, they were up on top of a ridge with thickly-wooded ravines on either side, especially steep to the right. They had gone about ten kilometres beyond the tip of the eagle's wing when Friend spotted the lorry coming towards them. There had been little enough freight on the main highway, and to see a juggernaut of this kind on a gently undulating mountain road gave Friend pause for thought. Perhaps it had come down from Russia, but if so why not take the main route down through Stepantsminda? It was quiet enough. He looked in his mirror again; the Mercedes seemed to have dropped back a little. That was good at least. There was no other traffic on the road. He looked to his side; Mira was dozing peacefully in her seat.

For a moment he lost sight of the lorry as it went down into a dip in the road. When he saw its headlights again, blazing uselessly in the afternoon sun, they were almost on top of him. The great machine jerked to its left, coming straight at them. Friend had only a split second to react. Instinctively he turned the wheel to the left, across the lorry's original path. He saw the driver's last-second adjustment, trying to turn right again to meet him. It was just what Friend needed to slew the trailer out of his way; the BMW's tyres squealed, then gripped. He missed clipping the tail of the lorry by the narrowest of margins.

Back in his own lane, Friend looked in the rear-view mirror. The lorry was out of control, skidding sideways down the highway. He heard its brakes screech and watched as it toppled over onto its side, blocking the road completely. Mira had woken up with the first squeal of the tyres. Now she looked over her shoulder at the chaos on the road behind. There was no sign of the Mercedes.

'So they have decided to kill us,' she said. 'Good.'

'Good?' said Friend. 'How is that good?'

'Because it means that my husband has also escaped them. If he were still in their control they would try to get me back first. Since they are not trying to get me back, he must have got away. He will meet us in Dirijan?'

'Yes. Maybe not straightaway. He has a long journey from Batumi.'

'Batumi? So that's where they've been keeping him?'

'Yes, they had him managing a hotel for them just outside the city.'

Friend explained to Mira about Kovalchuk's smuggling operation and the Silver Mountain Hotel.

'My poor Mgelis! He must have hated it,' she said.

'At least he had the hills to walk in, and some good friends in the monastery. I've seen worse prisons.'

'I expect you have. But I meant something other than his physical circumstances. All his life he has hated nothing more than being told what to do by anyone. His teachers tried, my family tried, even I tried for a while. He was always one of those people who live by their own code. You might think someone who earns his living as a smuggler, a criminal, would have no moral code. No, he has a very strong code, but it is his own, not society's. It's precisely because it's so personal to him that he hates doing anything against it so… so passionately. It's something visceral. So if the thing he has been told to do is against the code by which he lives, but he has no choice but to comply, I can imagine nothing more miserable for him. He would have been happier in a stone cell on bread and water.'

The road climbed steadily higher as they drove further north. Beyond Barisakho, where they stopped to refresh themselves with the bread, cheese and water Friend had brought with him, the landscape became ever more rugged, the trees disappeared further down into the depths of the valleys; all around was rough green scrub, gorse and rock. With every mile the bends in the road seemed to get tighter, at times zig-zagging up a slope, at others soaring precariously above a precipice. Dusk was no more than two hours away. It took nearly all of Friend's concentration to focus on the challenges of the road, stealing an occasional glance in the mirror when he felt he could afford to in case of any sign of pursuit. He saw nothing. Soon his breath became shallower and his head began to feel dizzy. Mira noticed the signs before he did.

'We should stop for a few minutes,' she said.

'No, we need to push on. The light will start to go before we get to Dirijan and this is no road for travelling in the dark.'

'It's also no road to be driving with altitude sickness. We're already a thousand metres higher than we were in Tbilisi, can't you feel it? It's about to get much worse. We'll be climbing up to the Datvisjvari Pass soon; that's another thousand above where we are now. We need to acclimatise or you'll pass out at the wheel.'

Friend shook his head to try and clear it. He wasn't thinking straight. His determination to make the rendezvous before nightfall was getting the better of his judgement.

'All right,' he said.

When they found a wider stretch of road Friend pulled over onto the grass verge. He stopped the engine and got out, wandering over to the edge of the road where he could look all the way down the mountainside into the valley beyond. It was spectacular, there was no other word for it. They had stopped at the point where the mountain range the road followed essayed a huge sickle-shaped curve to the east as it climbed towards the pass. The mountains sloped gently into the valley here, and Friend was captivated by the sight of a whole meadow of pink and white rhododendrons spread out over almost a kilometre from where he stood. He gazed off towards the south-east where a line of high peaks reached skywards; somewhere among them was the mountain where the wolf's breath had brought the great blizzard down upon him all those weeks before, and the little shepherd's hut where he had waited out the storm. It was an effort to tear his eyes away from the view and lead them back along the road they had driven, searching for any sign of pursuit. After five minutes he had seen no sign of any other vehicle, nor any sign of life or habitation anywhere in the valley or on the mountain. He and Mira might have been the last pair of human beings left on earth. He glanced back at her, over his shoulder. She was standing next to the car, doing deep-breathing exercises, drawing the mountain air into the depths of her lungs and holding it there for four or five seconds, before letting it slowly out in a long, controlled breath. Friend turned back to the car and opened the boot, drawing out the kitbag he had brought with him. They were in the mountains now, and it was time to change out of his city suit.

CHAPTER TWENTY-ONE

HUNTED

Friend could push the car no faster than about thirty miles per hour as they wound their way through a series of hairpin bends that took the road up the steep slopes of Datvisjvari Pass. The road was rough now, unmetalled, narrow and rutted and more like some mountain track laid out for hikers. There was little room for error with steep screed slopes hemming them in on the left, and a sheer drop to the valley floor on their right. Every bump and judder sent Friend's heart into his mouth.

'I don't suppose we have any vodka with us?' asked Mira.

'Vodka? No, there's some more water if you're thirsty.'

'Pity. It's customary among the people here to drink three toasts before you travel through the pass: one to God and the ancient deities of these mountains, another to our ancestors and a third to the patron saint of travellers.'

Friend smiled at her.

'It's a nice idea,' he said. 'All the same it's probably better if I keep a clear head on this road.'

'It will be better once we're over the pass. On the other side the road gets straighter and descends a little. It will be easier to breathe.'

Then Friend saw the car parked ahead, pointing towards them on the outer edge of another hairpin where the road widened into something like a viewing point. He slowed to a halt and looked in the mirror again. He didn't like what he saw.

'What is it?' asked Mira.

'A car up ahead. Looks like he's waiting for us. Another two coming up fast behind. No way to get off this road here. They've got us trapped I'm afraid.'

'What should we do?'

'You get in the back and lie on the floor, your head behind my seat. If they only see me at first they may think it's the wrong car, at least long enough for me to get past them. I'm not sure they've spotted us yet.'

Mira climbed into the back and lay still as she felt the car jerk forward. Friend kept the car at a steady pace, not wanting to look as if he were rushing. He was fifty yards from the car now and could see two men inside the front seats. There was no movement from them yet. Forty, he heard the engine start; thirty, one of the men got out of the passenger side door, he saw him raise an arm. Fifteen. Friend dropped the BMW down a gear and hit the accelerator as hard as he could, he felt the wheels bite the dirt underneath and the massive torque propel the car forward. At the same time the nearside passenger window shattered and he heard a burst of fire from an automatic weapon. He felt the sting of a shard of glass cut into his cheek and a sudden, dull pain in his right arm, just below the shoulder. He looked down and saw the tear in his shirt, the blood seeping down towards his elbow. It would have been worse if Mira had still been in her seat; three or four shells had burst through the window into the top of the passenger seat, leaving the stuffing sticking out of it and blowing the headrest clean off its supports.

'Are you all right?' he asked.

'Yes, I'm OK. Are you?'

'Flesh wound. Nothing serious. We're past them, but they're in pursuit and we can't go very fast until the road straightens out. Stay there and keep your head down. There might be more shooting.'

Friend heard two more bursts of gunfire from the car in pursuit, but both were wide of the target. He kept going, the car bumping and rolling with the road. It would be hell to aim a weapon from a moving car in these conditions, he thought. Scoring anything like a direct hit would be sheer bloody luck.

Up ahead he saw another hairpin approaching, and just like the one before it widened at its apex to allow tourists to park and photograph the view. He heard the roar of an engine behind him; the other car was trying to use the extra space to get alongside them. Another burst from the gun and suddenly the windscreen had gone; Friend felt cold mountain air buffeting his face. He picked up Yuri's pistol from where he had placed it on Maya's seat and fired off two quick rounds in their general direction, then dropped it and got both hands back on the wheel before the car slewed out of control. It was almost too late; the momentary imbalance of having only his left hand on the wheel combined with the recoil from the pistol had the BMW jerking left, right and left again. He felt a jolt as it touched fenders with the car alongside. They were almost through the hairpin now and ahead Friend could see the road narrow again to a single track. He waited a second, trying to judge the moment right, then gently applied the brake. In a second the other car was right alongside him. He hit the accelerator and edged the wheel to the right once more, hearing the clash of metal on metal. There was a squeal of brakes and then he was away down the long straight stretch that followed. In his wing mirror he watched as the other car struck a standing rock which marked the road's edge, then reared up and toppled over, disappearing down the side of the mountain.

'We're through,' he said, through the roaring wind.

'Good. It should be just another eight or nine kilometres to Dirijan.'

'I hope we can shake off the rest of them before that.'

* * *

Dusk comes early in the mountains and the afternoon sun was beginning to dim. Friend picked up some speed along the straighter stretch below the pass, but the rough, narrow track still restricted his pace. His arm was beginning to ache badly but there was no time to stop and bind it up. He wasn't losing too much blood anyway. Worse was the stinging in his eyes from the wind and dust through the open windscreen. He squinted through the pain and kept them open for any sign of further trouble ahead. He half expected another ambush.

But it was the landslide that nearly got him.

It was just around a left-hand bend, half obscured by an outcrop of rock until it was almost too late. He skidded to a halt just inches in front of it; a fresh pile of rock and earth brought down by melting winter snow. Mira was shocked by the sudden halt.

'What's happening?' she cried from the floor.

'Road's blocked.'

'By another car?'

'No, by rocks. Natural causes this time.'

Mira shifted her position so that she was kneeling up between the two front seats.

'Oh, God,' she said, 'it will take us at least an hour to shift that.'

'We've got ten minutes at best.'

'And your arm!' she said, looking at the blood flowing down his shirt.

'It's nothing. Needs binding up but it'll be fine. Look, here's the situation: we can't shift the blockage in time, and we can't get the car around it. The drop's too steep. I don't like the odds of going back to face them or staying here to shoot it out. I've only got six rounds left in this gun and no spare clips.'

'So what do you suggest?'

'Make it look like we had an accident. We came around the corner too fast, tried to avoid slamming into these rocks and slid off the road down the hillside. With any luck they'll waste some time looking for the bodies before coming after us. In the meantime, we try to make it to Dirijan on foot. Okay?'

'Okay,' Mira shrugged.

Mira grabbed the kitbag with the remaining food and water out of the boot and Friend reversed a few metres back along the road. At the last moment he remembered to collect the first-aid kit from the glove compartment. Then, with the car in neutral, he got out and together they pushed it towards the edge. It went over easily, bobbing gently at first down the hillside until the gradient grew steeper, where it picked up speed, pitched forward, struck a rock and tumbled end over end to the valley floor, splashing finally into the shallows of the Arghurvi river. They stood and watched it go. Friend looked around the scene. There were no skidmarks from the tyres, no debris from any impact. It wouldn't be likely to distract a professional for very long, but it was the best they could do. The air still reverberated with the noise of the car clattering downhill, but Friend thought his ears could pick up the sound of a distant engine.

'Come on,' he said, taking her by the hand. 'We need to get off this road.'

* * *

If there had been only one car coming after them, they might have got away with it. As it was, the pair of matching Hyundai SUV's came round the bend at pace, and only just managed to avoid the landslip as Friend had. Four men got out and walked to the edge of the road where they looked down the hillside to where the BMW lay in a tangled mess of steel, glass and undergrowth. They were dressed for the mountains, in sturdy walking boots and padded jackets; one of each pair carried an automatic weapon slung across his shoulder. It did not take them long to decide what to do. Two of the men began to scramble down the bank towards the wreckage of the BMW; the other two walked calmly around the landslip and made their way steadily up the road towards Dirijan and Shatili, their eyes scanning the hillside below as they went for any sign of movement.

Friend and Mira had not waited to see what they were up against. There had been no trees on the hillsides since long before the pass and only the natural undulations in the terrain, or the occasional boulders left there aeons ago by a retreating glacier, could offer any kind of cover. Neither was to be relied on. Their only hope was to keep ahead of their pursuers until darkness fell. Friend wanted to get clear of the road, so he led Mira further down the valley towards the river, until she spotted a faint track in the grass, and dragged him by the arm.

'Come with me,' she said. 'This is my country, my husband's country. I know somewhere we can hide.'

The path tracked the river, parallel to the road but protected from view by overhanging rocks and scrubby vegetation. They saw no sign of their pursuers, but Friend guessed they would not be far behind. For about an hour they walked, stopping once for Mira to apply a dressing to Friend's wounded arm, until dusk was well advanced and the green mountains had become immense blue shadows all around them. Then Friend glimpsed a jagged silhouette ahead, its outline still clear against the indigo sky.

They scrambled up a short, steep bank and found themselves on a wider dirt track. If they turned left, Friend surmised, they would find themselves back on the main road. To the right he could see what looked like a series of tall, stone towers.

'Come on,' said Mira, grabbing him by the hand and leading him towards them.

A low moon came out from behind the clouds and by its light Friend could see the skeleton of a village, all jagged stone and empty window frames, its houses a series of defensive towers each scrambling skywards to catch the light.

'Khevsureti is full of these places,' said Mira. 'Old villages abandoned and left to rot. Some of them still have one or two older people living there. Sometimes they live there just for the summer and then go down into the valley for the winter. But in some of the villages the only people who ever come are the tourists. They come in a bus, stay for an hour to take their photographs, then they go. This is one of those places. No-one ever comes here at night.'

'Why did the people leave?' asked Friend.

'The young people left to take jobs in the cities. Then the older people who stayed just died one by one and the village died with them.'

'Do you think we'll be safe here? Won't they come and search it?'

'Maybe they will, but if they do they'll search the houses or the church and they won't find us there. I have a better idea.'

The village straggled uphill either side of the track which wound itself gently around the gradient. Looking back over his shoulder, Friend glimpsed the flickering light of a torch somewhere back down the road. They didn't have much time.

At the top of the hill the road ended in a small, squat stone church: a simple rectangular building with a plain wooden door, its roof crowned with an orthodox cross. Mira led him past the side of the church down a narrow path which gave on to a churchyard bordered by a low stone wall. They climbed over it, crossed the far wall in the same manner and scrambled down the slope behind. Friend could see nothing but scrubby grass, small, bristly bushes and the looming mountains beyond. Mira stopped by a small hump in the ground and turned to him.

'Do you have a knife?' she asked.

Friend reached into his jacket and brought out a pocket-knife. Mira took it from him and began poking around in the earth with it.

'They're not easy to find in the dark, and this is quite a short blade.' She paused, hands on knees. 'No,' she said, 'this isn't it.'

She walked further down the slope to another hump and began prodding at that with the knife too. Suddenly she struck something metallic. She dropped the knife and began feeling around the hump with her fingers. Friend heard a click and watched in astonishment as Mira lifted the hump off the ground as if it were fixed on a hinge. He came closer. It *was* fixed on a hinge: a lid concealing an opening in the ground wide enough to take the shoulders of a well-built man. Around the opening was a rim of metal.

'Get in,' said Mira. 'If you feel around with your feet you'll find the steps.'

Friend did as he was told and climbed down into the steel cylinder. It seemed to widen out in the middle before narrowing again at the bottom. It must have been about twenty feet deep. He heard the click as Mira closed the lid and followed him down. At the bottom there was no room to lie down, but enough for them to sit side by side with their knees up to their chins. If they had to stay there all night it would not be very comfortable.

'Don't worry,' Mira said to him, 'there should be just enough air. There are a few little vents around the rim at the top.'

'Where exactly are we? What is this?' he asked.

'There are a dozen of these in this meadow,' said Mira. 'They started their life as *qvevri.*'

'Qvevri? I thought they were supposed to be made of pottery.'

'They are.'

'And can you make wine this far up in the mountains?'

'No, you can't. The winters are far too severe for the vines and they don't get enough sunshine in the shadow of these mountains. These qvevri came from a winery near Telavi. After the end of the Soviet Union some crazy American bought the place dirt cheap and tried to install modern methods. He thought he could mimic the function of traditional qvevri using these big steel vats which could hold much more wine. Cheap, mass-production, of course. Only he didn't take into account the chemistry. Ceramic reacts with the wine in a very different way from steel and the wine he made was terribly sour. Nobody would buy it. So, after a few years he gave up and sold the place at a loss.'

'Let me guess, your husband bought it.'

'Yes, the Khan is also a vineyard owner, although he has a manager in place to run it. He returned it to traditional methods and had these useless vats moved up here.'

'Where they make for useful hidden storage for the goods he is smuggling.'

'Quite right Mr Hunter.'

Friend opened up the kit bag and brought out the last of the bread, cheese and water for them to share and asked Mira for the pocket-knife so he could cut them. Mira felt around in her pockets, at first casually then with growing anxiety.

'I must have left it up there!'

'Well, if they find it, they find us, probably.'

'I'm sorry.'

'Never mind. I'll just have to go and get it. You put it down by the rim, didn't you?'

'Yes, you can probably reach it with your arm without getting out completely. There's a safety mechanism under the lid: release that, then just lift the lid up gently.'

Friend winced at the metallic ring of each rung as his boots made contact, the sound echoing around the little steel chamber like a chorus of bells. He reached the top and felt around in the darkness for the catch. After a moment or two his fingers found what felt like a spring mechanism of some kind. He played around with it and suddenly felt it release; there was a gentle click and a sudden coolness around his face as the airflow increased. He put both hands up to the lid and pushed.

It was like being a submarine captain, Friend thought, peering out into the darkness above and hoping the enemy wouldn't spot the periscope. He pushed the lid open a little further and heaved his upper body into the gap. Then he stopped. The beam of a torch danced around the churchyard. He watched as it shone out into the field, swinging around into his line of vision. Friend slid back into the gap and pulled the lid shut above him. He held it there in position, not daring to close it properly for fear the click would sound across the churchyard to where the enemy lay in wait. For two, maybe three minutes, he held himself quite still, waiting for the approaching stump of footsteps, the wrenching open of the lid, the spray of bullets down into the vessel below. In the darkness beneath him, Mira crouched in silence. Not daring to speak.

At last Friend could bear the wait no longer. He lifted the lid upwards, as slowly as he could, millimetre by millimetre, until he could peer cautiously out. Darkness met his eyes, darkness and a silence broken only by the rustle of some small animal in the undergrowth. He wished the thing actually did have a periscope: he only had a 180-degree angle of sight. If anyone were behind him further down the meadow he could have no way of seeing that it was unsafe to come out. But there was nothing he could do about that. His lifted the lid higher and raised his body into the gap once more, thrusting out his arm and searching around with his fingers. At first there was nothing but grass and small stones, but then he had it. He grasped the knife in his fist and wormed his way back into the hole, closing the lid tightly behind him.

For the next two hours Friend and Mira tried to sleep. The vents might prevent them from suffocating but there was only just enough air in the vessel for the two of them. As the night drew on it became uncomfortably hot and they wrestled with their outdoor clothes and wriggled their bodies to try to get more comfortable and cool. They ended up back-to-back, their feet braced against the metal, chins resting on their knees as they dozed. Friend tried to avoid looking at the luminous dial of his watch too often. Talking worried him; the metal walls seemed to amplify the sound of the human voice and send it reverberating back and forth. He had no idea how much insulation the turf above them would provide against escaping sound. But there was one question he had to ask.

'What time is sunrise?'

'Sometime around six-thirty at this time of year, I think.' She kept her voice low but didn't whisper as Friend had done. 'It should be safe to talk,' she continued. 'The earth will insulate the sound unless we're shouting or banging against the metal.'

'Do you want to talk?'

'We don't seem to be sleeping much. What else can we do?'

'What do you want to talk about?'

'You?'

'Surely we can find a more interesting subject.'

'Like what?'

'Like the Khan, for example. Tell me about him. About him and your family.'

'I don't think that's so interesting.'

'Not interesting? Everyone I speak to says he's the greatest bandit ever seen in this part of the world, a legend known to every single person in this country, and you say he's not interesting?'

'I'm not sure I like the word bandit.'

'All right – outlaw then. Will that do?'

He felt her shoulders shrug.

'He might be a legend to everyone else, but to me he's my husband. Mine. He belongs to nobody else.'

'You might let me know what I'm risking my life for.'

He meant it more as a joke than a real attempt at getting an answer, but he felt her back heave as she drew in her breath and he knew that if they had been facing each other his face would have felt the sting of her palm again.

'You are an infuriating man, you know that?' She hissed the words as she released her breath and Friend felt the tension leave her body.

'I have heard that before,' he said.

'What do you want to know?'

'About you, Mikel and Tengiz. How it all started?'

Mira shifted her position slightly, either to get more comfortable or to give herself a moment to collect her thoughts.

'I was twelve. Mikel fifteen, Tengiz about the same. Maybe a year or two older. We were never quite sure and neither was he. He'd been in orphanages for most of his childhood and was already in trouble with the police even then. Nothing violent, he wasn't a hooligan. Just a bit of thieving. My father was a good man. He took an interest in the poor and disadvantaged of Georgia, especially the children. I don't know how Tengiz came to his attention, but he saw something in him, a potential of some kind, that he thought he could bring out.'

'Who were his parents?'

'Nobody knows. Tengiz doesn't remember them. Apparently, he was found wandering in the mountains half-starved and dressed in rags. He would have been about eight years old at the time. He couldn't read or write and barely spoke, but he did seem to react to the name Tengiz, so that's what they called him.'

'What about his surname, Armazishvili?'

'He made it up himself. I've never heard of anyone else being called that. It means "son of the moon god", more or less.'

'Very dramatic.'

Mira laughed and held her arms across her chest as she tried to hold it in and avoid making too much noise.

'That's not all he made up. He told the other boys at the orphanage that he was raised by a she-wolf, like some Roman demi-god.'

'So even then he was working on his legend,' mused Friend.

'Oh, I think it was more of a defence mechanism. Some of those orphanage boys can be very tough. But that's where he got the name from, he told me, the boy raised by a she-wolf descended from the moon god Armazi. The nickname of *The Wolf* stuck with him ever since.'

'What was he like when he came to your family?'

'Beautiful and wild. I think I loved him from the first. My father gave him security, comfort, an education – he was very smart, you know – but he couldn't tame the wildness, the restlessness in him. You couldn't keep him indoors for more than two hours at a time. Sometimes when his patience ran out during lessons he would just get up and hop out through an open window.'

'Your father must have found that frustrating.'

'At first he did, but then he came to accept Tengiz for who he was. In fact, there was a bond between them that was probably stronger for the fact that my father in the end hadn't tried to force a change of personality, to try and turn him into another Mikel. And he gave Tengiz something important: lessons in human decency, in leadership and in family loyalty. I think a lot of his personal code comes from what he learned from my father. He was only with us for three years, but they were important years. No man before my father had ever sought his respect, or offered him love. Six months later my father died. He had a heart attack. It was very sudden. Tengiz was in hiding at the time, the police were after him for something. I forget what. He still came to the funeral. He was more upset than anyone, even my mother and me. He turned up out of nowhere, climbed down into the grave on top of the coffin and cried. All across the churchyard you could hear these great wailing sobs, the scraping of his fingernails against the coffin lid, as if he was trying to claw his way inside. Then from somewhere at the back we heard a shout of warning; the police had arrived. I saw his head jerk up from inside the grave, then before we knew what was happening he had jumped out, darted off between the mourners, vaulted over the cemetery wall and made his escape.'

'Sounds like an upsetting scene.'

'Not at all. It was rejuvenating; life reborn out of tragedy. My mother and I looked at each other and our tears dried up at once. Mikel didn't like it at all. I almost laughed when I saw his face.'

'Mikel and Tengiz didn't get on, then?'

'No. They never took to each other. I wouldn't say they hated each other but there was no warmth, they were too different, and Mikel didn't have the kind of flexibility of mind that my father had. He couldn't see the goodness in people unless it was the kind of goodness he recognised in himself.'

'Which meant?'

'A strict code of civilised behaviour. There's nothing wrong with that, of course. But Mikel couldn't see beyond it. He never learned to appreciate the variety in human nature.'

'So what changed between them? What turned coldness into hate?'

Mira was silent for a long time. Only by the rhythm of her breathing could Friend be sure that she hadn't fallen asleep. He wondered what truth she was wrestling with; what confession she contemplated in this darkened tabernacle to the strange rescuer whose job was only half complete.

'It started with me,' she said at last. 'Tengiz was my first love, my only love. My mountain wolf, wild and untameable. How could I resist him? Mikel didn't like it of course, but he hoped I would grow out of it. Find a nice boy from a good family and settle down. I wouldn't have got over it, of course, but perhaps Mikel would have got used to the idea only then the other thing happened.'

'What other thing?'

'My father's death. He had high blood pressure, but he took medication and we all thought it was under control. When he had the heart attack we were all stunned. He just got up from the dinner table one evening saying he didn't feel too well, walked across to the sofa, sat down and a minute later he was dead. You can't imagine what a shock it was. Mikel was devastated. He blamed Tengiz. He thought that all the stress of getting him out of trouble with the police over and over again had worsened his blood pressure and led to the attack. From that point on he really did hate Tengiz, and when I ran away to join him in the mountains two years later, he determined to destroy him. I was just seventeen.'

And then Mira began to reminisce about her life in the mountains, the nomadic existence moving from one centre of operations to the next, as the youth born of the she-wolf turned himself into the Khan, King of the Mountain. And, with his chin propped on his knees and in the heat of the cramped metal vessel with the hypnotic rhythm of Mira's narrative, Friend slowly felt the tension of the day begin to abate; he could almost feel it dripping from the ends of his fingers, from every follicle of his hair and out through the very middle of his back where his body touched hers. His eyelids flickered and dropped.

* * *

Friend climbed the steps to the top of the vessel and eased the lid open. It was still dark, but only just. As he pushed the lid back, he turned to look across the valley and saw the mountain peaks silhouetted against the deep azure of the morning sky. There would be about twenty minutes left before dawn.

Friend closed the lid behind him and began to skirt around the edge of the churchyard and the village, trying to stay between the buildings and the sun. There was no sign of life. No movement, nor any sound. The absence even of a cock crowing or a dog barking, the clatter of a dustbin being raided by a fox or squirrel made it clear this place was no longer one of human habitation. He edged slowly around the side of the village until he could see the outline of the track leading back to the main road. There was a man standing there. He could smell the cigarette smoke before he saw him, crouching down by the side of the road, looking back towards the village. His automatic weapon was laid across his knees.

Presumably the other man was somewhere among the stone towers. And what about the other two? Back on the main road to cut off any escape that way? There was no way of knowing. He considered using the knife, but quickly abandoned the idea. Even if he could kill the man before he reached his gun and the noise of rapid fire brought the enemy down upon him, without knowing where the enemy was he had no way to judge his next move. It would be a senseless killing. Silently, Friend turned and headed back the way he had come.

Mira held her breath as the lid above her slowly opened, only to let it out in relief when she heard Friend's urgent whisper: 'Come on up, quick! We haven't got much time.'

Stuffing Friend's water bottle into a coat pocket, she left the empty kit bag behind her and scrambled quickly up the steps. Friend helped her out and then the two of them hurried down the slope away from the church and the village beyond, only stopping when an outcrop of rock hid them from the buildings above. They sat and caught their breath as they watched the morning sun creep up between two great peaks across the valley, its warm, blinding light shining in their faces.

'Well?' Mira asked, impatiently.

'They're still there. I saw one of them on the track out of the village. His friend is probably somewhere among the towers. As for the other two, who knows? We can't go back to the road, anyway. It's much too risky. Do you know another way to Dirijan?'

'Of course. There are plenty of old smugglers tracks around here.'

'Then let's go now. While the sun is low they'll struggle to see anything in this direction.'

Mira led the way. She took him down to the river where they refilled the water bottle. Then they tramped along the rocky shore for a few hundred metres until they came to a small ford. On the other side of the river they picked up a narrow track, little more than the impression made by human feet in the stunted grasses, which led back uphill. For an hour and a half they climbed steadily until the sun was high above them and any advantage they might have had from its low position earlier was long gone. When they paused for breath, Friend looked back across the valley for any sign of pursuit. There was none. His eyes searched the mountains beyond for the line of the main road. Was there the movement of something there? A momentary reflection of the sun on the metal body of a car moving along the great rock wall beyond? Possibly. But lower down in the valley where their pursuers would surely be had they picked up any spoor there was nothing and nobody to be seen, just the churning foam of the shallow, rocky river, bright green grass and grey stone. No living thing, not even a sheep or a goat, could be seen.

The path reached a small peak, then ran along a narrow ridge with steep drops on either side. Friend found it hard to imagine smugglers carrying heavy bags of contraband over the route, or forcing nervous mules along such a razor-sharp path. He felt his head for heights, normally steady, being sorely tested. Mira pressed on nervelessly. At last the ridge opened out into a wider pasture and they crossed a meadow deep with spring flowers, undulating gently across a plateau between the mountains. They stopped for a water break. It wasn't much further, Mira assured him. They had been on the road for four hours and the sun was beating down directly above them.

Gradually the meadow rose up towards another peak and the grasses gave way to scrub and scree. Mira seemed to find the going easy, to relish this return to a former way of life, on the run from danger, relying on her wits and local knowledge. *She feels no fear,* Friend realised, *because this is her home, her natural state. In the mountains. Hunted.*

It was another hour's walk in the early afternoon sun. The road, little more than a rough mountain track, emerged out of nowhere, winding up into the hills and disappearing between two great peaks of rock. And then he saw the village. It appeared almost camouflaged; its squat stone houses and gently pitched rooves formed of stone and slate of an identical colour to the surrounding rock. They seemed to grow out of the roadside like a forest of stone mushrooms. They passed a shepherd on the way, who gazed curiously at Friend and then, recognising Mira, doffed his cap in respect.

Wearily, the two trudged up the winding road through the village. As they passed, the villagers stuck their heads outside in curiosity, many of them recognising Mira at once. Friend felt a hubbub of conversation bubbling away in their tracks.

'Where is the Falcon meeting us?' asked Mira.

'I was told the farmhouse by the top pasture.'

'Further up the hill then. It's not far.'

It was the last house in the village, a wooden structure like an English barn-conversion adjacent to a small meadow which ended beneath a sheer wall of rock rising up to a high peak beyond. In the middle of the meadow Friend saw the incongruous sight of an old Soviet helicopter, a peeling red star still visible on its fuselage. It was barely recognisable as an MI-8, probably 1970s vintage, and Friend was just wondering whether it might still be serviceable when first one, then two goats appeared from inside its fuselage and began nibbling at the stunted grass.

The unlocked door was in the centre of the building and walking through it Friend and Mira entered a large, galleried hall which rose double-height to the roof. Great iron chandeliers hung down from the roof on chains. The place seemed silent and empty.

'Mimino!' Mira called out. 'Vakhtang! Are you here?'

A door on the right opened and a tall, thin, unshaven man with a fringe of grey-white hair around a bald skull came in. He looked tired; his clothes might have been slept in and smelled faintly of last night's drink. Or perhaps it was this morning's. He greeted Mira fondly.

'Mira, thank God! I didn't think I would ever see you again.' He held out his hands and his bony face creased into a smile.

'It's good to see you too Mimino,' said Mira, answering his Georgian greeting in Russian, then cupping his elbows gently with her hands and allowing him to kiss her on both cheeks. 'You are well?'

The Falcon tilted his head to one side in a gesture of humility. 'The years pass, we all age,' he said, switching to Russian too.

'That we do. This is Mr Hunter, from England. He helped me get here.'

The Falcon turned to Friend, his expression cautious but respectful.

'Welcome to my home, Mr Hunter. You must both be hungry and tired. There is drink and food in the kitchen. Come through. I'm sorry I couldn't have laid on a better welcome.'

Friend and Mira followed the Falcon back to the door by which he had entered. He held it open and gestured them through. The table was set with bread, cheese, cold meats and a large flask of cherry-red wine. But that wasn't all. Standing in the middle of the well-appointed kitchen was Josef, chauffeur and right-hand thug to Senka Kovalchuk. In his hand was a long-barrelled revolver and he was pointing it straight at Friend's stomach.

'Like I said, I'm sorry about the welcome,' he heard the Falcon say.

A stifled scream behind him, and Friend turned to see Kovalchuk with one arm around Mira's shoulder, a knife held to her throat.

'Hello again, Mr Hunter. Journalism become a bore?' said Kovalchuk.

Slowly, Friend reached down and pulled Yuri's gun out of his waistband. He placed it carefully on the table and raised his hands in surrender.

CHAPTER TWENTY-TWO

A COFFIN FOR DIMITRI

Survivability can be measured. It is a matter of distances, angles, degrees of visibility, degrees of force. Timing and decisiveness. Friend's body was motionless, but his eyes were watchful and his mind a frenzy of analysis. He knew he could expect no mercy from these people. He knew the process involved. In training they called it PIOSEE: problem – information – options – select – execute – evaluate. Often you could forget about evaluating. Either what you executed worked, or you were dead. Pilots used the same method. And just like a pilot trying to guide a stricken aircraft down to a safe landing, situational awareness was vital.

And so Friend watched. He watched as Josef's face broke into a smile, the bristles of his moustache rising like the spines on a porcupine's back, his black eyes twinkling. He watched as Josef passed his gun from right hand to left, moving along the left side of the table towards Friend. Friend stayed still, didn't step back. Josef moved steadily, easily; he moved with assurance. He had swapped the gun over so he could pick up Yuri's gun with his stronger right hand. His own gun was held in his weaker left. That was important. He came closer. Friend hadn't moved; he was still close enough to the table to reach down and pick up Yuri's gun without effort. But Josef was waiting for that move. An opponent with a gun will always expect you to challenge him with a gun. He is also subject to two major points of vulnerability: over-confidence and distraction. Friend stiffened the edge of his right hand, pulled the thumb back. Three feet. Three and a half at the most. That was what he needed. Friend kept his hands high, reassuring Josef that he wouldn't make a grab for the gun.

And now it was too late for that anyway. Friend could see the triumph – over-confidence - in Josef's eyes before he turned his head away a fraction as his right hand reached out for the gun on the table. Distraction. Eyes and mind together focusing on the gun he was about to pick up; reaction time for the gun already in his left fractionally increased by the need for the brain to refocus and send a signal in the opposite direction. Josef's chin moved a few degrees, exposing the left side of the neck. Friend saw the point he needed to aim for. Taking a half-step forward, his right hand flashed down hard, the force of shoulder and hip behind it, his mind visualising a strike through the target object. The contact was satisfying. Josef's eyes widened momentarily before the brain, starved of oxygen, shut down. He was dead before he hit the floor.

The follow-through left Friend off balance for a fraction of a second. Unable to grab Yuri's gun with his flailing right hand, he straightened up and reached for it with his left. He turned to face Kovalchuk and Mira. Nothing had changed in the last few seconds: he still held her tightly across the chest, a knife pressed to the front of her throat. But there was something missing.

His eyes still upon them, Friend dropped to his haunches and reached for Josef's gun. After a moment he turned his head to look for it, and there it was. In the Falcon's hand. Pointing towards him.

* * *

So this is how it ends, thought Friend. A half-baked rescue plan for a so-called damsel in distress that would never have got so far as it did without the lady's own resilience and local knowledge. An executioner's bullet in the back of the head. And for what? To help the greatest criminal in the modern history of the Caucasus regain his primacy? To avenge Nia Dadiani and atone for her death, as he had never been able to atone for those others? Dodds, Higgins, Hindson, Parnaby, Jobling. Magniac was right: he could never bring them back. Who was he to think he could right the world's wrongs? He couldn't even right his own. And it had brought him to this: to a pointless, lonely death in a high mountain pasture three thousand miles from home. Let it be quick at least.

His hands were cable-tied behind his back, the Falcon dragging him by his shoulders, his heels scraping along the ground. They went out beyond the farmhouse to the pasture where the helicopter stood. He looked back and saw Mira, Kovalchuk behind her, Yuri's gun at her back. Their situation was desperate but still she looked calm, stern, determined. Even now, there was no sign of fear. Friend tried to get some purchase on the ground with his feet and pull himself upright, but the Falcon simply forced him down again and dragged him even more roughly. They bred them strong in the mountains. They squelched through the short grass, still damp from melted snow and spring rain. The Falcon dragged him halfway across the little field, then dropped him at his feet.

'On your knees,' he heard Kovalchuk say.

Friend struggled upright, then knelt there with his head bowed. There were no options left. This was it. Finished.

He heard the two men's footsteps softly in the grass; the Falcon walking back to guard Mira while Kovalchuk stepped forward to perform the execution. For him it had become personal. Friend breathed in and looked upwards at the face of the mountain, stark grey rock against blue sky. High above him, an eagle floated on thermals.

They say you never hear the shot that kills you, and Friend's first thought was that there had been two. He heard them distinctly, just a fraction of a second apart. Then he heard the echo rebounding from all the way across the valley and realised it had been just one shot after all, the sharp crack of gunfire striking the sheer wall of rock beyond the pasture and reverberating around the mountains. It was only when Senka Kovalchuk's dead body hit the ground beside him that he knew he was still alive.

The bullet had struck Kovalchuk behind the right ear and had taken most of his forehead with it on the way out. The dead eyes still blazed with anger. Friend looked over his shoulder and saw Mira standing with her arms extended, frozen in a perfect marksman's pose. A whisp of smoke drifted from the barrel of Josef's gun.

The Falcon loped slowly towards him. He reached down and picked up Yuri's gun from the grass, then pulled Kovalchuk's knife from the dead man's belt. He hauled Friend to his feet and cut through the cable ties on his wrists.

'Thank you,' Friend said.

'I had to get him away from Mira first,' said the Falcon, obviously feeling an explanation was called for. He stuffed the cable ties in his pocket, then leaned down and roughly began to strip the brown tweed jacket from Kovalchuk's corpse. He stood up and examined it in the mountain light, checking, Friend supposed, for bloodstains.

'Nice bit of cloth,' he pronounced at last. 'No sense burying it with him.'

'What about the shoes?' Friend asked.

The Falcon glanced down. Kovalchuk's feet were expensively shod in burgundy grain leather chukka boots. He slowly read the maker's stamp on the rubber sole: 'Edvard Grin. Good?'

'Very good,' said Friend.

The Falcon nodded. He laid the dead man's jacket carefully on the grass and set to work on the shoelaces.

Mira hadn't moved. She had lowered the gun but held the rest of her pose: legs braced, eyes fixed on Kovalchuk's lifeless body. Friend walked slowly up to her, gently took the gun from her hands and threw it away into the long grass. Mira shivered and looked up at him.

'It's over?'

'It's over.'

It wasn't over. A sound was growing; a sound that had first touched the fringes of their consciousness moments earlier as the echo of gunfire died away and the mountainside returned to something that was not quite silence. It had grown without them noticing, like the wind that had blown at Friend's back weeks before on another mountain, until at last their conscious minds acknowledged it and said: *listen, and turn, and see.*

For up the road from the village came the sound of singing: a crowd of people, men, women and even children, marching and singing as they advanced. Prominent at their head was the tall, loping figure of Stephen Magniac. Alongside him, as if leading a holy procession to church on a saint's day, walked the hooded Father Gachechiladze. But ahead of them both, walking with steady, purposeful strides, a hunting rifle held loosely in his hand, came a short, stocky man with thick dark hair and a pockmarked face. Dimitri Chopuradze was no more. Tengiz Armazishvili, the Wolf, the Khan, the King of the Mountain, had returned to claim his kingdom.

* * *

The Khan was standing over Kovalchuk's body, Mira just behind him, her hand on his shoulder. What was he thinking as he stared into the dead man's eyes? *Do you remember, Senka, how I warned you that the wheel would turn? Was it worth it, the power? Did the rush it gave you make up for this sad, lonely death on a mountainside beneath the melting snows? Were you ready when it came?* He turned away and walked up to Friend.

'Looks like I need to order a coffin,' he said. 'But I'm glad it's for him and not you.'

'I have your wife to thank for that.'

'I have her to thank for so many things.' He placed a hand on Friend's shoulder and pulled him into an embrace. 'You will always be welcome in this place, for what you have done.'

The whole village had gathered on the high pasture; perhaps even more people than the village itself contained. There would be allies, fighters and friends from all over Khevsureti: the Khan's rag-tag army of smugglers and scoundrels. They were not simply milling around, Friend realised, something was in preparation. The Khan and the Falcon were deep in conversation, the priest was moving among the crowd, issuing instructions, offering blessings. Further down the road three large SUVs were advancing slowly up the hill.

Mira was standing next to him.

'Where did you learn to shoot like that?' he asked.

'Here. Or somewhere like here. Give me a good rifle and I can shoot the cork from the neck of a wine bottle.'

'Yes,' said Friend, 'I expect you can.'

They were silent for a moment and Mira watched as her husband moved among the crowd, the Falcon at his side.

'Those two have been friends since childhood,' she said. 'Both of them on the run from the law since they were twelve or thirteen, picking pockets on the streets of Tbilisi, rustling livestock up in the hills. My husband's empire was built by the Falcon as much as it was by the Khan. I've never known a friendship as close.'

'I thought he was on the other side for a while.'

'He had to shift alliances. Temporarily. Don't be so hard on him. His family were also threatened; his wife and daughter. The Khan could offer him no protection. That is why he betrayed us to Kovalchuk. No man in Georgia has a greater loyalty than to his family. Not even to the Khan.'

'And when I killed Josef, he saw a chance to put things right. Will your husband forgive him?'

'There is nothing to forgive. He knew the position. They hadn't been completely out of touch since Mikel's men took me. He knew he could trust the Falcon once the odds were evened up. Kovalchuk made a big mistake coming here himself.'

The crowd was gathering again, organising itself into marching order. Friend saw Stephen Magniac striding towards him up the hill.

'Charmed life, Laddie. Forgive me if I've mentioned that before.'

'What are you doing here?' Friend asked him. 'I thought you'd gone back to your vines.'

Magniac clapped him on the shoulder.

'I realised the only way this crazy plan of yours could work would be to get both armies in the field against the enemy. I remembered Dimitri saying he would go to the monastery once things kicked off, so I drove out there, picked him up and helped him to gather up everyone he could on the way.'

'So I see. Thank you.'

Magniac shrugged. 'I talk a lot of sense, but when it comes down to it I'm just as big a fool as you are. Bigger, probably.' He looked around. 'Is there a telephone anywhere around here? I should really call Tamara and let her know we're all right.'

Friend nodded towards the helicopter. 'The radio in that old thing is probably your best bet, if you ask the goats nicely.'

The procession moved on, higher up into the mountains beyond village and pasture, to where the snow still lay among the peaks. They passed over into the next valley, from where they could see all the way to the Russian border, far to the north. Most of them travelled on foot, but a few had mules and for the Khan and his entourage, Friend and Magniac among them, there were the three SUVs. They stopped where the vehicles could go no further: beneath a low peak which led, via a narrow ridge, to a higher, snow-covered peak beyond. The air was cold and sharp and their breathing became short. They must have been at nearly three thousand metres above sea level.

It was only when one of the other two SUVs opened its doors and a portly figure stepped out, dressed in a well-cut suit, hands tied in front of its waist and its head entirely covered by a plain jute hood, that Friend understood why they had come. Two men held the hooded figure there, gripping its arms tightly, as the Khan walked calmly over to them and removed the hood.

Mikel Qorghanashvili gasped in the thin mountain air and blinked in its harsh light.

CHAPTER TWENTY-THREE

THE BRINK

The tightly-wound threads of Mikel Qorghanashvili's life had unravelled rapidly over the course of twenty-four hours. He had been coming out of a business lunch in Tbilisi when Kovalchuk called him with the news that Mira had slipped away from her guards with the aid of a man on a motorcycle. It had taken little more than an hour to pick up their trail thanks to a spot of luck and the co-operation of the local police, but by then Kovalchuk had reported the worse news that the Khan had gone missing from the Silver Mountain Hotel. His response had been immediate:

'Find them and kill them both,' he said.

Qorghanashvili had always known it would come to this. Holding the wife of a powerful man captive was never going to work on a permanent basis. At some point there was bound to be an attempt at escape, perhaps she would be killed in that, or in the next one, or she and the man (he could not bring himself to think of her as her husband – had they ever even married?) would cease to be of use to him and have to be eliminated. Yes, she was his sister, but any affection he'd had for her had died a long time ago. All he had left was his desire to demonstrate his power to her, his success; how right he had been and how wrong she was.

Having both of them go missing at the same time meant there was only one solution possible. The difficulty was that with the

Khan on the loose it was hard to be certain of the loyalty of his people. They had belonged to Qorghanashvili for some time now, but once they heard the news there was no way of telling which way they would jump, except for the few over whom he had a personal hold. But those were too few.

So Kovalchuk's Presnenskaya thugs it would have to be. They would head north, of course, to try and reunite the Khan with his people. That would give Kovalchuk's men something to work with: there were not so many roads leading up to Khevsureti and not so many people to hide among when you got there. If Kovalchuk failed, then there would be some cause for concern. A revitalised Khan, reunited with his people, would be a powerful enemy, bent on revenge. But Kovalchuk would not fail. He was a brash, impertinent young pup, but he was good at his job.

And that, at last, would be the end of the Khan. It was strange that Mira thought it was all so very personal to him. The truth was that nothing was so very personal to Mikel Qorghanashvili. Mira had been dead to his heart since she took up with that bandit, she along with their parents who had brought him into their household. The whole business had turned his heart to stone; he had vowed that never again would anything wound him as this had. It was true that revenge against the Khan and Mira had been sweet, but he had not pursued it for revenge's sake alone. It had been a matter of business strategy: he needed the Khan's connections, his machine to supplement his own. That had been it. He had never devoted one ounce of effort to revenge. Even in his early days at the Ministry, when he had been involved in the efforts to bring the Khan to justice, he had concealed his knowledge of the Khan's identity from the authorities. And now justice would come for the Khan through Qorghanashvili's own order. Perhaps it was fitting that it should be him at last. Their destinies seemed to be entwined from the very first.

Qorghanashvili went home and waited by the telephone for the news. By nightfall he had received a report that Mira and the

Englishman had been forced off the road and had taken to the hills just north of the Datvisjvari Pass. But there was still no news of the Khan. Kovalchuk's men had tracked him to a nearby monastery in the hills outside Batumi, but they had found the place empty. Even the monks had gone, though there were signs of recent habitation. He dined at home alone and when, as he lingered over a cigar at the end, Kovalchuk called to report that there was no further sign of any of the fugitives, he began to feel the first stirrings of concern.

Qorghanashvili realised he needed some fresh air to clear his head before bed. So he slipped out of the side entrance of his mansion and began the ten-minute walk to his local church. He was not a particularly religious man, but he sometimes found peace and solace in the religious atmosphere. Perhaps that was also why the Khan frequented that monastery of his. Qorghanashvili walked swiftly on his pudgy legs, casting the occasional nervous glance over his shoulder. There was nothing to suggest he was being followed, just a growing sense of oppression creeping over his soul. A sense that would have been heightened still further had he heard the telephone call his butler made when he saw him leaving home.

The church doors were never locked. It was a small place, square-built with a single dome in the centre tucked away down one of those numerous narrow streets hidden behind Tbilisi's grand boulevards. He made his way down the aisle to where a series of painted golden icons hung on the wall, bent to kiss one of them, then crossed himself and retreated to a nearby chair. There were only two other people inside: a very tall, fair, foreign-looking man with a beard and a mop of wild hair, dressed in an old khaki combat jacket, and one middle-aged priest he had not seen before. The foreigner sat quietly, while the priest went round the church calmly extinguishing the candles. He sat and composed himself for a few minutes, until the priest came over to him.

'You seem troubled, my son,' he said quietly. 'Is there anything I can help with?'

'No, father. I don't think I have seen you before?'

'You have not. I am Father Gachechiladze. I come from Khevsureti, but lately I have been near Batumi.'

'So what are you doing here?'

Qorghanashvili heard a movement from behind him and turned to see the tall foreigner moving towards them.

'What is going on?' he cried.

'Please remain calm, Mr Qorghanashvili,' said the priest. 'I bring you greetings from an old friend.'

'An old friend? Who?'

'The Khan.'

Before Mikel Qorghanashvili could give voice to the scream that rose in his throat, he saw the flash of a pistol from beneath the priest's robes and felt the foreigner's powerful arms around him as the gag was stuffed into his mouth.

* * *

Hooded and bound, Mikel Qorghanashvili was bundled into the back of a vehicle and driven away. They drove for several hours without speaking and there was no way for him to tell in which direction they were going. He tried to sleep, but the rolling of the vehicle as the roads grew steadily rougher and the fear that rose in his heart prevented it. As the air grew colder, he tried to tell himself it was just the chill of night, but he could not suppress the thought that it was mountain air he now breathed. The air of Khevsureti.

When the vehicle stopped and they lifted him out he could hardly stand, so stiff were his legs. They leaned him up against the side of the car, holding him tight by the arms. Then the hood was whipped off his head and he saw the Khan standing before him, the Khan and the mountains beyond and a crowd of people standing solemnly in the mist. Two of the Khan's henchmen emerged from the crowd, carrying between them the motionless corpse of Senka Kovalchuk. He recognised the thinning hair at the top of the head. One green sock dangled loosely from the end of a foot. The men walked slowly to the point where the green meadow met nothingness and calmly heaved the body into oblivion. There was no sound as it fell, no sign of its landing. Why waste time and energy on a burial? Why waste money on a coffin? Let the carrion birds pick the bones clean. Mikel Qorghanashvili knew at that moment that he was to be a guest at his own execution.

'Mikel,' the Khan said gently, leaning forward and kissing his foster brother respectfully, once on each cheek. Qorghanashvili squirmed, but the men held him tight. The Khan turned impassively away and beckoned for the others to follow. Two guards jostled Qorghanashvili and he wrestled with them for a moment, then spoke urgently to the Khan.

'Wait, Tengiz! You think I could escape from here? At least let me walk on my own two feet.'

The Khan stopped and turned around, then gave a nod and walked on. The two guards loosened their grip and Qorghanashvili followed on under his own steam. They walked only a little way further before the Khan stopped, and when he saw why, Qorghanashvili began to feel sick. The mountain fell away completely, as if cleaved in half by a giant axe; snow, grass, earth and rock carved away to leave a huge, sheer cross-section of mountain, perhaps five hundred metres or more, until the chasm ended in a pile of boulders and a little stream. He gazed down at it for just a second, then looked away in horror. Somewhere down there lay Kovalchuk's broken body. His own would soon be joining it. At least Senka had been dead when they tossed him over the edge, but would he be? How many seconds would the fall take? What thoughts would go through the mind? He looked back at the villagers, huddled together against the wind, waiting to see the end, and wondered what they were all doing here.

'They need to see justice done,' said the Khan, reading his thoughts. 'They need to see that the Khan's enemies are vanquished and that his word is law again. Then they will know where they stand, and their loyalty to me will be as great as it always was in the past.'

The two men stood together on the brink.

'We have had a long journey together, you and I, but now it must end,' said the Khan.

'Then let it end quickly.'

The Khan shook his head.

'I want to understand why. We, who have your sister in common, your father and mother like my own, could have been family. Instead you treated us like enemies.'

'Family? You came into my family like a cancer. You killed it. When you left there was nothing left worth salvaging.'

'I was young and wild. Your parents understood that at least. So did Mira.'

'And you are still wild. You're no different, Tengiz. You still don't see how you hurt my parents by your crimes.'

'I loved your parents. Your father especially. I came to his funeral if you remember.'

'Oh, I remember. You gave a very touching display of grief until someone shouted out that the police were arriving, then you got up and ran for your life.'

'True,' said the Khan, wistfully. 'But what did you do for them? Do you think they would be proud of the son they raised?'

'Of his public success, certainly. As for the rest, they are not here to see it. Neither will I be, very soon.'

'True again.' The Khan drew a deep breath into his lungs and when he spoke again it was no longer in conversation. It was a pronouncement of sentence. 'Mikel Qorghanashvili: five hundred years ago, an ancestor of yours guided the Persian army through the mountains into Georgia and betrayed his King. You have proved yourself a worthy successor. You deserve the same fate. Do you have anything to say?'

Qorghanashvili laughed scornfully.

'What right have you to judge me?' he said. 'The great Khan! Your own judgement will come too one day.'

'But not today, Mikel. Let it be done with.'

At a signal from the Khan, one of the guards held Qorghanashvili by the shoulders, the other by the ankles. He let himself be lifted from the ground and the great, fat body was swung, left to right, right to left, once, twice and at the third time with a great heave he sailed into the air above the precipice. For a second he seemed to hang suspended in mid-air, and as he did so Friend thought for a moment that Qorghanashvili's eyes met his own. But they were dead eyes, empty of thought and expression, belonging already to the world beyond, as Nia Dadiani might have said. Slowly, the dead man's eyes closed and the body began plummeting downwards, half a kilometre to its grave. No-one heard the sound of it landing. The body of Mikel Qorghanashvili simply disappeared out of sight. Days later, Sebastian Friend had the sense that it might be falling still.

That sense seemed to be shared by the watching crowd; a strange silence reigned around the mountain. But then, as if by a single will, a cheer of jubilation rose up. Tengiz Khan turned away from the precipice and met their cheers with a head raised and proud. A smile broke across his sombre face. The usurper was dead. Dimitri was dead. Long Live the Khan!

'It is a traditional death for a traitor,' said Mira quietly.

'He was also your brother,' said Friend.

'He had not been that for a long time.' Mira smiled and gave Friend's arm an affectionate squeeze. 'But all that is over now. You have given me back my life, and my true family. Now we go back to the village to celebrate. Come.'

The crowd was beginning to move back down the hill. Sebastian Friend and Stephen Magniac held back for some moments before following.

'She's right, you know,' said Magniac at last. 'You did it. You rescued a hostage, reunited a family, released Christ-knows how many other people from the pressure this syndicate was putting on them. Qorghanashvili and Kovalchuk won't ruin any more lives.'

Friend didn't reply. He was still staring out across the brink, his mind lost somewhere in the distant mists where bodies fell endlessly through bottomless chasms. That was the problem with regrets: you could drag them to the edge of the abyss and throw them over it, but they never hit the bottom. They were still there, levitating in space, their eyes locked with yours. Better turn your back on them if you could.

Magniac clapped him smartly between the shoulder blades with one huge hand.

'Wake up you silly bugger. Don't you get it? You beat them, Laddie. You won.'

The realisation came slowly. Magniac was right, in his way. It wasn't victory, but it was at least a resolution and, in its own very Georgian way, a kind of justice. A Khan's justice.

Stephen Magniac smiled as he watched the light return to his friend's face, a light which he, in his innocence, mistook for satisfaction in a battle fought and won.

END

Author's Note

Tengiz Khan was first conceived in outline as far back as 2018. Originally, I had intended to travel with my wife to Georgia to complete my research on the ground. However, first the intervention of Covid and subsequently the birth of our daughter meant that this journey remains a distant dream; a dream I find all the more appealing after working on this book. One day, I will walk those hills.

Three particular individuals made a notable contribution to *Tengiz Khan*. Firstly, I must thank Lucy Balmer Hooft for her kind and detailed scrutiny of the manuscript and the many useful recommendations that helped bring the book's locations to life. Lucy, who at one time was based in Georgia, is also a wonderful thriller writer; do check out her Sarah Black books: *The King's Pawn* and *The Head of the Snake.*

Huge thanks are also due to Major (Retired) Paul Martin of the Royal Regiment of Fusiliers. Paul's comprehensive knowledge of the experience of army veterans transitioning into civilian life was invaluable to me in fleshing out Sebastian Friend's history and adding depth to his character. It's a subject Paul knows well due to his work supporting ex-Fusiliers making that difficult transition, often encumbered by profound physical and psychological wounds. Little did I guess when I first met Paul on the terraces supporting Gateshead FC how much he would influence this story.

Lastly, my old friend Ben Williams has my gratitude for telling me the story of an ex-mercenary he once encountered in the wilds of Thailand. It was a funny, but slightly unnerving tale that slowly developed into a scene for this book – the first seed of the narrative that was to become *Tengiz Khan*.

Safe House Books is an independent British publisher of spy fiction which is reviving quality espionage for a new audience.

www.ingramcontent.com/pod-product-compliance
Lightning Source LLC
La Vergne TN
LVHW020539100826
845148LV00010B/1532

* 9 7 8 1 7 3 9 7 5 4 0 5 1 *